All Else is Folly

Susan leant against the mantel, looking down into the fire.

"Louis," she said slowly, "you and I did all our talking years ago. We talked too much, and we burst our marriage wide open. It doesn't leave anything to be said now. We're finished with each other."

"But you're not giving either of us a chance, Susan."

"We've had our chance long ago. I've made up my mind to marry again. And this time I've got my eyes wide open . . ."

Available in Fontana by the same author

Daughter of the House
Edge of Glass
Corporation Wife
The Tilsit Inheritance
The File on Devlin
Sara Dane
I Know My Love
Blake's Reach

CATHERINE GASKIN

All Else is Folly

Collins

FONTANA BOOKS

First published 1951
First issued in Fontana Books 1959
Thirteenth Impression January 1977
Fourteenth Impression August 1977

© Catherine Gaskin 1951

Made and printed in Great Britain by
William Collins Sons and Co Ltd Glasgow

THIS BOOK IS FOR
GEORGE AND CATHERINE MAHONEY

CONTENTS

FRIDAY   *page* 7

SATURDAY   46

SUNDAY   73

MONDAY   110

TUESDAY   170

WEDNESDAY   202

THURSDAY   228

Man shall be trained for war, and woman for the recreation of the warrior; all else is folly.

FRIEDRICH NIETZCHE

FRIDAY

I

From the moment the plane touched down Susan knew something was wrong. There was the weakness in her knees and the way her mouth had gone dry, and afterwards, while the luggage was being examined, there was that little silence of strain and apprehension between herself and Paul, all pointing to the fact. She knew she would be nervous, of course, but that didn't wholly account for this fluttering of panic, this sensation of events moving past too quickly for her to get a grip on them. She hadn't known fear quite like this before.

And because he was in love with her, Paul knew about it also. While they waited for bags to be loaded into the car, he slipped his arm through hers in that familiar gesture of assurance. She let her finger-tips rest on his palm. Before she moved forward to get into the car she increased the pressure slightly on his hand. All this was done without their looking one at each other, but somehow it re-established the contact which had been broken when Susan first looked down while the plane circled over London, and had known what she was coming back to.

The car began to move off. " Cigarette ? " he said.

" Thanks." As she bent towards the lighter he held, the police guards on the gate were only a blurred impression of dark uniforms.

Because she realised that she must be honest with him, she suddenly spoke her thoughts aloud. " I'm afraid, Paul."

He didn't fuss ; didn't even turn in her direction. " You don't have to go through with it. You needn't see him if you don't want to."

She flushed, and didn't care that he might notice it. "Louis would say I'd run away."

He said quietly : "Does it matter what Louis says ? "

Foolishly, even now she told the truth. "It used to matter very much."

He flicked his cigarette impatiently and some of the ash scattered across his coat. He didn't brush it aside, but sat staring straight ahead at the wide, flat road, at the prim, over-nest suburban dwellings which lined it. Later on there would be tall factories, self-consciously modern, and smug behind their stretches of green lawn. This was all too familiar, even after the absence of years. He turned sharply to Susan.

"It's six years," he said. "He will have changed."

She was sure of her words now. "Not enough. He's still going to be the same Louis—clever, charming, damned superior, and just human enough for me to have loved him." She added quickly : "I'm afraid of him."

He tried to compel her to deny it. "You're not afraid of him, Susan, but of the person you've imagined him to be."

She said firmly, as if it were a lesson she had learned to repeat : "I have never imagined Louis to be anything but what he is. He is just himself, no excuses, no apologies."

"Then he probably thinks of you that way. He may be afraid, just as you are."

"No." She shook her head. "Louis has never been afraid of anything in his whole life. No fear of God or of the devil—he didn't believe in either. No fear of life or death, and no respect for them. A person needs to be afraid of something, but Louis had no fear."

The ash of her cigarette had grown long while she talked, but she made no movement, and he knew she had something further to say. "We quarrelled about that in the beginning —I suppose he thought me a coward. But after that it seemed impossible for either of us to see the other's point of view. We were like strangers, never understanding each other—never even trying to understand. It was like a wrestling match which just went on and on—and both of

8

us afraid of losing a point. It wasn't marriage, it was just bedlam. In the end we wore each other out."

She said finally : " It's humiliating to have failed so completely. We made such a mess of it—such a damned awful mess."

They lapsed into silence, while the car pushed its way through the traffic which was thickening at each artery to the main road. Paul wanted to question her. All the years of not asking questions irked him now, and he wasn't able to begin. Humiliated . . . he wondered if she meant that exact word. Susan didn't exaggerate, but after all, the final victory had rested with her. She had scored the last point of their battle in leaving Louis and coming back to America. She had left the child as well. Perhaps that was what she had meant by humiliation. He began to understand that she had been nursing—incredible that he had not seen it before —the thought and memory of failure, and it had burst into unhealthy ripeness in the past hour. He looked at her—so serene and cool ; she didn't appear frightened—not in the least. This fact, above all other, gave warning to him.

He turned so that he could see her face more fully. They had reached Hammersmith Broadway, and her head and shoulders were outlined against tall, dark buildings, and the traffic piling up at the south and west entries. It was a habit of his to look at her when she was unaware of it ; something he lapsed into whenever the opportunity came. He knew, with a touch of misgiving, that it was something he could not easily learn to do without. He liked to allow his eyes to rest on her, dwelling on each detail of her dress and grooming. She dressed her hair sharply back to reveal the wide cheekbones, and didn't care that her mouth was large and wide. She was beautiful because of these things, and she had a beautiful body—disciplined, in perfect proportion. There was seduction—conscious or unconscious he had never decided—in her body.

Very clearly he could remember the day, more than four years ago when she had come to him for a job. One of his editors had introduced her, and she'd asked, boldly enough, for a position on his biggest women's magazine. He had admired the confidence which made her do it, and he had given her the job. Six months after he'd ridden his own hunch and made her fashion editor. He'd waited then for the results of his own recklessness to trip him up, but she'd come through even as he hoped she would. He gave her a sharp rise in salary. Susan hadn't thanked him. She always know her own worth, and that, he understood, was different from having a price.

At last he stopped looking at her. Individual privacy was something very precious between them and he knew he didn't live up to the rules when he stared at her like this. Perhaps he should tell her about it. Rules were meant to be broken sometimes—perhaps he wouldn't tell. They loved each other, but there was no licence in their loving, no taking for granted. Better to keep this private piece of Susan to himself, to possess quietly, to take out and re-examine time and time again. As if to confess and still withhold this small deception, he placed his free hand across hers, lying so still in her lap. Then he turned once more towards her, this time to watch the bars of pale autumn sunlight which alternately invaded and retreated from her face with every swinging movement of the car.

She moved her hand under his and gripped it quite firmly. Each gesture like this surprised him. However many times it was repeated, when it came it was still unexpected.

Now they were in the wide, sunlit canyon of Kensington High Street, and she said suddenly : " It grows so much more difficult than I imagined." Needing the reassurance he could so easily give she turned to him. " I wonder why suddenly I have this fear that things may go wrong."

" There is nothing," he said, " to go wrong. The divorce comes up for hearing in two months, and after that there's nothing but to wait until it's final. As long as you're careful to avoid what they call ' collusion,' then there's not a thing to go wrong. Not a thing."

" There's Midge," she said. " Suppose he doesn't agree to let me have her ? I don't believe he's capable of spite . . .

but then I'm not sure. How can I know in what way these years have changed him? I think it's that I'm afraid of—the unexpected in him."

"In Paris," he said slowly, "it didn't seem possible that you could be afraid of Louis. If you felt this sort of danger we shouldn't have come."

She said urgently: "The very fact of being in Paris made it impossible not to come."

His brows creased down heavily. "You went to Paris to look at fashions. That was business."

"This is business of a more desperate kind. I think," she said steadily, "that if I'm to have custody of Midge it will be only because I've talked to Louis . . . because I've persuaded him to let me have her."

His voice became louder, so that the driver permitted himself a second's glance in their direction. "Do you think," Paul said, "that any of the decisions will be left to you? If Louis wants the child, he'll keep her, and there's not a thing you can do about it. If you get Midge, it will be by his gracious consent." His voice still retained a thin edge to it, but she had seen his shoulders relax, and knew he was making up his mind to be patient.

When silence fell between them once more, she took up the thread of thought she had been following when the touch of his hand interrupted her. Paul had been patient for a long time now, and only he could have appreciated the urgency of her demand that they cut short their stay in Paris and come over to London. It hadn't been easy to leave it behind. Paris had been incredibly lovely in this season when the first leaves had begun to drift down, and she, who had never seen it before, fell wildly in love with it. Every moment which could be spared from the *salons* was spent with Paul discovering its charm and beauty. He taught her the Paris he had known before the war, when he had been a correspondent for one of his father's papers, and it was not the Paris of the tourists. She remembered it as a dream of spires and roof-tops with bits of the river threaded through like pale grey ribbon. Susan knew she loved Paris as only the Americans seem able to love it; she allowed herself to slip into its life-stream with complete abandon, not withholding herself, but revelling in its sounds and colours and odours, making the mistakes that countless Americans had made before her, and not caring about them.

Now they were entering a city whose landmarks were beginning to stand out for her, a solid grey city, standing beneath faintly coloured autumnal skies, with tall houses stretching towards occasional patches of pale sunlight. They were coming to arrange the final details of a divorce and there were going to be petty wranglings over the child they called Midge, and whose real name was the absurdly old-fashioned one of Alexandra Charlotte.

These were but the broad outlines; this was what, in Paris, she had thought simple and uncomplicated. But now, small shadings were creeping in to colour the picture. Louis seemed no longer merely the vague figure whom she had done without for six years in New York; disconcertingly he was coming to life as a person with a disturbing power to shake her confidence and security. Perhaps he would look at her in just his certain fashion, and she would know over again that sensation of naïveté, of knowing nothing while he was rich and full with his experience. She wondered had he known of this trick of staring with smiling ease and of making others immediately aware of everything about them which was ordinary and unglamorous.

One couldn't readily picture Louis against a new, peace-time background. He had fitted too well, with stock-type accuracy, into the tumult and chaos of war. Even their meeting had run along the conventional pattern of the period. His brother, Racey, had introduced them in a night-club, and they had danced until she was exhausted, because the air-raid had lasted all through the night. In the packed, smoke-filled room they had talked and laughed, and it had been incredibly wonderful to walk home in the dawn, with the mad brightness of many fires still in the sky, and to feel the beginning of love. They had breakfasted together, the three of them, in her flat, and afterwards they had left her with the breakfast dishes still scattered on the table, to get a train back to their R.A.F. station. There had been much laughter, and they were as careless and unthinking as two boys with a day of idleness ahead of them. But she had known from their talk that they expected to go on operations that night. It was no more to them than the performance of a simple routine.

That evening became, in memory, like many others. She grew accustomed, as time went on, to coming home from the Embassy and finding one or the other, even both of them, waiting at the flat to take her out—or when the time was short, to eating a meal there and listening to her records. Strange to think, that with the two so much alike it was difficult to pin-point a difference between them, she had loved Louis and regarded Racey with amused affection. As if to oblige her, he had remained amusing and charming, tried laughingly to make love to her, and had approved when Louis asked her to marry him.

Not more than a few months after they met they had been married in a half-shattered church in the village of Hythebourne where Louis lived. The day of her wedding she had met his parents for the first time, and despite Racey's assurances, she knew they were disappointed and alarmed. They accepted the arrival of an unknown American into the family with characteristic calm but no warmth, and the situation had never altered.

She shared life with Louis with the peculiar intensity which war seems to demand. They expected much of each other, expected, perhaps, that each should provide for the other the relief from the strain which their natures craved. Knowing each other too little, and loving too much, they had failed.

She struggled against the familiarity of the places passed and the onward rush of the car, to hold her attention on that period of their marriage. It was suddenly important, if she were to face Louis, to bring out of a protective memory and the dimness of the past years, the true reason for their failure. At Hythebourne, where she had waited during the months before Midge was born, the loss of understanding between them, the complete absence of any unity of thought, was frighteningly apparent. Louis came to her with the regualrity of a religious duty determinedly performed, whenever he had leave, and these days were lived through in a state of crashing tension. Mere words, unimportant and sometimes unnecessary between those who love, became double-edged, and actions were observed and remembered to be brooded over when he had gone back to the air-station. She could recall clearly, even now, the agony of discovering, through those months, that to love Louis was not enough. One had somehow, out of the brief hours of seeing him, to beget an understanding and a sympathy which made possible, even tolerable, all the rash words, the silences, the small obstinacies. The war and the brevity of his leaves, gave them no time for that kind of adjustment. They found no relief in talking of it, because the rift was too intangible to bear the strain of words, and time itself presented no opportunity, and in the end even the desire for understanding left them.

After Midge's birth she had settled to caring for the child, and planning for the moment when she would be old enough to take to London. Return to the flat in Carlton Mews now presented the only salvation of the marriage. Alone once more, and away from the atmosphere of decay she found at Hythebourne, they might reach out to each other to strengthen the bond of their love with sympathy and patience. The thought brought hope, and she waited for the time to pass with a sense of urgency.

The plan, when she told him of it, met with complete and final opposition from Louis. There were no arguments to convince him that the physical dangers she and the child faced were infinitely more to be desired than the slow strangulation of their love here at Hythebourne. Anguish over his inability to recognise the fact made her inarticulate ; she could find no words to tell him of the misery of the lonely nights, and the days filled with activity which the house and the two old people who inhabited it seemed never to recognise or appreciate. Looking at his smooth, handsome face, and his eyes which sometimes regarded her blankly, she wondered how she might describe the sensation of oppression, of time and all the past lives lived out in that house bearing down upon her. Caught in the routine of more than a hundred years, she was no longer an individual, but the person who was called Louis' wife. To remain there began to represent in her mind an annihilation of self.

In the weeks that followed Louis' decision she had tried to lay before him the evidence of her revolt. But she presented it to unseeing eyes, spread it before a mind so absorbed with the fervent worship of flying, half-dazed from the repeated tensions of operations, that he had no time or inclination to discover it. He expected her to settle to the routine of Hythebourne, which only his occasional presences made bearable, denying the right of the personality he said he loved to express itself within its chosen sphere. She prayed that his blindness might be relieved by one flash of insight, but it never occurred. From the moment she gave up hope she planned escape. She bore the almost insuperable difficulties of finding a passage to New York with a patience which her bitterness had made more dogged. Her flight from him and Hythebourne brought a deep and abiding sense of peace, so that it was impossible to feel guilt or remorse for an action which now appeared justified.

For six years there had been no sign from Louis, no message or letter, and it might have gone on that way for the rest of their lives, if she had not decided that she would marry Paul. She had written to Louis, and finally sent a formal request through her solicitors that he should start divorce proceedings on the grounds of her desertion. Even this brought no personal reply from him; it seemed to Susan that he treated it as he might treat an annoying request from a stranger, something to be turned over to his lawyers to deal with as quickly as possible. Each time she thought about it, the subtle overtones of contempt in his behaviour stung her. Louis had always had such a vast contempt for what he considered beneath him. There was punishment in such silence, the sort of cruelty which only Louis could be sure would wound her. He had not forgotten her, nor forgotten how she had hated and feared any suggestion of the impersonal in their relations. He knew what she had expected from marriage, and in withholding it, he understood too well what he inflicted upon her. Not even the dignity, the slight courtesy of a note to acknowledge the fact that she was coming to London in order to see him. She hadn't believed that the end of a marriage could be so completely bad, so evil.

But long ago, when she had decided upon this step, she had doubted that any relationship, any intimacy, even one so strained and precarious as that established between them, could be completely blotted out. It didn't seem possible to forget Louis, any more than she could forget the swift period in London, five months of danger and life lived at a fierce tension. Their brief love had moved along to the accompaniment of crashing bombs, and sometimes, watching the flames from incendiaries in the night sky, like cigarettes pin-pointed close to one's eyes in the dark, she had wondered how such a love could survive when the tumult and noise was over, when there was no more excitement and danger for Louis. They had lived from hour to hour, and loved desperately—he over-stimulated by his worship and pursuit of daring and mad courage, she fearful and trying to hide it from him. It had ended disastrously, as swiftly as it had begun.

They were turning into the Park and she noticed how the autumn colouring had already laid a tentative hand on the trees. They were still summer green, and yet expectant, as if they waited with certainty for the frost and wind which would presently tip them unceremoniously on to the grass. She wasn't pretending any more that she didn't see the difference here in London. No need to point it out to Paul. He, who had also known London during the blitz, would see it perhaps better than she. Ordered lawns and flowerbeds, and women with fashionably long skirts walking their dogs, and even the glimpse of a scarlet Guard uniform she had seen up by Knightsbridge Barracks—all this was surely London four years after the war. It was a city she recognised instantly.

They were in sight of the hotel, and turning out of the Park she began to think of the leisurely bath she would have, and then a cocktail later with Paul. Perhaps there was even time to phone Louis' solicitors to arrange an appointment for to-morrow morning. So much time would be lost if she had to wait until Monday. A week was all they had planned in London; she knew now, as she felt the pull of her old affections for the place renewed, that it was a dangerously long time. Better, perhaps, as Paul said, not to have come . . . safer, wiser. It was difficult to know what, in the end, was the safest, the wisest thing to do.

II

As Susan turned from the reception desk her glance fell on Louis.

He sat in the lounge, a glass on the table before him, his face half-turned away from her, and even after six years she hadn't forgotten how he held a cigarette, and smoked so quietly, with eyes half-closed like a cat's. Even in the bewilderment of that first moment it shocked her to realise how well she remembered.

He hadn't seen her. Instinctively she clutched Paul's arm, an alarming sense of panic driving her to seek the swiftest escape. She wasn't ready to face him; she needed the bath and the cocktail, she needed the support of so many trivial things before she could talk to him calmly. She knew the treacherous weakness in her knees was fear she couldn't drive away.

Paul was gazing at her now, an expression of inquiry upon his face. The bell-hop waited cheerfully for them to start towards the lifts.

She ran the tip of her tongue across her lips. It was a

familiar gesuture, when she was disturbed. "Louis is there," she said dully.

He looked beyond her. "Which is he?"

"By the entrance. He's alone."

He nodded slowly. "What are you going to do?"

She said miserably: "I can't talk to him now. I'm not ready."

He took her arm and drew her to the end of the desk, out of hearing of the clerk and the bell-boy. "Look, Sue, you probably know best because you know this guy, but if I were you I'd see him now and get it over. He's obviously waiting for you. In another few minutes you'll be having a call to your room from him."

"Yes." As if trying to gain time, she said slowly, "Will you come with me?"

"No, Sue."

Silently she questioned him.

"This is your show," he said.

She didn't say any more, but he saw the tip of her tongue on her lips again, and noticed now she ran a hand across her hair, and pulled lightly at the edge of her jacket to straighten it. He saw it as a sort of mental squaring of her shoulders, and suddenly, feeling her loneliness and panic, he touched her hand briefly.

"I'll be waiting upstairs."

The lounge was crowded. Only a few single vacant seats remained, besides the one facing him. He didn't notice her coming, and she actually stood above him for about ten seconds before he raised his eyes. Then he stared at her blankly. After another small age she saw his eyebrows begin to lift inquiringly. She struggled desperately to remember what she had decided to say, but it was quite gone. She said at last, weakly: "Do you mind if I sit down?"

He sprang to his feet, as if the words were unexpected, and pulled out the chair. "I'm sorry. Please do."

She sat down and looked at him, and saw his own eyes fixed on her unblinkingly. God! Why didn't he say something? Why didn't one of them say something? Another thirty seconds like the last and she knew she would get up and walk away.

Suddenly he said: "Would you care for a cigarette?" It was said not abruptly, but a little impersonally.

"Thank you." She was pitifully grateful for its proffered refuge, for the respite which the taking and lighting of the cigarette would offer her. He leaned over and lit it slowly, as if he also were marking time, seeking for words, though not in quite the same way as she. She looked at him quite closely while he held the lighter to his own cigarette. He had altered hardly at all, features just the same, hair as dark and brushed straight back. Nothing changed that one could pinpoint, unless one noticed his eyes, kindly and a little puzzled, and his hands relaxed and steady—different from the hands she remembered. Hardly changed, and yet a difference somewhere. She couldn't tell exactly.

He pushed the ash-tray towards her. "Do English cigarettes give you a shock? Most Americans don't like them."

"Any cigarette is good after a journey. Almost as good as a bath."

"Tired?"

"Tired enough."

He smiled, a friendly, odd little smile. "Then would you like . . . ? Look, let me get you a drink."

A waiter was quickly at his side, removing his own empty glass, and bending to hear Susan's order. "Gin and French," she said faintly.

"I'll have the same again."

"Rye and dry, wasn't it, sir?"

"Yes, that's right."

Louis was looking at her once more, smiling again and saying: "I'm waiting for my wife."

The shock of it kept her silent, once she had controlled her first impulse to cry out. She ashed her cigarette when it didn't need it, and in her agitation, nearly stubbed it out. She repeated his words over to herself, felt herself saying them and trying to find their meaning. She fumbled and groped, almost committing herself to speech and then retreating, and at last the truth of small facts began to add up. Louis had greeted her as a stranger might—a friendly, smiling stranger. His odd remarks which hadn't made sense now had a full, unpleasant meaning. He knew her as little as he knew the dozens of other people crossing and re-crossing in the foyer. To him she was no more than a woman who had come and sat down at his table ; a woman no different from any other.

Only his smiling unawareness of her identity prevented her from blurting out the truth immediately. Suddenly she didn't want to see the smile wiped off his face. She wanted to continue talking to him, experience for a little time longer his new friendliness and ease. Obviously he couldn't remember her and there was an explanation, but that could come later—when they'd talked a little more. She didn't look at him directly when she said : " Aren't I intruding then ? Hadn't I better go ? "

He laughed softly, a small, pleased laugh. " That's not possible. You won't find another seat here. And besides, you haven't had your drink."

" Surely you're not being fair. If you're waiting for your wife, you shouldn't have suggested a drink."

He smiled lazily. " Don't go. I'm always fascinated by an American accent."

" I'm not staying just for you to listen to my accent."

He leaned forward suddenly, his outstretched hand almost touching hers. " Look, I needed someone like you badly just at the moment. I'd like to tell you exactly why, but I'm afraid you'd be amused."

It was difficult now to disguise her own eagerness. " Probably my sense of humour is a little better than that."

" I'm sorry. That was wrong, of course." His face twisted strangely, and Susan saw the first sign of weariness and pain in it. He wasn't smiling now. " I just felt I had to talk to someone about it, but it's so difficult to begin."

She said in a low voice : " Why begin ? One sometimes

regrets pouring one's heart out to a stranger." She couldn't have explained why she said it. It was like a warning to him, almost an appeal not to break down his defences, not to make himself vulnerable. She wanted Louis back on the old ground. It would have all been easier that way.

The drinks arrived then, and when the waiter had gone, he raised his glass to her in a slight gesture. " Well . . . here's to all the people who come along at the right time."

" Providing it is the right time." If only he would understand what she meant. What colossal, stupendous folly to sit here allowing him to continue—listening to him.

" Are you always like this ? " he asked.

She sipped her drink. There was very little gin in it. " Like what ? "

" It's difficult to say exactly. Detached . . . cool. No, that's not what I mean either. Wise—dispensing a little wisdom like dribbles of good wine." Then he laughed, looking at her to see if she laughed also. " That's foolish, of course. You must think me foolish."

" No, not foolish. Unwise, perhaps. You're waiting for your wife—remember ? "

" Well . . . that's it." Again there was that expression of weariness and pain, a nervous twitch of his lips. " You see, I haven't seen her for six years, and when she comes, I'm not sure that I'm going to recognise her."

Susan looked down at her hands, feeling sick and cold. She had nice hands, well-cared for, and usually they gave her satisfaction to look at them. Now they were treacherous, traitorous things, which might tremble if she didn't clutch desperately at the glass. She began to wish madly that time could be pushed back ten minutes—only ten minutes. She would be standing again beside the reception desk, seeing the awning space of floor between herself and Louis. If she could traverse it again it would be in a different way. At that time Louis had been a stranger to her—he was that no longer. There had been weariness and fear in his face, and Louis, self-sufficient, fearless, collected, had sought help from an unknown woman. This was an incredible change, and ten minutes had revealed it to her. Oh, God! she thought desperately, get me out of this somehow, don't let me commit myself any more. She was praying suddenly, whispering the words inside her brain . . . 'Deliver us from all evil.'

"Six years doesn't alter a person all that much," she said.

"Oh . . . that! The change won't be in her but in me. Since I saw her last I've had a bullet in my skull. There have been whole chunks and pieces of my life I can't remember a thing about. Being married is one of them."

She couldn't say anything. 'Forgive us our trespasses . . .' Had she trespassed against Louis? Was every act of hers from now on to be adjudged small and mean? How did he feel about divorcing a woman he didn't know? She knew, of course. Hadn't she seen the fear, the weariness, the tightness in his face? He was feeling just as she would in the same circumstances. They had come even thus close together.

He said quickly: "Look, I'm sorry. I didn't mean to make you uncomfortable."

She looked up. "I know that."

"I don't think about it much any more. I forget that it embarrasses other people. I'm used to it now. It doesn't bother me any more—except at a time like this. That's why I wanted you to sit here and talk to me. It makes waiting a lot easier, you know."

"Glad if I can help." She hated the thin little platitude which escaped her. This was worse than lies. Paul liked her because she was truthful; she wanted now to be truthful to Louis.

"You are helping, you know, but like all nice people you don't want to intrude. Well, suppose you forget about me and enjoy your drink."

"Let's be fair, shall we? This isn't any ordinary drink, or any ordinary conversation." It was all making her sick, but for some stupid, impossible reason she went on: "You can't expect me to talk about the weather when you're waiting to keep an appointment with an unknown wife."

" It's not an appointment. She's not expecting me. I'm
sitting here solely because if someone walks through those
doors whom I can remember—even faintly—then a whole
chunk of my life is going to slip back into place. That's all.
A fairly long shot, but it might come off."

" What if it doesn't click ? "

He shrugged. " Then I'm no worse off, am I ? " With
hardly a break, he continued : " Have another drink ? "

" Thanks. I don't think I will." She wanted badly to get
away from him. He had never possessed the power before
to make her feel mean and petty. He used it now with
unconscious force.

" Why not ? Have I bored you ? I didn't mean to." He
wanted her to stay. He won the point, as he had done so
many times before. Yet it was not quite the same as all
those other times—an appeal, not a demand. " Won't you,
please ? "

Troubled, she allowed him to order another drink. This
was such madness ; why did she not put an end to it ?
What had happened to all her rationalised planning of how
this interview should have gone. The enigma lay in Louis.
He had taken charge of the situation with strange, un-
predictable hands, and had whisked it to and fro where he
pleased. She had followed dumbly, unable to do anything
else. Without trying to stop herself, she said at last :
" You're a curious man."

He was genuinely surprised. She liked the way his eyebrows lifted, humbly, yet confidently seeking an explanation. " And why ? " He was inclined to be amused as
well.

" And why not ? You've just told me something most
people wouldn't tell their greatest friend. And I'm a
complete stranger."

He laughed outright now. She saw suddenly, amazingly,
that he was enjoying himself. " But haven't you ever met
anyone you know instinctively ought to have been your
greatest friend ? "

Forgetting the evil combination of circumstances, forgetting, even, that this was Louis, she laughed also. "That's a complete untruth."

She continued to laugh until she remembered that she would have to relate all this to Paul. The thought sobered her; her conduct was inexplicable. Why in Heaven's name didn't she tell Louis the truth and be done with it? The interval caused by the arrival of the drinks gave her a little time. She knew that when she went upstairs she would have to say to Paul: 'I didn't tell Louis because I liked him so much as he is, that I didn't want to see him change back into the person I knew before.' As baldly as that. She felt better because she had put it straight in her own mind. There was a certain amount of self-respect to be regained by being honest, even thus far.

She said to Louis: "What else did you think?"

"Can I tell you?" There was a strange eagerness about him. "For one wild moment when you stood in front of me I thought you might be my wife. But then I knew I was wrong, and I felt slightly foolish. I suppose I felt like a child who's been expecting to get as much in his Christmas stocking as all his brothers and sisters put together." For a moment he paused. "No one's ever bothered to tell me what my wife looked like. I haven't even got a photograph of her. So I'm not altogether to blame, am I?"

She coloured, and hoped he wouldn't notice it. "No, you're not."

"Thanks." Then he grinned. "It seems to me I'm making an awful play for your good opinion. Why?"

"Increasing the tourist trade obviously. You're probably a member of the Chamber of Commerce."

He didn't laugh. "It's equally obvious you're not a tourist."

"Then what am I?"

"I don't know. I won't bore you by trying to guess, either. Do you live in New York?"

"All of the year except the summer."

"What do you do in summer?"

"Go home to Maine. I have a sort of farm there." It

didn't matter about telling him any of this. Louis had never known of it, never cared. Or had there never been time to tell him? Somehow there hadn't been time for much else beside their lovemaking and quarrels.

"What's 'a sort of a farm'?" Louis pushed his drink aside.

"Well . . . two cows and a few chickens and a stream to fish in. And Agatha."

"Who's Agatha.?"

"She's looked after me since I was a little girl, and she cooks like an angel. There's only Agatha and me left." That wasn't quite true. Paul had come with her to the farm the last two summers. Agatha had worshipped him. She cooked for him all day. Difficult to think now of the farm without Paul.

"Only Agatha and you left." He repeated the words slowly. Almost unconsciously she whispered them back to herself. They began to sound like a dirge, a mournful little couplet as sad as the first patter of autumn rain after a beautiful summer. She wanted to go on talking about the farm, about the hurried week-ends spent there, and Christmas when she went to church with all the people who'd been sitting in the same pews as long as she could remember. Louis had never heard about all this—about her agile, sharp little grandmother Katie who'd been alive at the time she'd married. Katie had never forgiven her for not marrying an America; she had gloried wickedly when Susan had come home without Louis. Katie hadn't wanted Susan's half-English child either. Yet Susan had loved the sharp-tongued little Katie with all her heart. They'd loved and hurt each other unceasingly.

She brought her mind reluctantly back to her surroundings, tapping one finger-nail lightly on the glass. "When this is finished I must go."

"Yes," he said, "I know." She wondered exactly why she was disappointed in his answer. Paul would place his finger on these inconsistencies. He would know better than herself why she had acted like this. All the small dishonesties

25

of this interview would be revealed ; what she couldn't face, Paul would face for her.

Her words made it seem as if she had already withdrawn, and momentarily a small cloud of silence fell upon them. Louis, forgetting the woman for whom he waited, wished she would not go away. Not for a second did he think he ought to try to stop her, ask her to stay. There was a quality remote from reality in their meeting. It seemed, fancifully, to him that they had marked time together during this half-hour. Very soon she would move on, unknown and nameless still, out of his sight. He did nothing to prevent it.

She stood up at last. He rose also, slowly. " I'm sorry you've got to go," he said. " I've enjoyed talking to you."

She said untruthfully : " I'm glad you found someone to talk to."

It seemed to both of them that they should have had more to say to each other, but a strange embarrassment choked their words. She said finally : " I hope you'll see your wife," then immediately wished the words unsaid.

" Thanks a lot . . . for everything."

They didn't shake hands, but he smiled at her. It was the first time Susan had ever seen Louis smile like that. It warmed her strangely, and in the face of it, her deception was an insult. " Give my regards to New York," he said. " I expect I'll go there some day."

" I hope so," she said formally.

He watched her as she walked away, and he saw too, the heads of many men in the lounge turn also to watch her. He offered a silent, motionless salute to the retreating figure, a good-bye murmured under his breath. Then he sat and ordered himself another drink. He didn't want it, but he had to do something, and the pushed-out, vacant chair and empty glass on the other side of the table was something he didn't want to notice too much. When his glass was also empty he got up and strode towards the reception desk. The clerk who slipped along to face him had a glassy, inquiring smile. Louis glared at him. " Has Mrs. Taite booked in yet ? "

The clerk ran his pencil down the list with a dummy-like motion. " Yes, sir, she has. Shall I ask the switch-board to get her for you ? "

" No, don't bother." Louis turned his back and walked towards the door. It was growing dark outside, and the traffic moved past in a noisy stream. He paid scant attention to it. On the corner of Piccadilly he bought an evening paper, and cut across the Green Park towards Carlton Mews.

III

PAUL WAS waiting in Susan's room when she arrived. He motioned her towards a chair, but instead she took a cigarette from his proffered case and remained standing. He lit it for her, then dropped into a chair himself. " How did it go ? "

" Not too badly."

That was a lie, but she didn't know how to begin to tell him what had happened. She laid the cigarette down in an ash-tray and reached for her dressing-case, wondering why she postponed the moment of her telling. The sharp sound of the locks springing back emphasised the silence in the room. She began laying the bottles, one by one, in a meticulous row under the mirror. She always considered that a room began to look like her own when the familiar bottles and jars were laid side by side in this way. A small phial of perfume, Paul's last gift to her in Paris, caught her gaze. She picked it up and uncorked it, holding it level with her nose, and looking backwards at Paul in the mirror. When she was certain his attention was fixed on her she said : " Louis didn't know me."

He sat upright. " What do you mean ? "

" Just what I said. Louis didn't know me from any other woman in the room. He thought I sat at his table because there was no other seat."

27

"Hell!" he said. And then, incredulously, "Are you sure, Susan?"

"Quite sure. He was friendly and charming, and he bought me a drink. But he still thought I was a stranger."

He stood up and came towards the dressing-table. She dropped her eyes and recorked the phial, taking up another bottle at random and unscrewing the cap. Paul stood beside her; she still didn't look at him in the mirror. "Susan, what have you done? Didn't you tell him who you were?"

She said tightly: "No."

"And in Heavens name why not?"

Unexpectedly, she didn't resent his questioning; she deserved anything he cared to say to her. But she couldn't answer him immediately.

He repeated in a very low voice. "Why not, Susan?"

She turned and faced him at last. "Because . . . oh, Paul . . . he told me was waiting for his wife. He hadn't seen her for six years, and he couldn't remember what she looked like. How could I tell him after that?"

He dropped back a step, and then, as if thinking again, moved closer and put his hands lightly on her shoulders. The hair which swept straight back from her forehead was level with his mouth. "Was it very bad, Sue?"

This time she said: "It was just hell. Lousy."

"I should have stayed with you. It would have cleared things up a bit."

"No, it didn't matter. I won't be seeing him again. He can go on thinking I was just a stranger he bought a drink for."

He gripped her a little tighter. "Why won't you be seeing him again?"

"How can I'. . . now?"

"How are you going to avoid it? Didn't he come here just to meet you. He'll probably be on the phone in a minute or two. What are you thinking of, Sue? You can't get out of it as easily as this."

She felt enormously weary, and knew her mouth was sagging in just the way she didn't want it to. There was so much explanation still to be gone over with Paul. " But he didn't come to meet me. . . . I don't think he'd care if he never met his wife. He was sitting there because . . . well, because he hoped that he'd recognise some woman as she came in, and that recognising her might bring things back into focus a little."

" What things ? "

She explained patiently : " He was wounded in the head after I'd gone back to America. He can't remember me."

He felt the droop of her shoulders under his hands, but he had no room for pity just then. Susan, in the short time she had been away from him, had slipped back into another world. She had passed through an experience he had not shared, and he was afraid. He had the feeling of being shut out, gently but unmistakably shut out. Susan had to be forced back to him in some way. He said : " You talked to him for a long time."

" I told you he bought me a drink." She wished it was all over. She would be having a bath, sorting things out in her own mind, while the steam swirled above her. Or better, perhaps she wouldn't think about it at all, just relax in the warmth and softness.

" Tell me something, Susan," he said more gently.

" What is it ? "

" When you were down there with him . . . did you think of yourself and the woman he was waiting for as different persons ? Did you, Sue ? "

Of course he had seen that ; she had known Paul would see that. She said : " I think I did."

His hands dropped from her shoulders and he went back and sat down again. She watched him light a cigarette, and it was with that air of reflectiveness which she had witnessed hundreds of times before. Paul always did it like that when he wanted space in which to think. " It simply means, Sue, that you still care very much about what Louis thinks of you."

" No . . ."

He cut in : " Yes ! The point is that he liked the woman he met down there, and—consciously or unconsciously—he doesn't like his wife. So now you've made up your mind that you won't see Louis, because you don't want to be associated with the woman he dislikes as his wife. It's as simple as that."

" Nothing's so simple as that, Paul."

" In this case it is. Louis attracted you enough to make you want to hold his good opinion. If you really wanted to be free of him you wouldn't have cared a damn."

" Does all this matter very much ? "

" That's my line, Sue. You answer it yourself. You want to have your kid, don't you ? "

" Yes, of course."

" Then you've got to see Louis—as his wife."

" Paul, I can't. I can arrange things through his solicitors. Besides, he doesn't intend to see me. It's not just a matter of my choice." She had turned her back to the mirror in order to face him, and in it he studied the arrangement of her hair. Even with the tired droop to her mouth and shoulders she was extraordinarily attractive, he thought. Louis, he knew, would have felt that also.

" O.K., Sue. It's your show."

Susan, about to turn away from him, halted. She was fearful because Paul's support seemed to be withdrawing from her. " Why did you say it like that ? "

He drew at his cigarette with a slow, patient movement. " Because that's how it must be, Susan. If you think you're right . . . well, go ahead. This is the part of your life I don't know anything about, and it's not my business to advise you."

" Paul ! You can't think of it like that." She crossed to his chair swiftly. He moved over and she seated herself on the extreme edge of it, laying her hand on his arm. " Isn't this the best for me to do ? It's so much easier to go away and not see him again."

He put his arm round her shoulder, drawing her closer, feeling her body relaxing against his. " In the beginning it is, Sue. Then afterwards you'll start thinking of the change in him, and wondering if it was permanent or only first impressions."

She stiffened a little. "I didn't say he'd changed."

"A guy doesn't have to be very smart to guess that. He was different from the person you'd led me to expect. After all, I didn't know him. What you told me, you believed yourself. And he didn't turn out like that, did he?"

Her hand gripped his arm, very tightly. "But all that doesn't matter. It's got nothing to do with you and I."

He put his hand out swiftly and tilted her face towards him, holding it too firmly for her to resist. "It matters a hell of a lot to me. It's taken two years for me to get you as far as divorcing him, and when it's over, I want Louis to be finished also. I'm not the sort who plays second fiddle to another man. You know that, Sue."

She shivered slightly. "But I don't understand what good it will do if I see him again."

"If you see him again you'll know whether you want to go through with this divorce or not." He released his hold abruptly, but she remained facing him.

"Is this an ultimatum?"

"Could be. But I didn't intend it to sound like one." He caught her body swiftly in his arms and began to kiss her. She moved slightly in his clasp, and relaxed again. He went on kissing her until all thought of Louis slipped from her, until she was aware only of the reality of her person enclosed in his arms. He didn't often use this means to settle their differences, and now he was regretting this occasion. She responded so readily, was warm and relaxed in his arms, as he had known she would be. While he was kissing her, Susan was no longer very attractive, but very beautiful. She had a talent for making love, like wearing clothes. She was at her best then, a best which he could only appreciate by learning of it.

They stopped kissing very slowly, gradually, as she liked

31

to do it. Susan was never to be hurried in her love-making; he had learned that long ago.

They had dinner at a small restaurant which had been Paul's favourite during the early days of the war, and it was Susan who brought the conversation back to Louis.

"I can't make up my mind what to do. If I could find out more about him—about the accident—it would be easier. He told me almost nothing."

Paul turned from his study of a group of men who were seating themselves on the other side of the room. "That's Jock Peterson there—used to know him in Paris," he murmured. "What were you saying, Sue?"

"About Louis—I'd like to know what happened to him. How much he can remember."

"He has a brother, hasn't he?"

"Yes."

"Contact him. He'll be able to tell you."

"No. I don't want to see Racey."

"Why not. You didn't quarrel with him too, did you?"

Susan laughed quickly. "No one quarrelled with Racey. He and I used to have blazing rows, and then go out and have a drink together and forget about it. I was with him when I first met Louis."

"And Racey—what's he like?"

She shrugged, looking down at her soup. She had yet to get used to English food. "Much the same as Louis. They were both crazy about flying."

He raised his eyebrows. "Is that all?"

She nodded. "Practically. It seemed to me that was all they lived for. Racey was night-flying when Louis and I were married, and he came up to London between ops. to be best man." She laughed suddenly, but Paul didn't miss the light ring of harshness in it. "I've always thought since then that Louis was secretly envying him having to go back."

He said savagely: "Easy, Sue. You're letting all this get you down."

"I'm not," she snapped. "It's quite true. Louis never let me believe anything else but that he grudged the time he had to spend on leaves, every minute he wasn't in the air."

"My God! Well, why did you get married?"

She laid down her spoon abruptly. "Don't you think I've asked myself that hundreds of times? And there doesn't seem to be any answer. I suppose because it was war-time . . . and I thought I was in love with him. And for him, well . . . his life might end any second, and he wanted the thought of a woman at the back of his mind. I happened to be convenient."

"Hell, Susan. You didn't think this at the time, did you?"

"Not right away. But it didn't take long to get round to that point of view. You see, I was just a sort of good-time girl for both of them—Louis and Racey. I kept on driving for the Embassy after I was married, and when I'd get back to the flat in the evenings I'd always wonder which of them was going to be there, which one was going to take me out dancing and give me dinner and pretend not to hear the sirens. It was like being married to both of them," she added reflectively, "only I didn't go to bed with Racey."

Paul watched her and the way she remained gazing at the tablecloth while the soup was removed; saw, also, how slowly she began the omelette she had ordered. He wished suddenly that he might confront these two men, make them more than the phantoms they were now. Louis he had seen, and what he remembered was a dark, good-looking face with the trace of English coldness Americans had learned to distrust. It was a face which now he ached to punch for the pleasure of seeing a look of surprise break over it, to see its slight disdain slip away from it foolishly, weakly. Susan was avoiding his eyes, and her face was white and strained by the very memory of the person who had sat in the lounge that evening. Paul had known his type often before. Living in London during the blitz he had discovered all there was to know about them. They

33

faced death with off-handed courage—lack of imagination he had called it in his reports—and at all other times they were coolly, complacently English, almightily sure of themselves and everything they did. They made him sick. He wanted to cut away from the whole thing, take Susan back to America, marry her and keep her so busy just being married she wouldn't have time to think about either of them—Louis or Racey. But first she'd got to be helped out of this mess. It was making him sick, too.

" You'd better see Racey, Sue."

She roused herself to some faint protest, but subsided before the words were formed. He saw her shoulders slip downwards, and that angered him more than anything. " All right," she said.

She was afraid. She was holding back her fear because Paul couldn't understand what he was suggesting she should do. It was more terrible, more frightening than anything she had imagined. To see Racey would be pure hell. A meeting between them would bring back in its savage truth the misery of the early days of her marriage before she had learned what to expect from both of them. They had been so alike those two—Louis and Racey. Scarcely any difference except that perhaps Racey, of the two, had seemed more human—never quite possessing Louis' indifference to danger and death. Racey had held her close when the bombs were falling, and sometimes, when the dance-floor had shaken beneath them, had reassured her with brief, swift words. With Louis it was different. For him the prospect of death had held as little novelty, as little awe, as sitting down to drink at a table with a stranger.

She shivered with the memory of it. It was into those recesses of his mind she had been unable to penetrate, and since he never gave of himself more than his body, their marriage had ended with uncomfortable relief on his part and frank dismay at its failure on hers.

Never before had she sat with Paul through a meal so silent. She knew him well enough to know that it wasn't anger which made him so, but the fact that he had recognised her confusion and had left her to get her ideas straightened out. A blind, unreasoning decision to accept his plan of seeing Racey had now formed in her mind, and she wanted once more to talk. She pushed her coffee-cup slightly aside and leaned forward. " Got a cigarette, Paul ? "

" Sure." He watched her closely while she inhaled, saw the little lines round her mouth relax and disappear. He moved the tiny glass of colourless liqueur closer towards her. " Drink it up, Sue."

She sipped at it slowly. " This always seems to me to taste of wild oranges—although I've never had a wild orange in my life."

" You wouldn't like them. Tough and bitter."

" You're a realist, Paul."

" Yes. And a damn' good thing, too." He signalled for the waiter. " Sue, you've got to let me help you with this."

She nodded. " Of course." That was the one thing of which she was sure. Without Paul's support she would have left London that night.

" You must see Racey, and afterwards . . . well, it depends upon yourself what you'll do about Louis."

She nodded again, fighting the reluctance which slowly mounted in her. " There's Midge too."

Paul was paying the bill, and without looking at her he said : " Racey will know about her. He's the one to ask."

" Yes," she said slowly, rising to her feet. She was thinking, as he helped her with her coat, that he understood her fear quite as well as she, but refused to admit it. She held his arm for a minute, feeling and being comforted by his solidity. Paul had always managed to twist events to suit himself, and if only she was willing to stand by and allow him to arrange this, within a week the problem of Louis would be gone forever. She looked at his attractive, friendly face and lean body, wondering why the memory of Louis should come to her now, while she gazed at him.

He broke her train of thought abruptly. " Sue, I must

speak to Jock. Haven't seen him for years. Don't come over with me if you'd rather not. I expect you'd like some sleep. I'll make it as quick as possible."

She began to say 'yes,' then changed her mind. "I'd like to meet him, Paul."

He said doubtfully: "He'll keep us talking for a long time. It isn't easy to get away from Jock."

Susan looked over at the group. There were three men and they were talking loudly over their coffee. As with Paul there was the unmistakable stamp of the pressman about all three. She had never succeeded in defining it to her own satisfaction. What was it?—a young-old look, an alertness, an ability to grow tough when they needed to. All these were aspects of them, but not the complete person. Whatever quality it was, they, like Paul, had it. She experienced a swift desire to be drawn, even for a short time, into that fraternity, to be accepted with Paul, as a part of him.

She said: "Let's go over. I'd like to talk to them."

He didn't reply but took her arm and led her forward. As he noticed them approaching, a heavy, blond man rose to his feet. Unsmilingly, he greeted them. "Hi, Paul. Haven't seen you in years."

"Hi, Jock. Still over this side?"

"Sure," the other growled. "Can't get away from the bloody country. Every damned assignment I get is over here."

Seriously, Paul replied: "Stop whining, Jock. Everyone knows you get these assignments because you apply for them."

"Maybe I do," the blond man answered gloomily. "More bloody fool I." He stared unblinkingly at Susan.

"Jock, this is Susan Taite. Sue—Jock Peterson."

"Pleased to meet you," he said heavily. "Sit down." He continued: "These are pals of mine," and mumbled their names, which Susan forgot immediately. He jerked his head towards Paul. "This is Paul Berkman—someone

I used to know before he inherited a chain of newspapers. I don't know him any more."

"Shut up, Jock," Paul said. "You're getting sour."

The other poked a fleshy finger at him. "Don't know how to be otherwise in this bloody world." He drained his liqueur glass with a vicious gulp. "Might as well die of drink and be happy as live to be blown up by somebody's stray atom bomb."

Paul laughed and Jock glared at him. Abruptly he turned to face Susan. "You said your name was Taite?"

"Yes."

"I know a guy called Taite—Louis Taite."

She said faintly: "Yes. My husband."

Half-drunken laughter spilled out from him. His tired blue eyes were lost in fat creases. "Well, what d'you know? Someone told me he'd got an American wife." He added carelessly: "Don't live with him, do you?"

"No."

He nodded. "Heard that too." Then he stopped laughing. The blue eyes emerged from their thick creases. "Nice guy, Taite. He works for the firm who are publishing a book of mine. Editorial staff."

They all looked at her, expecting her to say something. "Have you known him long?"

"About six months. Nice guy. Knows what he's talking about." He looked round the table. "How about us all having a brandy?"

Paul was the only one who accepted. Susan noticed the satisfaction with which Jock regarded his glass when it was placed before him. "Yes," he went on, "your husband is a nice guy. He always tries to smooth me down when I go to see him. He doesn't always succeed, but he tries. Nice guy."

Susan saw that Jock was going to get tight—that he had sat down with that one purpose in mind, and didn't intend to budge until it was accomplished. She turned round and looked at Paul. He immediately rose to his feet

37

and began to draw out her chair. Jock put down his glass. "You going? Stay and have another drink with me."

"No thanks, Jock. Got to be pushing off."

"Well . . ." He struggled to his feet also. "Was nice seeing you," he said to Paul. And to Susan: "Glad to have met you. I've always liked your husband, you know. Nice guy. If you see him tell him that I said so."

As they walked away Susan could feel the words trailing after her like a thread of cloth. He was repeating them again, ". . . nice guy."

IV

THE FLAT was emptier than usual when Louis got home. It was always empty, blankly so, but to-night the emptiness had a personal quality, something which seemed to stare at him and frown and even murmur. He switched on all the lights in the living-room, and put a match to the fire laid in the grate. It didn't catch immediately. He used two or three matches more, muttering under his breath as he knelt before it. He watched the slow flame for a while, and when it was firmly established, the black cat came out of the kitchen and began rubbing around him, purring in its muted fashion. The cat had no name. Louis called it anything which came into his head, and the cat never took any notice. It didn't belong to him, and although it arrived in the mews one night and had for days after run into the flat whenever the door was opened, it never would belong to Louis. He felt that it merely bided its time with him, and that one day it would leave.

The cat remained by the fire while he went into the hall to collect the letters on the table, and it gazed unblinkingly at him as he mixed a drink. Louis knew he had drunk too much that evening, and wished the cat would stop staring at him, but it merely waited until he had seated himself before the fire with his letters and glass, and then it came and sat beside him. He knew it wasn't affection the cat felt,

38

but the need for human society and warmth. He stroked it absently, before he began slitting the letters.

There wasn't much. A bill, two receipts, a notice of a club dinner, and lastly, a letter from his father. He read this slowly, noticing the uncertain scrawl of the hand-writing, and how, here and there, he neglected to finish a sentence. '*Racey has been down again*,' he wrote. '*We see him quite often.*' Louis turned the page thoughtfully. Racey . . . the beloved son ; how the old man worshipped him. Land and money which could be ill-spared from Hythebourne had provided the runway and hangar for Racey's Proctor, and now the old man lived only for the week-ends when Racey came down to fly. Racey, the cherished one . . . it had always been like that.

The writing continued unsteadily : '*Charlotte must have a pony soon.*' The old man indulged Midge in the same way as Racey, capricious creatures, both of them, whose favour must be won. '*The child needs to ride and Goldi is too slow for her now.*' The note of complaint crept in. '*You should come to see the child more often, Louis. She misses you !*' This last was not wholly true. Midge, a strange little child, missed no one very much. She was shy, reserved, oddly precocious, immediately uncomfortable in the presence of anyone save her grandfather. Beyond the old man, Racey was her only other favourite. Midge was seven, and for the four years since her grandmother's death, she had lived alone at Hythebourne with the old man, and one man-servant. Bullied and scolded by a succession of cooks and housemaids, she was scornful of all these in her rather grand fashion. She was often rude and rebellious, but happy enough if left alone to the vast pile of books in the library, and the old horse, Goldi. The child needed a governess more than a pony, but no governess could be persuaded to stay in that house. The grandfather aided and abetted Midge in her rebellion. There was a strange passionate devotion between the two.

Louis shifted in his chair uneasily. Poor little beggar ; she'd have to go to school sometime, and it was going to be difficult to bring that about. His father would refuse to help, he knew, pointing as evidence to the fact that Midge could read as well as children twice her age, and that she didn't need a school yet. Louis knew all this, and it wasn't the rate at which Midge read, but the kind of book which fell into her hands that troubled him. He knew, vaguely, that other small girls weren't like Midge, but he didn't know what to do about it, or even in which direction the difference lay. It wasn't the way to bring a child up, spoiled and yet neglected, longing for, yet determinedly scornful of the care which other children of her acquaintance received. She had grown into a proud and rather pathetic little creature, with dull brown hair in long plaits, and her grandfather's changing, brilliant blue eyes.

He laid the letter down swiftly. Something would have to be done about Midge soon, in spite, or perhaps because of his father.

The cat jumped from the chair and looked at him angrily when he got up. If it had dared to, it would have spat. Louis said: "Look, cat, I'm going to work. You can have the chair to yourself now if you want it." Instead the cat turned his back and sank down before the fire, eyes closed.

Louis rather reluctantly moved towards his desk and got out the chapter he had been working on. He sat down and read the last page. It wasn't too bad, but it was several days since he'd worked on it. The thread was going to be difficult to pick up again. He screwed a blank sheet of paper into the typewriter, and swiftly tapped out the first sentence of a new paragraph. The sound of the machine in that quiet room was shattering. He read the sentence over, then blotted it out hurriedly. He tried it again and it wasn't any better than before. Then he grew angry and impatient with himself, because since he'd started writing this book he'd grown into the habit of not allowing his thoughts to come between himself and the sentences taking shape in his mind. The idea that his self-discipline had failed caused him to plough savagely on, writing at a foolish speed, cursing the typing errors and each small hesitation which held him back. When the page at last slipped from the carriage, he picked it up and reread it. A few minutes later he laid it down, resisting the impulse to tear it up. It wasn't any good at all. He slumped back in his chair glad to forget about it.

He should have known it was useless to try to work this evening. He still felt a shoot of anger through him when he remembered the clerk's empty efficiency in telling him that his wife had already registered. It was pretty bad to think he'd lived with a woman for more than two years and hadn't recognised her when she'd walked across the foyer in front of his eyes.

God, was the hellish period of blankness ever going to end, were the bits ever going to fall into place again? It was sickening to have to go on pretending that he knew as well as everyone else what had happened during that period. How many newspaper files had he now read in order to fill in the gap? And of his personal life nothing remained, not even a photograph. And in his child there was sometimes a fleeting likeness . . . to whom? . . . a memory just on the fringe of his consciousness. The woman to whom that memory belonged could be reached on the other end of a telephone line. And still he didn't go to it and call her.

He pushed the chair aside awkwardly and got up. There wasn't a thing he could do about it except go through with this divorce and hope that the woman who was his wife would cease to trouble his thoughts any longer, would remain as little a part of his life as she had been for the past six years. Racey had sometimes tried to tell him what she had looked like, what her personality had been, but somehow Racey's description had made her sound like a cover-girl, beautiful, impersonal—every man's sweetheart. And that couldn't have been his wife. No matter how different he had been then, he couldn't have married a woman like that.

Knowing well that he ought not to, he got himself

another drink. God damn it, what had she been like . . his wife ? Beautiful, they said, and American, aggressively American. Perhaps she'd been like the woman he'd bought a drink for this evening. But that woman hadn't been beautiful, not in a regular fashion. When she'd begun to talk—what little she had said—he'd seen something beyond beauty in her face. The too-large mouth that was generous and warm, and the lovely flowing lines of her body when she had walked away from him. Her beauty had lain in those things, as in the small frown of worry he'd noticed between her eyes, and the skin at the back of her ears which the arrangement of her hair had revealed. She'd looked tired and strangely distraught, and he'd noticed her fingers holding the glass tightly, as if she didn't want to shake . . .

It seemed a long time afterwards, and he had refilled his glass several times, when the quiet buzz of the phone started in the hall. He took his drink with him when he went to answer it. It seemed to take a long time for him to lift the handpiece into position. " Hallo."

" Hallo, Louis." This was Elizabeth's quiet voice. This was the woman who expected to marry him when his divorce was final. He had written Elizabeth into his story and had said she possessed beauty of a classical kind, with silver-blonde hair. Sometimes she looked so perfect he didn't think it was necessary to talk to her, but to just look. This annoyed Elizabeth.

" Louis, are you alone ? "

" I think so. There's something sitting in front of the fire, but I think it's only the cat."

He imagined, rather than heard the small intake of breath. She said tonelessly : " You're tight."

" Yes, terribly."

He knew she wanted to reproach him, and he knew also, that she was afraid. Elizabeth wasn't often afraid to say exactly what she thought. " You can ring me when you're sober," she said finally. " We might be able to talk then."

The click of the phone when she put it down was gentle, but quite decided.

He stood looking at it rather foolishly. He hadn't had any intention of being rude to Elizabeth, but he wasn't sorry. She had been right—he was tight, and while he thought of it, he raised the glass and drained it. The drink was beginning to taste bitter on his tongue now, but he didn't want to stop. Ideas weren't sharp in his mind any more ; they all had a pleasant blur on their edges, so that when he reached out for a telephone directory, he didn't quite register what he was doing. It was more of a trouble than he expected, finding the number, but he got it at last and dialled it. An operator's voice, brisk and efficient like the clerk's answered him.

He said slowly, his tones thickened with the drink : " I want to speak to Mrs. Taite."

V

PAUL REGARDED the door of the bathroom through a haze of smoke and half-closed eyes. Steam curled slowly round the door and had started to blur the mirror before which Susan's row of bottles stood like an array of child's toys. Her brush and comb were as she had left them after fixing her hair into an arrangement which threatened to tumble down about her ears each time she moved her head. He looked around the room and saw nothing else out of place ; only the steam making its way firmly through the smoke gave an indication of her presence.

He got up and crossed to the dressing-table. Even as he did so he was aware of a faint wonder at the back of his mind at the strength of this woman's attraction for him. He looked down at her belongings—she suddenly became defenceless before him, as if in these trappings to her existence she was capable of being judged. He ran his eyes along the line ; perfume bottles in an amazing variety of shapes, nail polish, lotions, creams, and at the farther end, dominating all, a plump, squat bottle of French Cologne.

He picked up the brush and removed a strand of hair, watching it idly as it settled in the wastepaper basket. Then he turned and walked towards the bathroom.

Susan was sitting on a stool, a bathrobe hanging loosely on her, drying her legs. The room smelt of bath essence and powder, and was like the row of bottles on a large scale. She looked up when he entered, and he saw that one side of her hair had escaped the pins and had fallen on her neck. It was a strange lop-sided effect, and he noticed how the small curls clung damply to her skin. Her body was very beautiful, white and soft, and he wanted desperately to bend and kiss the hollow between her breasts.

She smiled at him, and began to feel for her slippers. He pushed them a little nearer, and watched, fascinated, the movements of her thighs as she suddenly thrust her feet forward into them. She stood up and drew the bath-robe round her.

" Won't be long," she said.

He grinned at her reflection in the mirror. " Don't hurry. I like to watch."

She laughed, a pleased laugh, and he noticed there was no strain in it any longer. Now that those sickening moments in the restaurant were over, the spiritless droop to her mouth had disappeared. She looked happy. He stepped nearer and began to kiss a patch of still damp skin behind her ear. She twisted suddenly and put her arms about his neck. He kissed her on the mouth and pressed small, nibbling kisses on her eyelids, feeling her move closer to him, and all the despair and weariness of the past hours fell away from her. For the first time since the plane had put down that afternoon, she was the person to whom he was accustomed. He drew her body close and held her gratefully.

The sound of the telephone cut deeply into their kiss. Unwilling to break it he held her still. But her body began to stiffen in his arms so he withdrew, a dull kind of resentment beginning to mount in him.

She hesitated at the bathroom door for long seconds,

and he knew, almost, what she was thinking, what fear held her back. " Shall I take it, Susan ? "

" No . . . no, I'll get it." She moved across the room with a half-run, the bath-robe trailing behind. She caught up the phone and again a hesitation seized her. It was a long time before she spoke. " Hallo."

Paul watched her, and her face told him nothing except that she was listening. For perhaps a minute she waited and then slowly replaced the receiver. She slumped down on the bed, shoulders hunched, hands clasped between her legs.

" That was Louis," she said. " He waited till he heard my voice, then he hung up."

Paul came towards her, and now he was struggling not to betray his furious anger. " Are you sure ? "

" Yes," she said. " Quite sure." She bent forward and her head slipped down into her hands. He heard her give a little sigh, low and wretched.

SATURDAY

I

THE GENTLE swish of the rain against the window pane was like a mournful little *obligato*, a muted and reedy accompaniment to Susan's thoughts. She pressed against the window, watching the rain drifting in a heavy mist against the trees in the Park, and down below it lay in grey pools on the road. The stream of traffic was unending; the grey pools dissolved and re-formed with each passing car. Watching this for a time, watching the policeman who either halted the flow or hurried it forward, so that it resembled the sudden emergence of a swarm of black ants into a single, disciplined line, she managed to thrust her disquietude to the back of her mind. But it returned—the first subject in a musical pattern it reannounced itself loudly—and continued in increasing crescendo. She fought helplessly against its rising swell, beat at it, but it went on, louder and bigger, until its largeness was something from which she recoiled.

Paul entered, and the fierce momentum of her thoughts dropped away. He crossed to her immediately, and kissed her without a word; in silence they stood close together, listening to the sounds of the rain on the window beside them, and the far-away muffled echo of the traffic. Then, against her own, Susan felt his body stiffen, and knew that his moment of respite was finished. He drew away from her. She watched him taking out a cigarette case, wordlessly extending it towards her. She shook her head.

"Would you like me to get hold of Louis' lawyers?" he said.

She nodded in the direction of the phone. "Yes, do. You'll find them in the book. Lawley and Patterson."

While he flicked through the pages of the directory, she moved over to the dressing-table. Studying him through the mirror, she saw the thin cloud of white smoke from his cigarette drifting past his head. When at last he lifted the receiver and asked for a number, she sat down stiffly on the stool, folding her hands in her lap. She watched the ash on the cigarette grow longer while he listened. Across the room she could hear the steady burr-burr of the telephone ringing. He looked over at her.

"These people obviously work a thirty-hour week. Nothing doing until Monday."

"Monday? Oh, damn!" She rose impatiently, striking the dressing-table heavily with her body, and setting the toilet bottles jingling against each other. As she walked to the cupboard she fought down the panic which had been with her since the telephone call last night. She took a coat from its hanger, and Paul, watching, saw the two spots of colour which flamed in her cheeks.

"I can't waste another day," she said. "I'll get in touch with Racey."

He drew at his cigarette, and said gently: "Come here, Sue. I want to talk to you."

She didn't move. "What is it?"

He stood up. "About Louis," he said.

"Yes?"

"Are you quite sure, Sue, that you want to go through with this?"

The words left a cold little silence between them until she said at last: "Of course, I'm sure. Why do you ask?"

But all the urgency had departed from his face and voice. He stubbed out the cigarette carefully. "Perhaps . . . I'm a bit premature in giving my little speech. Better leave it till you've seen Racey."

She moved towards him swiftly. "Paul, you're not being fair. If you've got something to say, then I've a right to hear it."

He caught her gently by the arm. "Look, Sue, it isn't going to do any good to go over this again. We'll get

47

no further than we did last night. Both of us—we'll have to wait." He took the coat off her arm, and threw it across the bed. She looked at it vacantly, feeling both his hands holding her now at the elbows. His voice had been so quiet. She remembered that Paul's voice never grew excited : it was impossible to tell how he was reacting to a situation. Impossible to do anything for him with the certainty that it was right. How little or how much, she wondered, was it possible to understand a person and still love ? Without hope of an answer, the problem hung at the back of her mind.

She said slowly : " I'll see Racey. That will straighten things out. We'll know what to do then." Even in uttering the words they rang falsely. She had known for a long time—last evening when she had talked with Louis—that events were shaping their own course. She sensed a movement of the inevitable ; she being pulled with it, Paul standing out against it. It was all these things of which they were both aware, these things of which they should be talking, and didn't. Instead, she merely repeated her last words.

" We'll know what to do then."

He didn't answer her directly, and she knew he had guessed her thoughts. Even when he kissed her, the unvoiced knowledge was there between them, so that for the brief moment he held her in his arms, it was an embrace of desperation, a silent appeal against what he sensed was about to happen—what was happening now.

He released her suddenly and said : " I'll have to hurry, Sue. There'a a lot of people I've got to see this morning. Will you be free for lunch ? "

With Racey still in her mind she replied absently : " No. I shouldn't think so."

He dropped a final, light kiss on her forehead, and didn't question her further. " Then I'll see you back here in time for a drink before dinner ? Right ? " She nodded and smiled, and as he left her, she noticed that he had already taken out another cigarette.

When he was gone she looked round the room, realising that she hadn't any idea how he would spend the day. He was gone already; his own concerns had swallowed him up. But more significant than that—she had been left quite alone, He did nothing to keep her with him, nothing to prevent her wandering further into this maze of uncertainty. He understood the danger fully as well as she, but a lightly phrased suggestion to lunch together had been his only defence. His passionate insistence upon her integrity prevented more. She crossed to the window swiftly and pressed her face sideways against the pane. Far below, she could see the thin trickle of people emerging from the main entrance of the hotel. At last he came, overcoat and hat on now, his head slightly bent before the rain. He moved off towards Piccadilly with the certainty of a one-time Londoner. She pressed her face closer to the pane to catch the last glimpse of him. It was at once courageous and foolish of him to have left her like this. He was disappearing into the sprawling, mist-shrouded stretches of the city for a whole day, as much apart from her as if he had remained in Paris. And she, vulnerable and bewildered, the telephone call to Racey yet unmade, felt the day stretching before her like a grey wilderness. Anything could happen. Paul knew all this, and still he had gone and left her.

She moved at last across to the phone, and took up the directory. Taite A . . . Taite D . . . Taite G . . . Taite Horace—and Racey's number. Her finger slid farther down the list till it rested on Louis' number. He still had the flat in Carlton Mews. She wondered had it changed at all. Her own possessions had been in that flat; things chosen and matched at the cost of endless trouble and time. Her books and his had mingled in the shelves; she had chosen the ornaments and given them their appointed place, and he had never disputed her right to do so. Suddenly she knew a desperate longing to see it again, to see for herself if Louis had returned after she had gone and plucked out each separate thing that had been hers, if his anger against

49

her caused him to sacrifice her possessions. The desire to know these things mounted swiftly, but, impatient with herself, she cast it aside, and picked up the receiver and gave the operator Racey's number.

After a long time someone answered sleepily. It was a man's voice, but not Racey's.

She said crisply : " Is Mr. Taite there, please ? "

" Just a moment," the voice said. It was a pleasant, good-natured voice. " Who's calling ? "

She hesitated, looking for the right words. " Tell him it's Susan—Susan Taite."

Racey's voice came almost immediately. He was excited. " Susan ? "

" Hallo, Racey."

" Witch, I didn't know you were in London ! When did you arrive ? "

" Last night. Didn't Louis tell you I was coming ? "

He laughed softly—Racey's old laugh. " He certainly didn't. He knows better." He hesitated, and the laughter died away. " Sue, have you seen him yet ? "

" Well . . . yes, and no." Sue attacked him without warning. " Racey, why didn't you let me know . . . about his memory going ? "

He defended himself too swiftly. " What was the use ? It didn't make any difference to you in New York. He was dead against it. And, hell, Sue . . . you can't blame me for not knowing you were coming over. I can't be expected to guess these things."

" No . . . I suppose not." She was repenting her quick words. Haste betrayed so much of one's feelings, and Racey had always been skilful at probing. " Look, I'll have to talk to you about this. There's so little I know about him—about what happened. When can I see you ? "

" Witch, any time you say. What about lunch ? "

She wasn't prepared. It was too soon. " No, not then, Racey. A bit later. Tea ? "

" Susan, don't be stingy. I'm not the type for tea."

She said firmly: "It's got to be tea, Racey. I want to come along and see you. We've got to talk, remember."

His voice sounded fretful. "All right, but . . ."

She cut across him. "I suppose the address in the phone book is right? I'll come along about four. See you then."

"Susan, wait a minute . . ."

She hung up as if she hadn't heard.

II

IT RAINED all the morning—a light, unhurried rain which made little dreary pools in the pavements, and slanted down on the faces of the Saturday shoppers. Susan lunched alone, grateful for the quiet, the table in the corner, the anonymity one achieves in a crowded restaurant. Her body ached with a strange kind of weariness—the weariness of walking the streets and being a stranger in them, the futility of idleness when others were busy. London, grey and remote under the rain had failed to open out before her. She had wandered among her old haunts, and they had greeted her as very slight acquaintances, nodding, smiling thinly, a trifle unsure of her identity. Everywhere had changed. Cream paint and red and blue doors . . . trim gardens in the squares and the first leaves lying on the grass. The cleared bomb sites were car-parks. And here, in her favourite restaurant, the waiters were new.

She ate her food slowly, wondering what Paul was doing. The thought of Racey kept running through her mind, but she drove it out determinedly. It wasn't any use thinking what she would say to him. There was no need to pretend with Racey. When the time came she would say as much as she felt like saying, and no more. He would laugh at her, of course. Racey had always laughed at her when she wanted him to be serious. But she could make him tell her the truth. One could rely on Racey to tell the truth most of the time. Only when truth was inconvenient did he hedge around it with supreme skill.

It had stopped raining when she came out to the street

again. The morning shoppers were all gone. Instead there were cinema queues—long lines of people standing patiently in the pools left by the rain. Jermyn Street was quiet, St. James's Street empty. An occasional taxi cruised down towards the Mall. The Palace clock pointed to twenty minutes past three. Susan took the path under the dripping trees at the edge of the Green Park. There was no one sitting on the wet benches, and all the deck chairs had been stacked in piles. She felt the quietness to be deceptive, as if the city was waiting restlessly for the dusk to fall and the hum of business to start once more. It waited for the typists and the shopgirls who had departed at one o'clock to hurry back, take their places in the queues outside the cinemas and the Corner Houses. It waited for all the people to whom Saturday night was the point of the whole week. And even wet Saturdays couldn't make a difference.

At Hyde Park Corner she caught a bus which took her up to Marble Arch. She began walking towards Seymour Street, keeping her pace deliberately slow because it was still only ten-to-four. The block Racey lived in was large and undistinguished. Susan remembered that one of the Embassy Staff had lived here during the blitz. It wasn't hard to see Racey fitted in against this modern and impersonal background, living, probably, with someone else's furniture and china, and demanding nothing more than hot water whenever he wanted a bath and someone to come and make his bed in the morning.

She rode up in the lift and found his flat without any trouble. She could hear the sound of running water as she rang the bell. It ceased abruptly, and after about thirty seconds, Racey opened the door. Susan was unprepared for the sight of him, so completely unchanged against his changed background. Even without his uniform he was exactly as she had remembered him, more like her memory of Louis than even Louis himself was. She felt herself being taken in his arms. He kissed her hard on the mouth.

"Witch, you're more beautiful than ever! Let me look at you properly." He held her off a little.

Susan wanted to brush him aside gently as one might an over-demonstrative dog, but instead she smiled at him. " You haven't changed, Racey—not at all."

He laughed while he helped her with her coat. " No, I don't change, except for the worse." He laughed again, plainly not believing his own statement. His good-humour was obvious. It was easy to please Racey, easy to anger him also. He led her forward into a living-room where a tea-tray was already laid on a low table. Susan sat down on the lounge and he took an armchair opposite.

." Well, Witch, tell me all about it." He offered her a cigarette ; she took it and waited for him to light it before answering.

" Where do I begin ? " It suddenly seemed a colossal task to tell Racey everything which had taken place.

" The beginning, of course. Have you come straight from New York ? "

She drew on her cigarette. " Things had better come in their right order. In the first place, I've been in Paris— on business. And with my boss, Paul Berkman."

He laughed, unkindly. " What are you, Sue ? A kind of super private secretary ? " He laughed again as he saw her annoyance mount. She was more attractive when she grew angry.

She said quietly : " Shut up, Racey ! I haven't got time to play around. Paul Berkman owns a newspaper syndicate. I work on one of his magazines and I've been covering the autumn fashion shows in Paris for it."

Racey flushed darkly ; his eyes lingered on her suit and hat. " And what has Mr. Berkman been doing ? Buying you the models ? "

She reached unhurriedly for an ash-tray. " Paul and I are going to be married."

He didn't say anything at first. Then he got to his feet and leaned with his back to the mantelpiece. Susan was glad of the silence ; Racey always needed a little time to collect his thoughts—or to control them. Anything was better than his light cynicism—unhelpful, he was almost unfriendly.

At last he said : " That, of course, is why you're in London. The divorce."

" Yes. We've got to get things settled. There's Midge, too."

He said thoughtfully : " I'm glad you've remembered Midge."

Susan sprang to her feet and came close to him. " I don't have to be reminded of Midge."

" Quiet, Witch," he said casually. " I'm not blaming you for clearing out. It's a pity, though, that you did it in such a hurry. Midge is a nice little kid—but odd, definitely odd."

Her anger receded a trifle. " That's hardly my fault. Even if I'd stayed I couldn't have made much difference. As it was I had so little to do with her up-bringing. . . ."

" Yes, Sue, I know all that, but still . . . Well, you'll probably see Midge for yourself. My mother's dead, you know. Midge has been living at Hythebourne with Father and old Sydney these past four years." He began to chuckle softly. " God . . . God, she's a rum little kid."

Susan walked away from him and sat down. She could feel the nails of her left hand biting into her palm. This was all such a mess. She wished she didn't feel so frightened and so unequal to going through with this struggle. The whole story and six years was too much to recover in one day. Louis and Midge . . . the old man alone now at Hythebourne . . . and Racey leaning there against the mantel, smooth and conventionally handsome, smiling at her and at her bewilderment. She drew at her cigarette. It gave her some slight satisfaction to see that her hand was quite steady.

She said slowly : " Racey, I want you to tell me exactly what happened to Louis. Everything."

He stopped smiling. " It was one of those things you've got to expect to happen in war. It happens to a certain number—it might have been me."

Susan looked at him clearly. " No, not to you, Racey. Things like that never happened to you, did they ? " Even as she spoke she wondered why she had made that comparison. Six years ago there had been no essential difference between the two. But last night's conversation with Louis had marked a clear division. They were no longer an entity, two persons to be thought of as one. Susan edged forward on the lounge. Out of this meeting with Racey was coming the key to Louis' personality, an insight into something which had baffled and almost defeated her.

" Go on," she said. " I didn't mean to interrupt."

" It's the same story you've heard so often before, Sue. You've probably read it a dozen times, but that doesn't make it any the less true or real. It wasn't long after you'd gone back to New York. Louis was on a bomber escort mission, and he was shot down over France. We heard he was missing, and then, much later, presumed dead."

She held her body very still, listening to the words, seeking in them more than their limited meaning.

" He came back eventually, and then we got the story. He'd had a head wound, and the underground people had found him and looked after him. They couldn't risk a doctor coming, and he almost died. They kept him at a farmhouse all the time, until he could travel. Too long, I think. It began to get dangerous for all of them. Then in the end they gave him papers, and the farmer's son, a kid of fourteen, went with him right down to Spain. He was very ill, Susan, and the kid was like an angel."

" What happened ? "

" Louis went on, and the kid went back. God knows, he would have been safer to have come on with Louis to England, but he wouldn't. Didn't explain. Just left him and turned back."

She thought about it for a long time. Even presented in Racey's matter of fact phrases she could feel the danger and the loneliness. The incredible faith which had sustained life through such a succession of days. The long journey home through France and Spain—and Louis had been ill.

" Why," she asked, " didn't you let me know ? He was presumed dead, you say ? "

"We weren't sure, Sue. It was a tricky business. And then . . . there was Mother."

She jerked her head sharply to look at him. "You mean she wouldn't let anyone tell me? My God! What right had she . . . how did she dare . . . ?"

"She was an old woman, Sue, and ill. You can't blame her overmuch."

"Why? Because she thought I didn't care?"

He said smoothly and justly: "How were we to decide except by your own actions? After all, you had . . ."

She cut across him shortly. "Yes, I know. I had left him."

She leaned back, turning her gaze away from him. So even after she had gone, she thought, the old woman's anger carried a striking power, a power to hurt her now, after six years. There had been such a queenly, dignified tyranny in the old woman. Her word had ruled at Hythebourne. The habit of despotism is not easily broken, Louis' mother had not given it up, even in death.

Once more Susan faced Racey. "What was he like when he came back?"

He shook his head, coming to sit beside her on the lounge. "It was pretty bad, Sue. He was sent straight to hospital, and kept there. God knows how he managed to make the trip home. It was pretty grim. He didn't know me when he saw me first."

He stopped, but her impatience couldn't allow him a pause. "Go on. Did you have to tell him everything?"

"I told him as much as I thought he could take in. I didn't let the old people see him until I'd coached him a bit. He knew enough then to be able to talk to them sensibly."

"And me?" She caught impulsively at his arm. "What did you tell him about me?"

His eyebrows pointed upwards in two question marks. "Everything I could think of."

"Yes, of course." She released her hold and sank back again. "What else?"

Racey's tone was more gentle when he picked up once

more. " He began to remember things gradually. Bits here and there . . . school and college, flying and so on. When he left hospital he knew enough to keep the people round Hythebourne from being too much aware of what had happened. I suppose the pieces have been falling into place ever since."

" How much do you think he remembers by this time ? "

" Almost everything, I think. He's stopped asking me questions long ago, but I know he still has one or two bad moments when a complete stranger rushes up and claims him as a school friend, or a member of his squadron."

" Does he ever talk about it now ? "

" No, never. He's sensitive about it. Likes you to think it never happened."

She sat quietly and thought for a few minutes, putting Racey completely out of mind. Yesterday evening, Louis had told her of the accident as easily as he might have spoken of a burnt hand, something to be passed over casually. But Racey said he never talked of it. Not even now could she believe he had perpetuated a supreme piece of mockery in not recognising her. Where was the purpose in it, or the purpose in the telephone call last night ? If there was malice behind it, it was malice so subtle it stood more than one chance of failing to hit its mark.

She said slowly : " Give me a cigarette, will you ? " When it was lit she leaned back against the cushions. " Racey," she began slowly, " would you say that Louis knew what I looked like ? "

He shrugged. " I don't know. He used to ask me about you—what you looked like. He didn't have a photo, you know. But he hasn't asked me anything for a long time now. I couldn't say whether he's not interested any more, or whether he's remembered for himself."

She said then : " What did he feel about my going ? Did he hate me for it ? "

" How can you hate what you don't know ? "

That was the very worst of it, she knew. Louis could feel nothing for her—neither hate nor love. It denied her personality, transformed her into a shadow, a ghost. Once again she leaned forward and caught Racey's arm. "I saw him, Racey. Last night."

He nodded slowly. "Yes. I've been waiting to hear this."

She told him briefly. It was not the same as telling Paul. He faced her quietly and without interruption allowed her to finish. Between them was a knowledge of Louis such as Paul could never possess. In the simple telling the scene became clear-cut, never ridiculous or fantastic as it had seemed last night. In the end, when she had finished the short recital, there remained only one further question, and Racey voiced it immediately.

"And what you want to know is whether his not recognising you was a pretence?" He shook his head and his voice lacked his usual casualness. "That's something I couldn't decide."

The words dropped heavily, like stones into deep water. She said softly: "What shall I do? Racey, tell me what to do."

He sat watching her, expecting to see the corners of her mouth quiver. But they remained still, like the hand which held the cigarette, like the other, lying so peacefully in her lap. He watched her calm face, thinking how she had altered in these six years. This Susan was quiet and mature, a beautiful woman; the other Susan, the one he knew best, had been his kind, restless, vital, expending energy and love with extravagant hands. She had been beautiful too, but in quite another fashion. She had suited both brothers then— only it had been Louis who had married her. He wondered what Louis had thought of her last night, wondered if he had known that she was marked with the change of every one of those six years, that to know her one must humbly start from the beginning and learn all over again.

He drew closer to her. "Sue?"

"Yes?" She hadn't turned her head.

"Don't worry about it too much. It must work itself out in time."

She looked at him startled. " Time ? But there is no time. There's only a week. That's not real time—that's only days and hours and minutes."

She was acutely aware of the pressure of his arm as he drew her closer. " Leave time to itself, Sue. These things have a way of looking after themselves."

She made a passionate objection. " That's madness. How can I stand by and not worry when this decision must be made. Am I to see Louis or not ? "

He caught her shoulders then, holding her at arm's length. " What are you afraid of, Sue ? Which of them do you fear most—Louis or Paul ? "

" Why should I fear either of them ? "

" But you are afraid. You've come to me because you're afraid."

" No . . ." She uttered only the single word, then stopped because there was no reason to go on denying the truth of his statement. She clasped her hands together and rocked forward a little, head bent. She said : " I am afraid. I'm afraid of Louis because of what he may do to me, and of Paul . . . because I may lose him."

His hands still on her shoulders, he shook her lightly. " Witch, your old age has turned you into a fool. Don't you know that fear drives out sanity. Keep your head, for God's sake, or you'll lose everything."

She swayed back, out of his clasp.

He watched her for a moment longer, and when she said nothing more, smiled lightly, and stood up.

" Hang on for a bit. I'll get some tea." He began to whistle, a light, high tune, as he left the room.

Susan watched the long grey ash on her cigarette fall to the floor. She took two more draws, then stubbed it out, brushing the powder from her skirt as she stood up.

She was in Racey's place, back resting against the low, modern mantel, when he returned with the tea and hot-water jug. He still whistled the same skittish tune, breaking here and there when his own movements with the cups and saucers absorbed him, and then resuming. It was a strange little tune, sweet, high, and, heard now amid her bafflement and confusion, curiously moving.

" Racey, what is it . . . that tune ? "

He faced her, still bending over the tray but with eyes upraised. " Can't remember exactly. I used to know a ballet dancer. . . . I've sat and watched her dance to it dozens of times. I don't think I ever knew its name."

" The girl . . . what became of her."

His shrug was careless, unthinking. " I don't know. Lost touch with her years ago." He shrugged again, laughing this time. " Where do they all go, Sue—all the beautiful girls one used to know ? Precious, lovely, exciting creatures. Why don't they stay that way ? "

She said drily, as she came to sit down beside the tea-tray once more : " Very few of them can afford the time to hang round waiting for you to miss them."

" Quiet, Witch," he said, and laughed again. She was getting tired of him laughing.

They were silent while they drank the tea, neither making any attempt to touch the food on the tray. With Racey's face in profile, Susan studied it carefully, wondering all over again at the strange similarity between the two brothers—a similarity which had once been complete, and which now had limits. She was making a comparison in a way which had never been possible. The sensation that she walked on the edge of a discovery returned, and she broke the silence abruptly to question him. " Racey, what are you doing these days ? Do you ever fly ? "

He put down his cup quickly. " I've just been thinking about that," he said. " About something that might help you."

Susan replaced her cup also, waiting for him to go on.

" The point is, Sue, that I've got a job as liaison officer between an aircraft factory and the various civil aviation lines who take their crates. It means regular trips to the Continent and so on—I got as far as South America once, but that's by the way. Whenever there's a job to be done in France I go over under my own steam. The plane's kept down at Hythebourne because it's an easy hopping-off spot."

He stopped, and she said impatiently : "Where's this getting me, Racey ?" She regretted the tone a second later, for a shade of annoyance ran over his face.

"I'm coming to that. The point is I'm making my next trip to-morrow night. It means going down to Hythebourne first. Do you want to come ?"

Put to her like that, the question was unanswerable. The shock of it was like a visible curtain between herself and Racey, something which had cut her off and shut her into a world where decisions must be faced and made with frightening speed. He waited coolly on the other side, waited for what she would say.

Susan stood up and moved once more to the mantel, standing with her back to him, as much to remove her gaze from his calm detachment, as to hide her own face. She began to finger the small ornaments, one by one, her hands at last resting upon one she recognised. The memory came to her through long passages of time, and she saw the small Dresden cup and saucer once more in the place they had occupied in the drawing-room at Hythebourne. Racey had brought them here, he alone knew for what reason, for they were almost grotesquely out of place in that fashionably bare flat. Her fingers dropped away from the china quickly. They belonged at Hythebourne ; were not hers to touch or think upon. The house and family had always drawn back from her, half-distrusting, half-fearing her. Even during that wearyingly long period before and after Midge's birth when she had lived there, she had been a stranger, speaking a language and knowing a way of life which had scarcely been comprehended. To return to it, even for a day, seemed unthinkable. But what of her child, Midge, growing up against the background of Hythebourne and the old man's ministrations ? To have the child brought up to London for an interview would defeat its own purpose. To come suddenly upon the situation as Racey proposed, would be to strike the reality of it. There was a careful wisdom in his suggestion, tossed at her so lightly, like a challenge he thought she lacked the courage to accept. To see Midge in her everyday state, to capture a swift, true knowledge of the child, was surely half the reason why this trip had been made.

Susan turned to him and said steadily: " Yes, I'd like to come. What time are you going? "

She looked for surprise or approval, but he gave none. " I'd like to start about eleven in the morning. Perhaps we could get lunch at a pub on the way down."

She nodded, experiencing once again the sensation that events were moving beyond her control; they pressed forward to a climax not of her own designing.

III

FROM CARLTON MEWS Louis made his way through the wet streets swiftly. It had taken him a long time to reach this decision—last night, when he hadn't slept, hours lying still in the darkness; listening to the night sounds of the city about him slowly give place to the silence of the dawn; hours during the morning when he had paced the flat in a fever of self-questioning.

And suddenly the doubt and indecision had fled; he cursed the spent hours. He quickened his pace, and the wet, empty streets he traversed echoed with the sound of his steps. St. James's Square was deserted, save for a solitary car-park attendant. In the Green Park he followed the path which Susan had taken earlier; but then he crossed through the muddle of Shepherd's Market and finally broke through into Park Lane. He had very little hope that he would find her in the hotel at that time, but he never slackened his pace.

A rush of warm air met him as he entered the foyer. He checked with the reception clerk, then slowly turned and selected a chair, settling with infinite patience, to wait for her arrival.

Susan walked back to the hotel. It had begun to rain

again—heavier now, and more purposeful. She glanced regretfully at her splashed stockings, at the pools reappearing on the streets, the hurrying figures bent slightly under umbrellas. At Marble Arch the cinema queues stretched in long lines on the edge of the pavements. 1s. 9d. *Queue Here*, the notice said. The people stood patiently in the rain. The barrow boys in Park Lane offered her their wares with mechanical persuasion. She glanced at them indifferently, and suddenly the weariness and fear she had fought all the day overwhelmed her. In the midst of that press of people she halted, shoulders brushed on either side by passing strangers. At last she made her way to the kerb and hailed a passing taxi to take her the few blocks to the hotel. She noticed that her hands trembled as she paid it off, and mounting the few steps was a short nightmare. Inside, the soft warmth enfolded her; a trifle unsteadily she moved towards the reception desk.

Through the glass doors, Louis had seen her pay off the taxi. He was already standing as she approached.

She stopped short when she saw him, and for one second he thought she would fall. An incredibly swift shadow of emotion passed across her face, too swift for him to read it, and afterwards it was gravely composed. Her face was now as still as her body. He advanced towards her.

He said with deliberate quietness : " Hallo, Susan."

" Hallo, Louis."

There was nothing to be said in that first moment. He was looking at her with eyes of recognition, and everything in her wanted to welcome him back from the dead. But she could say nothing. His face also was grave, but somewhere beneath the surface there glowed briefly a trace of a salute to her, a kind of gesture of renewed friendship which was much more than his mere greeting. Between them, in the fixed gaze of their eyes, the distant and half-forgotten past slipped into focus, as if a strong light beat down suddenly upon it. The silence was more significant than any words they might have used; it said more for them—fear, astonishment, regret. All this was said for them, and still more remained.

Louis touched her arm gently. She struggled to remove herself from that long, fixated stare. "Let's go into the bar," he said. "It's quieter there."

As she turned slowly in that direction his hand fell away from her, a studied, careful movement which made her wonder if perhaps he feared to make too great an encroachment upon her person. In the bar they found a small table and he seated himself opposite her. There was no haste in his manner as he ordered the drinks. While they waited, he silently gave her a cigarette and lit it.

Suddenly, as he held the lighter before her, he smiled. It was like the beginning of something entirely new, a different hour, a different day. The frail cord of tension between them snapped, or was forgotten, and its ends slipped away unnoticed. She dropped her eyes to the table, but somehow she knew that he was still smiling.

During the pause when the drinks were placed on the table and he paid for them, she kept her eyes away from him. She clutched her handbag tightly in her lap, and with the tip of her toe beat a nervous, soundless little rhythm on the carpet. These were the moments before the curtain went up, the moments of uncertainty and hesitation. He broke into them in a low voice.

"Well, Sue . . . here's to us."

"And to hell with the rest of them." It had been their old phrase, something to laugh at long ago, and it slipped off her tongue with forgotten ease.

She sipped at the drink slowly, cold now, and shaken by this betrayal of her tongue. There was danger for her in every word spoken here, danger for her if he smiled again, a threat to her security in each resurrected memory. She began to long for the moment of release from him.

He allowed the silence to continue only a moment longer. There was the small sound of his glass against the table top and then he leaned forward. Looking at her, there was no hint as to her thoughts, no clue in that quiet, waiting face. Her fingers, curled about the stem of the glass, were still. In that brief moment he noticed again their peaceful beauty, just as he had seen it last night. He saw that they were strong hands, reposeful but alert, betraying her thoughts to no superficial scrutiny.

He asked the first question gently. " Why didn't you tell me last night, Susan ? "

She ran her tongue across her lips, gaining precious seconds. " How could I ? " she said at last. " I thought . . . in the beginning I thought you knew me. After that it was too late."

" But why, Susan ? Why ? "

A sharp recollection of the uncertainty and doubt of the past twenty-four hours came to her. Passionately, almost angrily, she defended herself. " How could I ? It was an intolerable position. I did the best I could."

Her face was flushed and troubled ; its calm had broken. He pressed his advantage swiftly. " The best ? I don't think so. You should have told me."

" How could I ? " she said once more. " You gave me no chance."

" There was plenty of chance. Did you lack the courage ? After all, I'm used to shocks . . . people I've never seen before suddenly claiming me, patches in my life about which I can't remember a thing. Think of it, Susan. Only just think of it, and it becomes so simple to say, ' I am your wife.' "

She held her head up and said quietly : " Are you angry about this ? "

" Angry ? No, I'm not angry. I just want to know why you lied to me."

" I didn't lie to you. You didn't ask me about myself —my name . . . nothing."

" For God's sake don't quibble, Susan. You know you could have told me." There were frown creases in his forehead and tight lines all round his mouth. It didn't look like anger in his face, but a kind of fierce invective against the circumstances which had led them to this.

She commanded his silence abruptly. " Then listen to me." For the first time she began to be certain; freed from humilating fear, no more anxiety. "Why wasn't I told ? Why did you let me arrive in London without knowing what had happened to you ? Which of us has the most need of courage. What were you afraid of in me ? "

" No . . . no, not that." The tone was patient, disappointed. " When I was first aware of your existence it didn't matter whether you knew or not. You were nothing to me. What can a man feel about a wife he doesn't remember ? Then . . . as time went by, it seemed not to matter in another way. I was indifferent ; I never thought I'd see you again."

She was silent and she was waiting to hear the end of it. He saw the waiting in her face, in her hands. She sat there waiting, withholding a decision, until he should be finished. He felt the sweat start under his collar.

" Then you wrote that you were coming. It was the one chance I had to make all the pieces fall back into place. Don't you see, Susan ? " He said no more, made no further attempt to put it into words. He drew his hand wearily across his eyes.

She did see it then—saw it as clearly as he had meant her to. There was horror and tragedy in the picture she saw, the one of Louis smiling at her yesterday, smiling at her with eyes which didn't recognise anything about her. He hadn't asked her to pity him when he had told her yesterday. She had felt interest in the situation, dismay at her own part in it, but no pity. Now it crept over her, and she crouched back in her chair, in a feeble, fluttering effort to escape it.

He looked at her again. " It didn't seem possible that I wouldn't recognise you. I counted on that."

He went on looking at her, wondering what she was thinking, trying to interpret correctly the lift of her eyebrows, the set of her mouth. He leaned backwards in order to see her face at a greater distance. He remembered her as she had come upon him yesterday, withdrawn, reserved, every part of her a stranger. She had been kind after a fashion—her own fashion. The face which regarded him now was no longer impersonal. Shadows here and there hinted at emotion—emotion he couldn't quite touch or reach.

At last she said quietly : " The blame doesn't belong to either one of us completely. People always make mistakes when they're not sure of the facts."

He knew that was as much as she was going to say. Calmly she had taken her share of the responsibility, leaving him his. He said: " I counted on it too much. That was a mistake. We might have avoided this if I'd been a little less sure."

Louis watched her as she leaned forward. Into her face there flowed an eagerness ; a sudden warmth, intimation of a desire to reach understanding.

" But perhaps it would have been worse to be prepared for each other." Slowly a flush mounted in her face. She stopped, and Louis knew that she would never finish what she had tried to say. He regretted it, but he could do nothing about it.

Susan picked up again, ignoring the pause. " I've just seen Racey," she said.

He nodded. " I thought perhaps you would. He told you all about me ? "

" We couldn't decide, Racey and I, whether or not you remembered me." She chose the words quite deliberately. " For myself, I couldn't believe it was merely a pretence."

He shook his head. " I'm not capable of such subtlety. Why would either of you imagine I had pretended ? "

Confused, she allowed her eyes to leave his face. " I don't know. Why does anyone pretend ? "

He said reflectively, almost as if he spoke to himself. " Fear is at the back of most pretence. Were you afraid of me ? "

" No, not afraid—uncertain. You've changed, Louis."

" You also. You've changed a great deal."

She raised her eyes to him, her fingers dropping away from the stem of the glass. He saw the first astonishment of their meeting return. Her lips fell slightly apart, and he could see the moisture on their inner rim. She started to mouth a word but no sound came. At last she said : " How much do you remember ? "

" All of it, I think."

She picked up her drink again and began to sip at it. He went on: " Racey used to tell me about you—some smart crack about he and I being your war effort. It didn't mean a thing to me. You don't know what it's like, Susan. I used to look at young Midge and wonder about you— how you talked, what you thought, what you did. Then after a long time I stopped wondering. I accepted you on faith. ' The eternal Susan ' I used to call you. You only existed in space, not in time."

He drained his glass and set it down again, carefully. There were a series of damp rings on the table surface, and he began to trace them with his finger, not looking any more at Susan.

" When I went home last night I couldn't stop thinking about you—it was a sort of tickle at the back of my mind. I started to drink. I drank too much. You and my wife were a bit mixed up. Somehow you got to be the same person. I was hearing your voice, but you were saying the words I imagined she would say. In the end I couldn't stand it any longer. I phoned the hotel, and asked for my wife. Unconsciously, I must have known, because I wasn't surprised when I heard your voice." He stopped talking, and looked at her.

Susan said gently : " Why didn't you speak to me last night ? "

He shrugged. " What was the use ? I wasn't in a fit condition to speak to anyone. I was tight. The moment you said ' Hallo ' I knew I had been right. That was all I needed."

"Didn't you think of how I felt after that phone call? It was a shock."

She saw a trace of laughter in his face when he answered. "Just at that moment I hadn't any charitable notions where you were concerned. Frankly, I didn't care what you felt. I didn't want to see you again, or talk to you."

"Then why are you here?"

He spread his hands flat on the table. "I told you I was tight last night. I felt differently this morning. After all, you didn't come to London for nothing. The sooner we get this over, the better for both of us."

She leaned back in her chair and looked away from him. She looked at the people perched on the bar stools, looked at the rows of bottles reflected in the mirror. She could even see herself in the mirror, and thought it strange that she didn't appear different, altered in some way, after this conversation with Louis. He hadn't changed at all. This was the same old Louis, getting tight when things disturbed him, making up his mind coolly and impersonally about matters which concerned herself, remembering now their married life, regarding it as something to be finished with as soon as possible. . . . Louis who never considered her feelings, Louis never afraid of decisions, never hesitating. There was no real change in him—a little quieter, more reflective—but beneath that he was still as she remembered him. The low murmur of voices filled the room, flowed over her; the barman handled row after row of polished glasses, and Louis sat there waiting for her to continue. She turned back to him.

"Yes," she said dully. "We must get it over. I'm leaving at the end of the week. There's a lot to do."

He shrugged. She hated the way he shrugged. "There's not much to be done. The only question we've to settle is what's to be done with Midge."

"Midge is our child—not a piece of luggage to be stored." Susan felt her body tightening with anger.

"You can hardly afford to talk like that, Susan. It was you who left her behind. Remember?"

Her anger was now something which hurt within her. It was anger against his cool control of the situation, his good-looking impersonal face, anger against herself for feeling this anger. She was silent for a moment, and then said evenly : " I want to spend some time with Midge. Racey is taking me down to Hythebourne to-morrow."

He said nothing. In his silence there was a victory to her. He didn't want her to go to Hythebourne. To go back to Hythebourne was to go back to the root of things. He said : " There's no need to make the journey. Racey can bring her back to London."

" No," she said. " I'll see her there. Racey's making a trip to France, and I'll stay overnight with her."

He said reluctantly : " You'll find Midge shy. She's not used to the idea of having a mother. I think she's always imagined they were persons who belonged to other children, and she didn't particularly need one."

Susan's anger mounted until it was a bewildering, maddening pain. She rose to her feet, pushing the chair jerkily across the carpet. Her movement was quick and Louis had no time to copy her. She leaned over him, enjoying for the moment the advantage of her position. " Tell me one thing straight, Louis. Do you intend to let me take Midge back to America with me ? "

He stood up slowly. He was taller and looked down at her now. " That will be something for you to decide, Susan. Go down to Hythebourne and see her there. If you can persuade yourself that she'll be happier with you in New York, then you can take her."

Then he stooped to pick up the glove which had fallen to the floor when she had risen, and handed it to her. She accepted it dumbly. He stepped back to let her pass, but made no effort to follow. She turned back to him. " Aren't you leaving ? "

" Not just at the moment. I'll get in touch with you here when you're back from Hythebourne."

" Yes, do." She made to turn away, then hesitated because some feeling of urgency, some need to communicate with him was holding her. Their gaze met, and she guessed that he too had caught a shade of her emotion. They waited for each other to speak, but the silence grew. Desperately Susan looked about her. The bar was more crowded now, the buzz of talk louder. All these were a wedge driven between them, forcing them apart. The uncertainty of this moment needed silence and peace to counterbalance it. A few seconds more of it and she knew she would turn and walk away.

At last he said: "I'm sorry things have gone like this, Susan. I didn't mean to come here with recriminations, but . . . I've messed it up a bit. I'm sorry about that."

She nodded. "I know . . . I'm sorry. Good-bye, Louis."

He halted her. "Susan, if you need me you'll phone, won't you. I'm still in Carlton Mews."

She nodded again. "I'm leaving fairly early in the morning. Perhaps I could phone you then. Midge would like to have a message from you."

"Yes . . . well, I'm usually at early service at the Abbey until about nine. Any time after then."

"At the Abbey. I didn't know you . . ."

"I don't spend all my time drinking, you know. Good-bye, Susan." She felt he had regretted his words, wished her to forget about them. But she carried them with her as she left him.

Louis watched her go, and, as happened yesterday, he saw the eyes of the men about him follow her progress across the room.

IV

UPSTAIRS, PAUL was waiting for her. It was like returning to a familiar country to feel his arms about her. She pressed close to him until his hand, seeking to turn her face upwards towards him, drew them apart. He looked down at her, frowning.

"Sue, what is it?"

"I've seen him again. I've seen Louis."

" Tell me about it," he said sharply.

He led her to a chair and poured a drink for her, but he remained standing, sipping his own, until she had finished talking. She was glad when it was finished; she leaned back in her chair and closed her eyes briefly. The interview with Louis no longer seemed important. Paul was important now; he was near her and she wanted to feel his arms about her once more. Without opening her eyes she knew that he had drawn nearer, and soon his lips were brushing her face. It was easy to forget about Louis this way.

They dined late at the hotel, and on a sudden impulse she had Paul take her to the Café de Paris to dance. It wasn't a success going there. Before the bomb which had wrecked it, this had been one of her favourite places in London. The new decorations reminded her of a gigantic white bedroom, and it typified too strongly the change since the time when Louis and Racey had brought her here to dance. With no thought of danger to add excitement, the experiment fell flat. She was surrendering her memory of London during the blitz for a knowledge of it in peacetime, neat, grey and austerity-ridden. And indifference and dullness in the faces of the people.

Without waiting for her request, Paul took her back early to the hotel.

SUNDAY

I

Susan woke early. Without even turning to look at the clock she knew it was early. The quality in the silence told her that much. She lay quite still, gazing about her. Through the partly-drawn curtains the morning light made a timid entrance. The room, save for the patch of brightness at the window, lay in tranquil grey shadow. She closed her eyes, but the first restlessness increased. At last she flung aside the bed-covers, conscious of a desire to talk to Paul—or anyone else. But it was too early for him to have awakened. Instead, she went to the window and looked out.

Down below the pavement was wet with dew. Along the cracks the moisture glistened faintly. In the Park the mist swathed the trees like grey head-scarves on old women. Somewhere across the waiting, Sunday-morning city a clock began to strike. Susan counted the strokes. Seven. The hours before breakfast were empty, and she was thinking that now Louis would be rising, would soon be setting out to walk to the Abbey. She looked down again to the damp pavement, the silent, deserted road, and back again at the clock. The hands had already moved to five minutes past the hour. To get to the Abbey in time for the service was, for her, almost impossible, but she closed the window sharply, turned and hurried towards the bathroom, slipping off her gown as she went.

The hands of the clock moved round swiftly. It was later than she wished when she caught up her handbag and scarf and left the room. A sleepy lift attendant answered her ring, and downstairs in the foyer, the work of the day had begun. A few cleaners stopped to look at her as she hurried past; the sound of their machines was shrill and deafening. A commissionaire, hatless and gloveless at this early hour, saw her just before she reached the doors, and sprang to open them.

Outside, the mist-laden air struck her sharply. She drew her coat closer, looking round for bus or taxi, but there were none. Even when she had reached Piccadilly the road stretched before her emptily. She was unsure now of the quickest way across to the Abbey, and wasted some moments in hesitation before cutting through the Green Park to the front of the Palace. Here there were the usual guards, and a policeman, but no one else. They stared solemnly at Susan as she started down the long silent stretch of the Mall. Over to her right the tower of Westminster Cathedral kept pace. The distance seemed longer than she remembered it, and as she walked she thought that no other city was ever quite so sleep-bound as London on a chilly Sunday morning. Nothing within sight stirred or moved. Even when she was through Admiralty Arch and into Trafalgar Square she could see no sign of a taxi. As she turned into Whitehall the sun began to break through fitfully. She gazed about her and saw how it washed the buildings with a pale light, and how, as she passed the Cenotaph, the stone shimmered whitely. A tram lumbering across Westminster Bridge broke the stillness. The sun had caught the face of Big Ben. Only the roof of the Abbey had yet been touched, and inside it was dim—and chill with the coldness of stone.

About twenty people knelt before the first altar, their faces turned away from her. The only light was above the young priest who read the communion service. She had never before realised how difficult it was to recognise one among many kneeling figures in a church. She moved forward softly, almost on tip-toe, until abruptly her feet brushed something on the ground. She looked down and saw that in the dimness she had blundered unseeingly into the wreath of red poppies which fringed the familiar black

74

marble slab. Never before had she passed it without a thought for the significance of the unnamed soldier who lay there; but on this autumn morning, unobserved in the quiet Abbey, she knew a kinship with him, grief as for a friend. Quietly she stooped and put the wreath back in position, then moved to a seat in the back row.

After a while she saw Louis. He knelt a few feet in front of her, and to the side. His hand on his forehead had thrown a shadow across his face. She gazed for a long time at the line of his shoulders, his bowed head, and when the service was almost over he glanced sideways and saw her. He gave her only a faint smile and then turned back towards the altar, but Susan was reassured. The light was growing stronger, and at the end of the service, the lamp over the altar was extinguished, leaving the building in its peaceful, uniform greyness. Louis remained in his place, and even after the soft noises of the people departing had died away, he stayed there.

Susan sat still. Her eyes moved from one monument to another, the walls, the altar, and finally to the roof. The roofs of old churches were like Bach's music, she thought. They were clear-cut, symmetrical, their lines flowing onwards, one into the other, like the giant polyphonic harmonies of a fugue. One arch, one pillar, to balance another—note against note, voice against voice, each part a separate melody, and moving along as a perfected whole. They were big. They had a largeness beside which lesser creations shrunk to insignificance.

She brought her gaze swiftly downwards, because Louis had stirred and was rising. He came towards her immediately. They did not speak, but he took her arm and led her carefully across the shadowy floor. Outside they paused for a moment on the step.

"I didn't expect you," he said.

She answered gravely: "I didn't expect to find myself there. It's not usually my kind of place." She paused, but then decided to go on. "I liked it, Louis."

Once more he took her by the arm and they began to

walk. "Come with me some week-morning," he said. "It's better then. The service is held in the little Chapel of St. Faith. I think you'd like that, too."

They turned out across Parliament Square towards Whitehall in silence, and as they walked Susan began to wonder about him. She glanced quickly up into his face, seeing there, in the lightly relaxed lips, in the bright eyes, the evidence of an unknown personality. Where, in all the danger-crowded days and nights, in the extreme craving for pleasure, had Louis kept hidden the part of him which could kneel so humbly before an altar, to whom quietness and peace were beautiful. For Louis and Racey both there had been no god but that of power and speed, no knowledge of fear or darkness, death, but no immortality. In contrast to that time, the man walking beside her was a stranger, but he laid his hand upon her as if he were a friend.

They didn't break the silence all the way up Whitehall and crossing Trafalgar Square. At the entrance to Carlton Mews Louis didn't even halt, but led Susan straight in, as if they had together been following the same ritual long enough to have made it custom.

She pulled at his arm abruptly, forcing him to stop. "Louis, I can't come in here."

He looked at her, his face puzzled. "Why not? I wanted you to see it. I haven't changed it at all."

She said passionately: "What makes you suppose I want to see it? I've finished with all this, Louis. It's not my life any more."

"In that case," he said coldly, "it couldn't matter less to you whether you come or not."

They faced each other, her height making her nearly level with him. The anger of yesterday was returning to her swiftly, anger which he seemed able to rouse in her without effort and for his own satisfaction. He still held her arm, but it was now a tight grip from which she couldn't break free. She waited, thinking what to do, and then suddenly she saw that her anger had been foolish, for he was now

76

smiling at her in a way which showed he had been un-conscious of it.

"You mustn't mind my getting excited over this, Susan. Sunday's the one morning I can have both bacon and egg for breakfast, and I rather wanted you to share it."

His hold had relaxed; he led her gently on again. She submitted because there was no point in making further protest. She allowed herself to be taken along, but all the time a fierce kind of terror was mounting in her brain. So many hurtful, bitter memories waited here for her. Did Louis have no memories of their savage quarrels, their ecstatic love-making? Had he no vision of the nights when she had lain here alone, when the planes had gone over-head, crying in the darkness, wholly consumed with fear for him, and love for him? Did he know nothing of the times when he had come home on leave wildly exhilarated by the danger and uncertainty of his existence, demanding her love, and laughing at her fears until she became ashamed of them? If he knew any of this he chose to hide it; his face was composed as he opened the door and stood back for her to pass.

Inside, she followed him to the kitchen. They had always eaten breakfast here, and she began to lay the table with an alacrity which dismayed her when she became aware of it. Things had changed, of course—new shelves, new paint, different china—but the routine itself was unchanging. She made the toast and coffee as she had always done, while he turned smoking bacon in the pan.

The talk during breakfast wasn't of the matters which concerned them both at that moment. Susan wondered why they each avoided mention of Midge, why each refused to speak of the future in terms of their personal lives. Over and over again she found herself about to speak to him of the divorce, and each time the thought was dismissed as soon as it rose. Why did they wait, she wondered? Why draw back like this? Why pretend? Yesterday he had said: 'Fear is at the back of most pretence.' Why were they afraid?

While Louis stacked the dishes in the sink, Susan wandered into the living-room. Here nothing had been changed. This might have been as much her room now as then. She sank slowly into one of the chairs and looked about her, aware that her knees trembled, and her wrists were weak with a strange kind of fear. She had a terrifying sensation that time had turned back upon her—one of those moments which seemed to have been lived through before. She pressed her hands together to still their trembling, and saw how each ornament had kept the place she had given it, her books were undisturbed upon the shelves. The silence was very strong in this room—a waiting silence. What was it waiting for? She felt betrayed by it; here, her doubt rose to the surface, more clamorous than ever before. Demoralised, she rose and turned to go, but Louis stood in the doorway.

"It's always been like this, hasn't it?" he said.

She didn't reply, but sank down again upon the seat. He walked past her, towards the bookshelves. "I used to wonder about you," he continued. "The books told me practically nothing—they're such a mixed lot. You liked ballet, that was all I could be sure of." He ran his hand along the books, but never looked once in her direction.

Without prompting, he began to speak of it. "It was a long time after the accident before I came back here. Perhaps I was afraid of it. I knew nothing of you—Racey had tried to tell me, but the real you, the person you are now, never came out of his description. Yes, I think I was afraid. I was afraid of what I might find out about my wife. I put it off as long as possible, but in the end I had to come. I looked at everything I imagined was yours. There were your books, your pictures, even some clothes you'd left behind. I knew what was my own because I could remember it being at Hythebourne. All the rest was yours, and I tried to build up a woman out of that."

She managed to stand up because she wanted to force him to turn and face her. "What sort of woman did you find ? . . . what did you make out of a pile of possessions ? "

He turned around slowly, as she wanted him to, and said gravely : " I liked what I saw. I wanted her to come back, so that I could see for myself."

She watched his face grow suddenly strained and anxious. " After that I questioned myself. I tried desperately to remember what it was that could have gone wrong between this woman and myself. What had I done . . . what had she done ? "

He paused and then said clearly : " Susan, why did you go away ? "

A sick distaste for herself swept through her ; there was no longer a clear answer to his question. Spiritlessly she turned and walked from the room.

In the hall she took up her coat and handbag. Louis had not stirred. She let herself out into the Mews, and the click of the door behind her was final and lasting.

" I can't say why I went. I don't know," Susan said to Paul.

They faced each other in his bedroom across an untouched breakfast tray, and a pile of half-smoked cigarettes. He was smoking now, and she saw his forehead drawn into fine lines. He had always looked like that in New York when something had gone wrong on the paper. ' God,' she thought, ' why do I do this to him ? What makes me do it ? '

" Paul," she said aloud, " you must understand that it was just an impulse. After all, this isn't an ordinary occasion. Louis still only half-remembers me. We left so much dangling in the air last night."

He pulled at the cigarette, and she thought that he looked ill and tired. He said at last : " Look, Sue, this is your show, as I've said before. I want you to handle it your own way. But, hell . . . I can't be expected to sit by and watch you make yourself miserable over this guy! Sure . . he's had an accident, and we all feel sorry for him, but he got along very well without you all these years, and I'll bet if we only knew it, he's got someone all lined up to step in where you stepped out."

Miserably she looked away. How sick she was of it all. She wished that to-day, instead of setting out with Racey, she was taking a plane with Paul back to New York. She could get nowhere with Louis. His enigma would have to remain forever unsolved. After their parting this morning in Carlton Mews she didn't very much care. It was better not to see him again, much better. Even Paul would agree on this.

She stood up and walked slowly round the room. "Paul, I've decided not to see him again."

"Louis?" He stood up eagerly, stubbing the cigarette out. He came towards her. "I'm glad of that. I wanted to ask you not to."

"Why? On Friday night you insisted I must see him."

He caught her lightly by the shoulders. "A lot has happened since Friday, Sue. A lot I hadn't bargained for in coming over here. Louis and Racey and the kid . . . they count with you, don't they? And all the time I've got to sit round like a fool watching you get more and more involved."

She burst out suddenly: "I wish you'd come to Hythebourne with me."

He shook his head. "Look, honey, you don't need me to defend you against your own kid."

His hands slid down her arms, and they stood close together for a little time. Then he leaned his face against hers, and she could feel his worry and doubt. Without his saying so she felt his need for her then as never before. It was a need removed from ordinary desire. She stood quite still, feeling his breath against her temple. Then he stirred, and she knew that it was time to go.

II

"How BEAUTIFUL you are this morning, Witch," Racey said to her.

"I'm not, you know. But if it pleases you to tell me so, then I'm willing to listen."

He grinned. "It always pleases me to be able to tell a woman she's beautiful. God shouldn't have made an ugly woman. It's an appalling waste." He continued in a lower tone. "Old what's-his-name said something about man shall be trained for war, and women for the recreation of the warrior."

Susan leaned nearer. "What was that? I didn't catch it."

"Nothing, Witch, nothing." He grinned again, pressing his foot down on the accelerator. The car responded with extra speed, and Susan settled back against the seat once more. They were well out of London by this time, and she was beginning to feel hungry. Racey's conversation had been amusing; he was clever in a light-hearted fashion, mercilessly critical of what he disapproved. The expression of his contempt had fallen about the heads of these drivers less able, less sure than himself. Susan pitied them; hesitant, slow, they didn't seem to belong in the same world as Racey. It annoyed him, she knew, to be forced to recognise their existence.

They ate their lunch at the bar of a tiny pub. The odour of the cheese sandwiches piled on their plates was strong and good. Racey paused suddenly over his beer. "Look, Sue, it isn't going to be all roses for you down at Hythebourne."

She nodded. "I wasn't expecting roses."

"I've phoned the old boy, but it wasn't easy to explain things. He hasn't known all this time that the divorce was going through."

"What have you told him?"

"I've simply said that you were in London for a couple of days and wanted to see Midge. No use upsetting the old chap before it's time."

"What do you mean—upsetting him?"

"Well . . . if you decide to take Midge . . ."

She cut in coldly: "You mean if Louis decided to let me take her.'

81

He flushed a little. " All right, all right—it's not my affair. All I want you to do is not to mention the possibility to him. He'll go off his head if he thinks Midge might be taken away from Hythebourne. He just worships the kid."

She thought about it in silence for a time. When the last sandwich was finished she questioned him again. " Racey, what have they told Midge about me? . . how much fiction have I got to uphold? "

" You can't dish out fiction to a kid like Midge. She's a sharp little beggar. We've always said that her mother didn't like living in England and went back to America. As far as I can see, she's always grown up with the idea that mothers weren't entirely necessary in the scheme of things. Being the ruling female at Hythebourne gives her quite an amount of satisfaction."

Susan wanted to protest, wanted to fight off the self-accusation which had begun to pile up about her. In a quick fever to escape she grasped her handbag and rose. " Come, Racey," she said dully. " We ought to be moving."

He drained his glass, and prepared to follow her, glancing then at his watch. " My God, yes. The chap I want to see is leaving Paris about nine this evening. It'll be too bad if I don't make it."

He drove faster then, and in complete silence. Susan wished he would talk again. Talk and laughter kept away the ever-rising vision of Louis, of Hythebourne, of the still unknown child, Midge. The towns passed quickly. She knew their names, repeated them softly to herself as she had always done on these drives, years ago. Habit and custom was reasserting itself with hateful sharpness, and worse than that, she had no means of preventing it. Over the last two miles she was aware of being afraid once more. She almost gave way to her despair as the familiar fields and lanes came into sight. Racey had increased his speed, for the landmarks passed too quickly. Round the next bend she would see the house.

But before the bend Racey stopped. The unexpectedness

of his act was an anti-climax. She listened unwillingly when he jerked his head towards a field on her right and said :

"We've pulled the barn down and made a hangar."

This was Hythebourne's largest field and was now given over to pastures on which a few cows grazed. Racey's hangar stood at the end closest to the house. The barn which had stood there had been decaying slowly, the roof leaking and covered with brown-green moss, the colour of the surrounding landscape. Often during the months before Midge's birth she had gone there to escape the atmosphere of the house, gone to lie for hours in the fragrant-smelling hay, thinking about the child who was coming, thinking about Louis, thinking, too, she remembered, about Racey. It was all gone now, swept away to make room for this trim, weather-tight structure. She was conscious of a sharp regret, so she merely nodded and said nothing. After a few moments Racey drove on.

They passed the first wall, then the dovecot, an elaborate stone building larger than a small house, where the apples were stored, and moved up the short driveway beside the wild stretch of lawn. Racey drew in, with that long familiar sweep of his, under a wall in the unkempt gravelled square in front of the house. She looked about her. This at least was unchanged—the warm colouring of the stone, the deep mullioned windows. Seen from this side, Hythebourne was a beautiful, gracious house, and only after one had gazed at it for some time did the signs of encroaching decay become apparent.

A deep Sunday quiet lay over the house. The front door was open, but there was no sound of anyone about. Racey got out of the car, taking the suitcases with him. Susan followed more slowly. At the door he paused and waited for her.

"Ring the bell, will you, Susan ? I haven't a free hand."

The chill of the unheated house struck her as she advanced. She turned immediately and closed the door behind her, at the same time glancing about, seeing the neglect, the need of repair and paint. For four years Hythebourne had been without a mistress and there was evidence of the fact in the shabby discomfort she saw about her. She shivered a little, recalling the first time she had entered this hall with a graceful, white-haired woman waiting to greet her.

They listened to the footsteps in the passage, and soon the figure of the ancient, stooping manservant, Sydney, appeared in the service door.

He gazed unblinkingly at her. " Good afternoon, Mrs. Taite."

" Good afternoon, Sydney. I'm glad to see you again."

He nodded gravely, but didn't reply. She wondered what he thought, what they all thought, about this visit. His face gave her no hint. He turned to Racey. " Good afternoon, Mister Horace. The master is expecting you. He would like to see you in the study."

" Mrs. Taite also ? " Racey raised interested eyebrows.

" If Mrs. Taite will be good enough to wait in the drawing-room, tea will be served shortly."

Racey nodded. " All right. But hurry it along, will you, Sydney ? I want to get off as quickly as possible."

" Very good, sir."

With a vague salute Racey left her alone with the silent, black-clad figure of the butler. He stood stiffly there, waiting for her to pass on. For a moment or two some breath of union existed between them. They looked at each other ; Susan wanted to speak to him, but had no words to say. The manservant knew about most of what was going on—about this dying house, about the old man who had not come to greet her, about her child, about the life being lived here since she had left it. She sighed, because she could not ask him. Her footsteps were lonely and loud as she moved on.

The drawing-room at Hythebourne had once been white and gold. Somewhere in this ancient family there had been an alien to this straightforward county stock, perhaps some fashionable lady fresh from the salons in London. There were Regency candle brackets on the walls, gilt-edged mirrors. The fireplace was a chaste white marble. Then a few generations of solid family tendencies had been superimposed. A huge Turkish carpet claimed the end portion of the room and heavy chairs stood about on it. The Victorian period, mercifully, had made little mark, but Susan thought it a sad room. There was the smell of disuse here, an impression, valid only in those first seconds, that life had left the room long ago and had never returned. The windows faced half-west, so the afternoon light flooded in, giving the place the sad and waiting atmosphere of an empty church.

Susan closed the door softly and moved to the already lit fire. She walked softly also, as if the silence itself was sacred. Unwilling to turn her back upon the room and the chairs and tables which stood about in attitudes of waiting attention, she leaned against the marble mantelshelf. The clock behind her ticked dully on, indifferent to her intrusion. She noticed with a strange detachment that her hands were clenched tightly ; the fear which had attacked her in the car had not subsided, but rose again and again in little rushes of added panic.

But she was cool enough outwardly when at last the door opened and she turned to face Racey and his father. The old man was vastly changed ; she saw that even in the first moment, judged it in the first fumbling steps towards her.

He faced her calmly : " Well, Susan ? It seems a very long time since we saw you last."

' How old he is,' she thought as she held his hand in her own. It was heavy and dry to her touch. His body had thickened in the past years, his face had a high purplish tinge, like a fruit upon which pollution had already settled. He looked weary ; his head, held stiffly on his shoulders in the familiar way seemed weary ; his hand felt as though he longed to let it drop listlessly to his side once more.

Between Susan and Lionel Taite there existed a strange relationship. Friends they had never been, for the old man and his wife had fiercely rebelled against Louis' marriage to her. But from each towards the other there gradually grew up a hard-won respect. In the many polite and coldly-worded battles of their acquaintance, neither had been the complete victor, and the memory of this tinged their meeting. They held off, each waiting for the first thrust from the opponent.

"I'm well, Father," she answered. "And you?"

"I manage," he said testily. "I manage."

They gazed at each other, and after a moment Susan recognised her defeat. Her defences were crumbling before the signs of his age. Under the disguise of his high colour the skin was thin and old, and the hand he now placed on the mantel near her shoulder was trembling. She pitied him, knowing that he would have scorned her pity. In fear that he would read her face and feel shame, she turned away.

With grave courtesy he indicated a chair. "Please do sit down, Susan. Tea will be here shortly." He himself remained standing, looking towards Racey. "I hope Horace that you told Sydney to bring Charlotte. Her mother will want to see her."

With his imperious habit of not waiting for an answer he passed his attention once more to Susan. "I expect you saw Louis while you were in London?"

"Yes," she replied. Then stung to anger she said boldly: "It was a shock to learn about his accident."

He didn't attempt to excuse himself. "We didn't think it necessary . . . advisable . . . to inform you at the time. When the danger was over it seemed even less so."

Well, that was it, Susan thought. With those words she was at last given her proper place in importance—the last one to be considered, the lowest place at the table. He had now come to view her in the light of a regrettable incident in Louis' life. Probably he hoped a divorce was on foot, so that his son, his family, might be rid of her presence. The child he had always regarded as belonging wholly to himself. Susan was no part of them, never had been. This visit would see the end of her. He might almost have uttered the words, so plainly his attitude proclaimed them.

They regarded each other in distrustful silence, and from the expression in the eyes of this red-haired woman he feared, the old man began to have his first doubts. Racey, still standing, shifted from one foot to the other with what was, for him, a surprising lack of ease.

The opening of the door saved Susan the necessity of finding something more to say. The three together turned and looked in that direction. Seeing them thus absorbed in her, the child hesitated, holding firmly to the worn silver handle of that high, white door.

Her aloof shyness and pride was evident in every line of the thin young face. She returned their gaze steadily, but two spots of betraying colour sprang into her cheeks. Susan saw that she was tall for her age, with narrow hands and feet. Then, triumphantly, she noticed her brown hair, done carelessly in plaits which hung to her shoulders, had more than a hint of red in it. It was a small thing but it gave her absurd satisfaction.

The old man stirred. Susan, glancing swiftly at him, saw that his sternness had broken. He was smiling at the child, holding out his hand towards her.

" Come along, Charlotte." His tones were at once pleading and possessive.

The child closed the door carefully behind her, and advanced towards them.

As she drew nearer Susan was conscious that she wanted to cry out, wanted to claim her before she came into the sphere of the old man's authority. She half-rose from her seat, but fell weakly back again, struggling to overcome the trembling of her knees, the treacherous numbness in her hands. She wanted to halt the child's progress, drew her close, look at her, touch the soft texture of her young face. Tendrils of hair escaped the plaits, and Susan wanted to put them in place. Most of all, the mistrust must leave the child's eyes.

But the old man was sure of his possession. He said gently : " Charlotte, come and shake hands with your mother."

It was a supreme piece of cruelty, and he perpetrated it with apparent innocence. Midge extended her hand towards Susan formally. "How do you do," she said coldly.

Helplessly, Susan watched as Midge moved on eagerly to Racey. "Well, Spider," he said, catching her about the waist and lifting her high. "Been growing a couple of feet, I see."

Midge laughed with pleasure. The sound broke strangely on that strained and tensed atmosphere. She kicked her legs wildly as Racey swung her to the ground again, childishly enjoying the new sensation. Her flush was brighter as she turned towards her grandfather once again.

He looked down at her fondly. "What have you been doing with yourself all afternoon?"

"Reading," she replied promptly.

He tried to suppress his pleasure in her then, shaking his head with false gravity. "You read too much, Charlotte. You should be out of doors most of the time. Where was your puppy? Could you not have played with him in the stable?"

She answered offhandedly: "We get bored with each other. He wanted to go to sleep."

The old man made small sounds of disapproval. But he glanced directly over at Susan and said: "Charlotte reads extremely well." It was almost a challenge tossed at her, to take up as she willed.

"What kind of books do you read, Midge?" she asked carefully.

"Mostly Grandfather's books," she answered. "Some of the words are hard, but I skip those."

Susan felt a sharp dismay touch her. She looked with pity at the child, who was only seven, and knew so little about the ways of children. She was a pathetic little mite, her dignity and solemnity at once appealing and tragic. She began to speak softly to her grandfather with grave confidence that she alone would receive his attention. But she was not unaware of her other listeners, for occasionally she threw a quick glance in their direction. She was still shy and more than a little afraid, Susan knew, but she made an incredibly determined effort to hide it.

At the appearance of old Sydney with the tea-tray, Midge stopped talking abruptly. It was as though the rattle of the tea-cups was sufficient cover for her, and she need no longer keep up her own pretence. While Sydney laid a small table before Susan, she slipped over to stand by Racey. He put his arm about her waist and lifted her on to the chair. "What is it, Spider?"

"Are you going to fly to-day, Racey?"

He nodded. "As soon as tea's over."

"When are you going to take me up?"

He squeezed her slight bulk, laughing. "When you get a bit fatter. I'm afraid you'll slip out of the safety belt."

Susan handed the first cup to the old man, who now sat close to her. The teapot still raised she looked across at Midge. "Aren't you afraid of flying?"

Midge's face underwent a curious change. The two bright spots deepened rapidly; her pale neck was stained crimson. Her eyes grew suddenly brighter and larger, as if by an effort she was forcing herself not to cry. It was a cry of outraged vanity when she said: "I'm not afraid of anything."

Susan laid the teapot down carefully. "That's a very brave thing for a little girl to say, Midge."

"It's true, isn't it, Grandfather?" She turned passionately to the old man.

"Of course, my darling, of course." He looked sternly at Susan. "I've never held with this modern business that children should be allowed to give way to their fears about every trifling thing. My own boys were never afraid of anything, and Charlotte's just the same."

Together, the old man and child, they faced Susan angrily, trying to wipe out the insult she had offered by the force of their displeasure. If Lionel waited triumphantly for a contradiction of his statement, he was disappointed, for she turned to Racey and said calmly: "Do you take milk?"

The old man grunted softly and subsided, thinking her a weak fool. Midge slipped from Racey's encircling arms and began to draw a footstool into place before a low chair. On this she placed her cup and plate, and began to eat bread and butter hungrily and in silence. In the breaks of a spasmodic conversation with Racey, Susan watched her constantly. The young face was composed and grave again; she was unconscious of the scrutiny, and more child-like than she had yet appeared. She was such a baby and so defenceless, yet the old man strove with all his powers to make her to his own pattern of arrogance and self-sufficiency. As she turned from refilling Racey's cup, Susan caught the single glance which passed between the grandfather and the child; it was a look which excluded the whole world outside of themselves, a look of devotion, almost worship. Susan turned her eyes away from them because she couldn't bear the strange intimacy she had briefly glimpsed.

With refilling cups, passing plates, murmured conversation, tea came to a slow end. Racey, impatient and silent during the last ten minutes, stood up eagerly. " Look, I've got to push off. Who's coming out with me ? "

The old man and the child rose together. " Of course, we're coming, my dear boy," Lionel Taite said.

He nodded briefly. " Good. I'll go upstairs and get my gear. Spider, will you see the cows are cleared off the field ? " With only a faint nod to Susan, he hurried from the room. Midge and her grandfather followed him immediately, the child pulling at her grandfather's hand, talking in a high, piping tone which betrayed her excitement. The sounds of their voices echoed in the passage outside.

Susan followed more slowly. She was beginning to wonder if perhaps it had been a mistake to come down here. The time was so short, Racey would return to-morrow morning, and in those few hours she must try to break through the old man's protective and jealous shell in order to reach her own child. What did Midge really think of her, under the cover of that disdainful aloofness? Had Lionel yet imbued her with his own dislike? A swift misery engulfed her as she thought of the unequal fight ahead. Lionel had so much on his side—the child's confidence and love, even her passionate impulses he could call to obedience. Her own efforts, of necessity, could be only feeble and poor in the face of it. She was well aware of the near-hopelessness of the task as she made her way to the big field.

By this time Lionel and Midge were well ahead and out of sight. She crossed the gravel court where Racey's car stood, and pushed open the high garden gate. This was the square overlooked by the front bedrooms of the house, and when Louis' mother had been alive, even with the larger part of it given over to vegetables, it had blossomed with colour almost the whole year round. Susan looked about now in dismay. The huge square was completely overgrown, with only a beaten path through the tall, feathery grass leading up to the stone dovecot. A few late insects hummed through the weeds and nettles, their soft scrapings reminiscent of the voices of the bees she had listened to during the summer when she had lived here. The garden had been beautiful then, soft and feminine— tall lupins and hollyhocks, and the heavy scent which came from the rose-garden when the wind blew. If she closed her eyes she could still hold the picture of Louis' mother, an old faded sunhat on her head, moving tranquilly among the flowerbeds, snipping, weeding, and when planting times came, working as hard as a man. A tall, handsome old woman, looking at her with faded blue eyes under the sun hat—a hat which, she told Susan one day in a mood of friendliness, she had once worn to Ascot. It had been veiled and flower-trimmed then.

Anger at the wilderness of neglect, the indifferent destruction of so much beauty, swept through her. How could they have been so careless, she wondered, as if the old woman's memory wasn't worth the effort to keep her garden in order. Susan walked on swiftly, trying not to see it any more.

Racey called to her as she entered the field where the hangar stood. As she waited for him she noticed that the apple crop had been taken in. The leaves in the orchard were brown. Racey drew near, swinging helmet and goggles in his hand, and she saw a curious glint of suppressed excitement in his eyes, much like that displayed by Midge and her grandafther. They were all the same, she thought. Every one of them—still crazy about aeroplanes and flying. They never could be different.

"Well, Witch," he greeted her. "What do you think of the offspring?"

"Oh, hell, Racey! What has everyone done to her? She's scarcely like a child at all."

He shrugged, but he was not unconcerned. "I know, Sue. But what were we to do? A kid as intelligent as Midge can't live alone with two old men for four years and not turn out a little peculiar."

She said, a little weakly: "What about a governess?"

He laughed, so loudly the sound echoed back through the orchard. "Haven't we tried? Susan, the governesses coming and going to Hythebourne keep the railway branch line working. They just won't stay. Can't say I blame them." He looked back to the overgrown garden with distaste. "In any case," he continued, "Midge doesn't do too badly. She goes over to have lessons with the Blakes every day."

She didn't reply, but gazed abstractedly along the avenue between the trees. There was a sweet damp smell of wood in the orchard; she drew it in sharply. She said gently: "Racey, why don't you care about Hythebourne any more? Why have you let it . . . go . . . like this?"

He regarded her a trifle grimly. "Because it's finished, Susan. It's finished. There's barely enough money to run it, and I won't let the old man spend any more on its upkeep. It will see him out his time, and then we'll be rid of it—as quick as we can."

"And Louis? Does he think this too?"

"Louis?" He laughed flatly. "Louis couldn't care less."

There was nothing to say to him. She told herself that she had expected these words, or ones like them, but they were none the less painful when they came. She wondered, in passing, why she cared what became of Hythebourne. This had been the scene of her growing unhappiness, from this as much as from Louis she had tried to escape. Once more she glanced back towards the ruined garden. So much had changed; there had been no time, as yet, to catch up with the change.

Conscious that he was watching her, she said quietly, in a tone of dismissal : " I don't think I'll come any farther, Racey."

He smiled. " O.K., Witch. See you in the morning."

" Give my love to Paris," she answered faintly, remembering with sudden pain and regret how beautiful it had been when she left it two days ago.

Racey bent over her, and, careless of the fact that his father and Midge could watch his actions, he kissed her warmly on the mouth. She felt his arms go round her tightly, drawing her very close. He had kissed her this way before, but it troubled her that his kisses should be remembered so clearly. He had no right to kiss her in this fashion. But Racey had never recognised any right but his own. She grew angry, but even her anger was helpless against him.

Releasing her, he began to laugh soundlessly. " Remember me, Sue ? " he said. " It's been a long time."

He walked away from her, and she watched him carefully. Arrogant and supremely sure of himself, like his father. He would be another just like the old man, and when he was also old he would be no wiser. It was difficult to think of Racey as ever being old or unsure. He had once courted death so extravagantly that it had almost seemed his one fear was of old age. She had not expected him, any more than Louis, to live through that dreadful period. But they had both survived to face a future that neither seemed to want. Hythebourne was not part of it ; that had been cast off. She wondered then, why she concerned herself with them. They would, all four of them, go on from this point.

and except for Midge, it was scarcely likely that their separate fates could touch her again.

Deliberately she took her eyes off him and looked back into the orchard again.

The sound of the plane at last drew her gaze. Racey had wheeled it from the hangar, and its engine now hummed smoothly, echoing back from the hill above Hythebourne. Midge had cleared the cows off the field, and now came running towards the plane. Susan stopped in amazement as Racey stood up in the cockpit, shouting something, and motioning wildly to her to go back. Susan saw with horror, that the child had almost walked unknowingly into the propeller, invisible to the untrained eye now that it was in motion. The old man caught the meaning of Racey's shouts, for he moved forward with surprising speed and grasped the child's arms, pulling her well clear of the machine. Satisfied, Racey took no further notice of them, and soon the plane taxied to the end of the field and turned into the wind. At the end of that long expanse of flat green it had dangerous frailty. The engine roared louder, and the plane came towards them with gathering speed, its wings tilting with each bump of the field's surface. Susan waited, with clenched hands, for the paralysing second before it was airborne. This moment had never grown less agonising for her with repetition. But inevitably there was that clear space between the undercarriage and the ground. She watched it rise higher, watched Racey salute the three figures beneath him, watched it circle the field, climbing all the time.

But there were sounds in the orchard behind her, and old Sydney was running forward, shouting and pointing at the plane. He emerged from the trees beside Susan just as Racey completed his circle. From the plane he raised his arm in a brief wave towards them, then headed off towards the Channel.

Sydney turned to Susan in a kind of despair. The short run had spent and almost exhausted him. She could hear his struggle for breath. " What shall I do, Mrs. Taite ? "

he gasped. " There's been a telephone message. I was to get Mister Horace to the phone. I was to stop him taking off." Miserably aware of failure he looked towards the plane, tiny in the sky, the sound of its engine rapidly fading.

" Was it urgent, Sydney ? "

" The gentleman said it was very urgent, Madam. He said I was to stop Mister Horace taking off and get him to the phone whatever happened." He gazed ahead sadly to the place where Midge and her grandfather were fussing together over the closing of the hangar doors. " Well . . . I must go and tell the Master," he said.

Susan walked back through the orchard. There had been a look of fear in the old manservant's eyes ; he was troubled far beyond any normal extent, agitated by a thought of something which seemed to threaten Racey. He had gone towards his master with no show of confidence, as if he too fully knew the other's age and helplessness.

III

SUSAN UNPACKED her suitcase in the room which had previously been hers. It adjoined Louis' bedroom, but the communicating door was now locked and the key gone. She spread her familiar bottles on the bureau, taking comfort from the fact that they also were alien in this house. Humming a snatch from a once-popular song, she shook her frock from its folds and hung it in the huge cupboard. It swung there forlornly, as if suddenly ownerless and unwanted. She looked at it and stopped humming, because all at once the sound had become lonely in that quiet room. The door leading to the passage was open, but the house also was still. She dropped her shoes dully on to the rack. It was dusty.

She turned back to the suitcase, and in defiance took up the tune once more. She couldn't remember the words— the time was slow ; she had danced to it long ago in London with Louis—or was it Racey ? The sound seemed to grow around her, filling the room, drifting out on to the stairs.

Her confidence swelled, and as she picked up her nightgown she executed two turns of a slow waltz.

As she wheeled round to face the door she halted abruptly. The nightgown began to slip off her arm, and she made a furious effort to grasp it. Midge was standing in the doorway regarding her solemnly, and Susan's fingers, suddenly nerveless, could find no hold on the thin silk stuff.

"Come in, Midge," she said faintly. She bent to pick up the nightgown, wondering how long the child had been standing there watching her.

Midge stepped inside and leaned against the door. It closed behind her with a crash which made the toilet bottles on the bureau rattle. Still leaning against the door she said: "I heard you singing. I wondered who was here."

Susan looked at her in surprise. "Didn't you know I was having this room?"

Midge didn't say anything, but moved forward to look at the things on the bureau. Its edge came level with her chest. She stood on tiptoe and reached out to touch the bottles. Without looking at Susan she said: "I didn't know you were staying here."

Susan dropped the nightgown back on to the bed. A dull kind of despair overcame her. It was so impossible to reach this child with her guarded face and strangely apathetic words. She watched as Midge began to finger the brushes, tracing slowly the design on their backs. Midge said suddenly: "I have some like this. Mine are silver—they belonged to my grandmother."

Susan remembered them as they used to lie on the old lady's table—worn silver, lovingly handled. There had been a tiny silver vase to match, in which all summer long stood a single white rose. Louis' mother had loved roses best of all. She said uncertainly: "I remember them. I used to see them on your grandmother's table."

Midge put down the brush quickly and wheeled in surprise. She opened her mouth to speak, but at the same moment another thought seemed to strike her, for the dullness fell once again on her face. Sullenly she turned away from the bureau and began to walk across the room towards the window. Half-way there she was halted by the sight of the dress hanging in the cupboard. Hesitantly she stood still, looking at the dress. Her reluctance broke suddenly, and she hurried towards it. Susan watched her hands exploring the grey silk, watched her stretch upwards to feel the frosty grey beads around the neckline. She fingered the pleated skirt, and at last dropped down to touch the grey suede of the shoes.

Finally she said, her voice ringing hollowly in the empty cupboard. " My grandmother never had a dress like this. Did you buy it in America ? "

" No. I bought it in Paris."

" It's beautiful," the child said, sighing. She ran a silk fold across her cheek, and dropped it regretfully. Now unmindful of Susan's presence she crossed to the bed where the suitcase lay half-unpacked. Close to her now Susan could see that her face was flushed. She laid her hands on the nightgown, examined it briefly and intently, and passed on to the other contents. She fingered stockings, underwear, dressing-gown, each item seeming to give her more curiosity about the others. Then tossing them aside she hurried back to the bureau and began to unscrew the tops of jars, of bottles, of perfume flasks, smelling each eagerly and passing on to the next. Then she replaced them all carefully, in their meticulous row, and faced Susan.

" Is it hard to get things like these ? " she said, pointing to the jumble on the bed.

" It depends upon how badly you want them," Susan answered slowly.

Midge said bluntly : " How did you get them ? Have you got a lot of money ? "

" No. I had to work to get the money to buy them. Everyone works for what they want, you know."

Midge looked at the pile, and they gradually began to assume a different aspect. In Susan's words, they represented so much work, and an extent of wanting them.

"Couldn't you buy them in England? Is that why you went away to America?"

"No. You can buy those things in any big city, and I didn't go away just because I wanted them. I was born in America. I couldn't get to like England very much, so I went back."

"Why didn't you like England?" Midge spread her hands, indicating the room, the house, the surrounding fields.

Susan leaned wearily against the bed. "It's difficult to explain, Midge. I lived here—in this house—for quite a long time, and I liked it, too. But a country isn't just trees and fields and houses. It's the people one gets to know."

A fine contempt began to break over Midge's face. "But that's silly! I don't like the Blakes very much—but I don't mind going over there."

"But Midge, they're just other people, they're not your family. Would you like to live at Hythebourne all the time if you didn't get on with your grandfather, or your daddy?"

"Well, didn't you like them? Didn't you get on with them?"

Susan, watching the child, grew pale with anxiety. These words were so dangerous, able to touch off whole piles of memory and bitterness. And who knew what bitterness the child had stored up for herself, and which was now coming forward to seek an explanation? It was sickening to see her standing there, excited, flushed, waiting for the answers, and yet to know that the truth would hurt and shake her, would do nothing to ease the pain of her bewilderment.

She began slowly. "It was difficult, Midge. Life in America is very different from here—the people have different ways. I wasn't used to them. Your daddy and I didn't understand each other very well. We couldn't agree on a lot of things. I thought we would all be happier if I went back to America."

The child flushed crimson. Her voice rose in a shrill scream. "That's not true! You went away because you

98

didn't like us. You didn't like me! My grandfather told me so—and it's the truth."

She turned on her heel and flung herself out of the room. Susan could hear her sob as she fumbled with the door-knob. The heavy door slammed behind her, and the bottles tinkled against one another.

After a long time Susan began dully to fold the under-wear.

Susan found Lionel waiting for her in the drawing-room before dinner. He rose stiffly to his feet as she entered and hastened towards the tray where Sydney had laid out glasses.

"Will you have some sherry, Susan?" he said, not looking at her.

She didn't want the sherry, but there was nothing else, so she agreed.

He handed her the glass, and her fingers, pressed against the stem, could feel the deeply-cut pattern. He inclined his own glass to her gravely. "Your very good health."

She reflected, that while he didn't like her, his treatment of her didn't lack the touch of good manners. They had little to say to each other, and after a few attempts to maintain conversation, they dropped the effort. There was a silence in the room which could have been mistaken for one of intimacy and peace.

Susan thought, as she sat there, that it might, after all, have been worth knowing the old man in a capacity other than that of an enemy. He was very far from being a fool, and when she had examined his library she had seen the extent and scope of his reading. It was a pity that they had never, in all the months she had lived at Hythebourne, been able to relax with each other for even one half-hour. The old man's disapproval of her, on the grounds that she was an American and an outsider, had never lessened. Yet with Susan the feeling had persisted, that, had the barrier once been removed, they could have been friends with ease and surprising swiftness. Oddly enough, even now the idea had not left her, though with only one evening before them, she did not see quite how it could be managed.

The old man glanced at her often as she stared into the fire and thought that she was an extraordinarily handsome woman. Her hair worn in that way, back from her pale face, and set off with the grey dress—her clothes had always been in good taste, even if they had sometimes made his wife purse her lips and wonder how much they had cost. What a pity she had never fitted in—never been the sort of person they had wanted for Louis. Too much rebellion in her, too much independence. She had remained aggressively American within the framework of an English family, and that sort of thing had never worked. Leaving Louis and the child like that had been the final stage of her rebellion. Better that it was over and done with, though it was hard on the child. Charlotte might have learned much from this tall, graceful woman sitting before him. In her own fashion Susan had been a good mother. American women were always so efficient. But if that efficiency had produced in Charlotte the same alien tendencies and ideas, then it was better that she had gone. Much better. . . . He looked at her again. She was really much too handsome to have lived quietly at Hythebourne. Women with faces like that attracted excitement and upsets. They couldn't help it.

At the first sound of the dinner gong Susan started up as if eager to break the long train of thought. Lionel went forward to open the door for her, and together they crossed to the dining-room. Sydney hovered silently over the dishes on a table behind the screen. As Susan appeared he hurried to seat her midway down the long table. There were three places laid, and the old man was already looking back along the passage and frowning.

"Send someone to fetch Miss Charlotte, Sydney. Children should learn to be punctual. She ought to remember she has dinner here on a Sunday night."

Sydney pushed in Susan's chair. "Miss Charlotte asked me to tell you, sir, that she wouldn't be down. She's not feeling well and has gone to bed."

"Not feeling well? She was perfectly all right a few hours ago. Is she ill?"

"A little over-tired, I think, sir. The excitement . . ."

The old man grunted and sat down heavily. "Children haven't got the stamina they used to have. At her age Louis and Horace would have been on their deathbeds before they'd have turned down a chance to come downstairs to dinner. Water, Susan?"

She pushed her glass towards him. "Do you think I should go and see her?"

"No . . . no. Charlotte likes to be left alone. Believe me, if she were ill she'd let me know. This wouldn't have been the first time I'd held her hand and told her stories to put her to sleep. She'll be all right." He began his soup.

Susan, remembering the child's face crimsoning with passion, knew well enough that this was one of the times when she would resent intrusion. Midge had gone away and brooded over their talk, over the miserable ending to it. It was very likely that this was her gesture of defiance, one small childish power which she knew she could exercise, and which would not go unnoticed. The knowledge of failure was very close to Susan. She plunged her spoon into the soup, wondering if the hours between now and the time of her departure would ever pass, and if, when she returned to London, it would be only with the thought of having done more harm than good by coming here.

It was at the moment when Sydney bent over his master to remove his plate that they caught the first sounds of a car on the gravel outside. Sydney laid down the plate again, his bent shoulders stiffening, a look of fear and anxiety coming into his face. He grew so pale that Susan's impulse was to go to help him. She glanced at Lionel, and the old man was sitting erect, in an attitude of listening, but his expression wasn't one of fear. The door-bell rang loudly through the house, and Sydney hurried away to answer it. Neither spoke as they strained to catch the sounds of voices in the hall. Suddenly Lionel leaned towards Susan. "What's happening? Can you hear?"

The words were impossible to distinguish, but the tone of the voice which answered Sydney's greeting was immediately familiar to her. She said slowly: "I think it's Louis."

He looked towards the door in surprise. "What the devil has he come at this time for?" He turned back to Susan, as if suddenly remembering a connection between the two. "Do you know why he has come?"

She didn't begin to answer, because the door opened sharply, and Louis entered the room, with Sydney close behind him. Lionel struggled to his feet, gazing at his son with a mingled air of pleasure and bewilderment.

"Good evening, Susan," Louis said. "Good evening, Father. Sorry to burst in on you like this. I tried to make it before dinner." He looked back over his shoulder at the manservant. "Sydney, could you get me some soup? I'm famished."

"Very good, sir."

When the service-door swung to behind him, Louis turned to the two at the table. He looked from one to the other gravely. "There's been a spot of trouble about Racey. I came down as soon as I heard."

His father sank back into his chair. With one trembling hand he grasped his napkin; his face was white and fearful. "Is it something to do with that telephone call Sydney took? Someone was trying to reach Racey . . . said he wasn't to take off."

Louis nodded. "I'm afraid so. I'll explain . . ." He broke off because Sydney had returned with an extra plate. Louis walked round and dropped into the place which had been laid for Midge. Silently he began his soup.

The old man watched him carefully, as if seeking from the bent head, the quietly moving hand, some explanation of his son's arrival.

To Susan, he seemed to have aged subtilely in those few moments. Awareness of a threat to Racey had struck at him and while he didn't seek to avoid it, he was bewildered and afraid. He sat, with hunched shoulders, indifferent to his surroundings and to the food which Sydney placed before him.

Susan kept her eyes away from Louis. She was glad, watching her still and calm hands, that they had not betrayed her. This further meeting with Louis was an alarming piece of circumstance, forcing her back into the situation from which she had fled that morning. Probably Louis would never again voice the question to which she had refused an answer, but in her presence there was an unspoken criticism. This morning, by refusing to meet his questioning in the Carlton Mews flat, she had given him command of the situation. She was conscious with every part of her that he still held it. There was confidence and a new kind of power in his attitude as he sat there, still and alert.

They hurried through dinner, and even Sydney, sensing all the things which waited to be said, hastened through the service with the speed of a young man. At last Lionel, unable to suffer his own impatience and anxiety any longer, imperiously declined cheese for all three, and shuffled round swiftly, even before Louis could rise, to pull out Susan's chair.

In the drawing-room the fire had burned low, and no one seemed to notice that it needed replenishing. The chill struck Susan as soon as she entered, but it was so much a feeling of atmosphere that she didn't think to glance at the grate. Sydney had already left the coffee tray, but none of the three made any move towards it. Louis closed the door, and came towards them, and now all the urgency of his manner was expressed in his walk. All his energy seemed to be concentrated on an effort to make them understand his words with a minimum of questioning. They took their seats, Susan and Lionel, one each side of the fire, and waited for him to begin.

He looked at his father, who sat calmly enough, his body erect, as if determined to listen in silence. "I'm sorry, Father, that you have to hear about Racey like this, but there's nothing else for it."

Lionel said quietly : " Tell me, son, what is it ? " Susan was stirred with pity and admiration for him.

"I had a phone call this afternoon," he began slowly. "It was from someone—a man—who said he was a friend of Racey's. I didn't understand in the beginning, because he began to tell me that he had been tipped off that the customs men were going to be at Hythebourne to-morrow when Racey lands, and they'd search the plane."

Lionel flushed alarmingly. "Why ? "

Louis moved closer to the fire and stared down at it, hands in pockets, not looking at either. "Because every time Racey makes one of his short trips, he brings back a cargo with him. He's been doing it too often, and now they've found out."

"Oh, God ! " the old man said. " Oh, God ! "

"The person who phoned me," Louis continued, "was obviously the one who disposes of the stuff when Racey brings it. He was going to try to reach him by phone in Paris to-night. That's his only chance. If he can't contact him, Racey will land to-morrow with his usual load. God knows what will happen after that."

Lionel crumpled suddenly, his head falling miserably into his hands. " What are we going to do ? " he whispered.

Louis didn't answer him, but went swiftly to a cabinet and brought out a brandy bottle and glass. He placed them on the tray and half-filled the glass, returning to his father and urging him to take it. He watched anxiously as the old man took the first mouthful. After a few minutes he took another sip, and then looked up at Louis earnestly.

" What are we going to do ? " he repeated.

Louis straightened. " I don't know," he said.

Susan shivered. The chill of the room, or the sound of his voice, had penetrated deeply. There was so much more at stake for the old man than just the punishment of his son. There was his love and pride, there was terrible anxiety. He was very old, and it was for himself and for what he would lose, as well as for Racey, that he grieved.

" The stuff shouldn't be difficult to hide, if only we're

given the chance. Lace and perfume . . . things like that. But there's nothing anyone can do if the police and customs men are on the field when he lands."

Lionel sat upright. " Then he must be warned. It's a matter of who reaches the plane first. If Racey could take off again . . ."

" I've been thinking of that myself," Louis said thoughtfully. " There's just a chance that it might come off. If he took off again he'd be in trouble for resisting the police, but at least he could get rid of the goods."

With one last gulp Lionel finished the brandy. Some of his fear had left him. " That's what we must do. Yes, that's it." He seemed pleased, happier. The knowledge, once faced, was much less dreadful than the nameless something at which Louis had hinted. Returning hope restored him temporarily. He gazed from one face to the other—from his son, with his dark handsome face grave and concerned, to his son's wife, pale skin and red hair across which the fire cast a strange light. It angered and bewildered him that he saw no reflection of his own enthusiasm in their faces. They had no faith, these two. They did not believe that there was anything to be done for Racey.

" Why," he demanded, " did Horace not tell me what he was doing ? How long has this been going on ? "

Louis heard the words with misgiving. " He's been doing it for more than two years."

" So long ? He's been deceiving me all that time ? " His voice quivered in misery. " I would have stopped it—he knows that. That's why he didn't tell me. . . . I would have stopped it."

Louis stirred in quick anger against his brother. " He gave you that," he said, pointing to the brandy. " Didn't you ever guess ? "

" That was nothing. Nothing ! " He waved his hand, dismissing the suggestion. " A few bottles of brandy each time he came back . . . that was nothing. No more than anyone tries to do when they're coming back from France. How was I to know there were other things ? What did you say—perfume, lace ? My God, what is Horace thinking of ? " He shook with a strange kind of rage, fearful for his son, yet hurt and angered by the deception. He looked at Louis. " Did you know about it ? "

" Yes, he told me about it a long time ago."

" You didn't tell me," he said. And then, imploringly : " But you should have told me."

" I hoped it would never be discovered. You need never have known."

" Only fools think they'll never be discovered," Lionel replied bitterly. " I know better than that what was in your mind. You hoped that I should be dead before this happened."

Louis said nothing. A deep silence settled over the group about the fire. They each of them had their eyes fixed on the ground, considering the problem, imagining what the morning must inevitably bring. But for Susan it had altered, from the moment of the first telling. She was now seeing it as something in which Lionel was the principal figure. She knew his hurt, his fear ; she felt an admiration for the way he faced it. For it was on him, in the end, that the greatest blow would fall. He would suffer more even than Racey. And that he realised this, she could tell from his face.

At last he stirred. He slipped his hand into his pocket for his watch. The routine of going to bed was changeless, even when he faced a night sleepless from worry. The anxiety he did not show now, he could give way to in private. He stood up slowly.

" Louis, the fire is going down. If you and Susan are staying any longer, you'd better see to it." He caught the mantelpiece a little as if to rest himself. " Good night, Susan. Good night, Louis. I wish you'd see Sydney before you go up, Louis. Breakfast ought to be a little earlier in the morning. We ought to be ready in case Horace is early."

They watched as he slowly made his way across the room. His walk was old and shuffling, but Susan was aware of the pride and discipline which would never leave it. The door closed behind him quietly.

She had expected that they would begin to talk as soon as the old man left them, but it wasn't that way. Louis put some wood on the fire, and touched it gently with the poker. Then he dropped into the chair his father had vacated. The silence between them was of a mixed quality, neither unfriendly nor intimate. She watched him for a long time. An autumn wind was stirring outside. Behind the securely drawn curtains she pictured the blackness of that untidy tangle of lawn. The wind would rustle through the long grass in the garden. It was an unhappy sound, like ghosts whispering together.

" What a bloody fool he is ! " Louis' voice, very human and close to her, was a shock.

" Racey ? "

" Of course. He's crazy to think they wouldn't catch up with him sometime or another. And of all times it had to be when you are here."

" Does that matter to you, Louis ? "

" Matter ? Of course it does." He looked at her calmly.

" Why ? " Immediately she wished the word unsaid. They were drifting back towards the mood of this morning, and she was unable to face it.

" Because I needed to be able to see you, talk to you, without having trouble like this to cope with as well. You do see that, Susan, don't you ? "

Fear drove her back from him. She rose to her feet quickly.

He rose at the same time, as if to stop her, but his hand fell back at his side. " Why are you going away, Susan. Why did you leave this morning ? "

She leaned against the mantel, looking down into the fire, staring at the log which Louis had placed there. It had caught and was burning brightly, the flames eating in at the ends, and curling slyly round the middle. " Louis," she said slowly, " you and I did all our talking years ago. We talked too much, and we burst our marriage wide open.

It doesn't leave anything to be said now. We've finished with each other, you and I."

" I can't believe that."

She turned and faced him directly, thinking that she had never seen him with this look before, this expression of earnestness and slight bewilderment. At the same time he was confident that she would break before it. " You must believe it, Louis," she said. " It is all ended now. It was ended long before we started the divorce proceedings. This is just the part that hurts a little—we're both humiliated because we weren't clever enough to make our marriage work out. But if we're really truthful we'll both admit that when I take my plane on Thursday, there'll be a sigh of relief on both sides. This is the sticky bit, but we'll be over it soon enough."

" Susan, you're not giving either of us a chance."

" We had our chance long ago, Louis, and we muffed it. I wanted you to give me a divorce because I'd finally made up my mind to marry again. I've known Paul more than four years. I've worked under him, and I understand that man through and through. I'm surer of him than I am of my own right hand. He hasn't got a vice or a virtue that I don't know about, and he can't pull any more surprises. Don't you see, Louis ! I'm sure this time—very sure. I'm going into this marriage with my eyes wide open. There isn't going to be any failure."

He didn't reply. His lips were drawn tightly, but she saw that it wasn't in impatience or anger. He was thinking about her words, and there wasn't yet a reply to them, or else he didn't think it worth while making one. He looked like his father now, she thought. Emotions tightly held in check, while his light blue eyes flickered over her. They were Racey's eyes as well, and Midge had them too. Peculiarly brilliant at times. They could also be icy, and colder than anything she had ever imagined. Abruptly she turned away from her study of him.

" So you see, Louis, why there's nothing we have to say to each other. You must make up your mind about Midge, because I want to know as soon as possible. Anything else will be just a waste of time. We've both got our separate lives to go on living once this is over, and the sooner we start, the better."

She left him then by the fire, and began to walk across the room. At the door his voice halted her. " Susan ! "

" Yes ? "

" Good night. Sleep well."

" Good night, Louis."

He watched the flow of her skirt about her hips as she turned again and opened the door. For a long time he stared at the place, seeing her as she had stood there with her head outlined against the white panels. Then he took another glass from the cabinet and poured brandy for himself. He took his father's chair again before the fire, sipping the brandy slowly. It wasn't of Susan's words that he thought, but of the way she had looked as she uttered them. A warm colour had stained her pale face : where her dress was cut away from her throat he had seen a little pulse leap. The flicker of the firelight had caught the red in her hair. But through it all, through the vision of her, the fumes of the brandy, the gentle crackle of the fire, he began once more to hear her voice : ' *There's nothing more to say to each other.*' The words, quietly spoken, seemed to echo round the room, whispered back at him from corners. He held the brandy close to his nostrils ; and he tried to shut out the sound.

Much later, Susan, lying still in the huge bed, became conscious of Louis' quiet movements in the room next to her own. She sat up, shivered as the cold struck her, and saw under the communicating door a pale streak of light. Then she heard him on the stairs, and in his room once more. A long time after the sound of his movements had ceased, the light remained there, a shining strip on the carpet. She lay awake until at last it was extinguished. Now as she lay in complete darkness, the sound of the wind in the garden pressed still closer about her.

MONDAY

I

THE SUN was shining when Susan opened her eyes. She blinked and closed them again, until the sounds of a stirring house about her forced her back into full consciousness. Now in the sunlight, the room was a brighter, more cheerful place. The silk curtains by the window moved lightly in the morning breeze; from the yard below there came the shrill cries of a child playing, and the shriller barks of a puppy. Listening to them, it was a long time before she remembered that this morning Racey was expected back from France.

The thought sobered her, and she got out of bed slowly, as though her body was unwilling to start the day's routine. She was aware that every part of her was resisting the happenings which she would force herself to face. Her thoughts went to Lionel, and she experienced a little of the agony of mind with which he must begin the day. His old body seemed to sustain so little life, and now it must be recklessly expended upon these hours of misery and doubt. She began to wish, while she gathered up her toilet things, that the day was ended, and whatever its events, that they were past. The rush of time and fear, and a new, obscure kind of dread, were all sweeping across her. As she left the room she suddenly knew the urgency of the hour, the need for hurry.

The bathroom at Hythebourne was a strange apartment. It was a perpetual threat to a stranger to the house, for the door opened inwards upon a flight of steps, at the bottom of which was a raised platform. On this stood the bath, and directly opposite was a door leading through into the dressing-room of the main bedroom. Susan could never imagine how it came into being, for it looked like an oversized and inconvenient cupboard. It was always icily cold, and the one window came level with the platform, so that when one sat in the bath one could look out over the stable-yard and fields. Susan locked both doors, tried the water and found it tepid. She spent as little time as possible there, but the breakfast bell was already sounding as she climbed the perilous little flight of stairs to the higher door.

She found her walking shoes outside her door when she returned, and someone, probably Sydney, had replaced the flowers which had stood on the bureau yesterday. Faint noises of the household came to her as she dressed and underneath, from the dining-room, she caught the occasional clatter of the dishes. There was no one to be seen as she walked down the stairs, but Midge's high-pitched voice came clearly to her. The child looked up unwillingly as she entered the room, as though reluctant to admit her presence. Louis and his father rose at once, but the old man's greeting, mumbled far back in his throat, was scarcely audible to her. Susan spoke quickly to Louis and Midge, and passed on to the sideboard where Sydney had left fish on the hot-plate. There was silence over the table when she sat down. Susan knew that only Midge had been talking as she came down, and now even the child was quietened by an atmosphere which she sensed, but could not understand.

Louis heard the car first.

Susan glanced in his direction the moment he laid down his knife and fork. His body did not move, but she had the impression that he stiffened.

His father glanced at him sharply. "What is it? Can you hear something?" He looked hopefully at them both. "Is it Horace back already?"

Susan had caught the sounds also. She shook her head. "No. It's a car."

They waited, in attitudes of listening, until it turned in by the dovecot, and then the old man stumbled towards the window to see it before it swept round to the front of the house. "There's only one man in it," he said. "Thought they'd send a pack of police as well."

He returned gloomily to his place at the table, but did not attempt to go on with his food. Midge wriggled down off her chair. "Who is it, grandfather?"

"I don't know, my pet. We'll see in a minute."

Louis looked quickly at his watch. "Midge," he said gently, "hadn't you better be on your way to the Blakes'. It's almost time."

The child answered promptly, looking towards the old man: "But I always stay at home the days when Racey is here. Grandfather never sends me."

Lionel gestured apologetically. "That's right, Louis. She never goes on the days when Racey is here." Then, a little more softly: "The child doesn't have much, you know. It makes a little excitement for her."

Midge watched her father carefully, waiting for the word of assent, though half-expecting to be refused. She was ready, Susan knew, to obey unquestioningly, whatever he decided.

Louis, impatient for the child to go, nodded. "All right, Midge. But you'd better run outside. We want to talk."

Midge nodded and slipped away from her grandfather. At the door she stayed, because it had opened before her, and Sydney stepped inside. Behind him the three at the table caught a glimpse of a man wearing a loose overcoat. Startled by his sudden appearance Midge sidled past, then broke into a swift run. They could hear the sound of her footsteps dying away on the stairs.

Sydney said gravely: "A Mr. Cutler from Customs and Excise to see you, sir."

The man stepped into the room and looked at them mildly. Seated there, to Susan's mind, they must have presented a solemn front of resistance, but he went on gazing at them mildly. He still carried his hat, a soft, crushed, expensive brown one, as if he had been unwilling to hand it over to Sydney.

At last Lionel said : " Thank you, Sydney. That will be all."

The door closed behind the manservant, and they all turned their attention again to the stranger. He smiled at them ; the smile, sudden and unexpected, worried them. He stood there with the ease and the simplicity of a close neighbour, and for that very reason he seemed to contain more menace. He might have been almost middle-aged, but he looked young, and his skin was firm and pink, as if he spent a great deal of time in the open air ; he had a thatch of very straight, very blond hair.

" I'm sorry," he said carefully, " to burst in upon you at breakfast time. I had no other choice." He looked at the old man, and said nothing more.

Under his gaze Lionel shifted unhappily. " Won't you . . . er . . . sit down ? "

Cutler nodded gravely, dropped his hat on a side table, and slipped easily from his overcoat. Susan noticed that his tweed suit, soft and loose-fitting, was well cut. With his strange but insistent politeness he said : " Do you mind if I pour myself some coffee ? At the pub down the road where I slept they only know about tea." Taking the silence for assent, he moved to the sideboard.

They watched in growing fear, while he poured the coffee, and came back to take Midge's vacated place. Here, in this new intimacy of the breakfast table, the threat in his easy movements, his quiet manners, seemed to increase immeasurably.

He stirred his coffee slowly, looking at the old man. " It's about your son, Horace, that I've come, Mr. Taite."

Louis spoke for his father. " Is there something wrong?"

Cutler faced the other, the look of mild surprise still on his face. " Yes, there is something wrong. I thought you'd know."

They remained silent under his accusation. He sipped at his coffee while they waited for his next words. The tension heightened perceptibly. Susan could feel her body grow tight and rigid, and looking across, saw Louis' hands on the table betray him. Lionel, too, sat with his air of fearful expectancy. His aged and thin face had flushed darkly.

Cutler continued, and as he spoke he stared down at his cup. "I've come down, Mr. Taite, because I want to examine your son's plane when he lands this morning."

Louis said quickly: "And why?" The words were unthinking, too swift.

Cutler looked at him, faint surprise on his face. "And why not? Your brother has been making trips to the Continent in his own aircraft. He has every opportunity of bringing goods into the country illegally. Why shouldn't I examine his plane?"

His gentleness made him more formidable. Susan regarded him, sitting there, seemingly absorbed in his coffee, and she knew that his presence carried a very powerful threat. His firm, clean-cut face was unshadowed and incorruptible. Unable to stop herself, she gazed at his hands; they were small and neat, like his body.

The old man spoke slowly, his speech blurred and hesitant. "What do you expect to find, Mr. Cutler?"

The other shrugged elaborately. "I hope I shall find nothing."

No one spoke any more. Susan was glad that neither Lionel nor Louis had troubled to deny Racey's guilt. They each sat wrapped in their own particular silence, and none of them mistook it for a silence of ease. It was the stillness of mistrust and waiting. Susan glanced uneasily across at Louis and then at his father. Neither took any notice of her. She knew, in those long quiet minutes, that each one of them was thinking about Racey. But their thoughts possessed no unity. Each might make a bid to save him, but each plan would fail because of a counterplan. There was nothing binding them together; their thoughts drifted about insecurely, and it almost seemed as if the quiet man, sitting in Midge's place, could read them at will.

At last there was no more to do. They had finished all the coffee, all the toast had been eaten; they could not drag out the seconds by passing the marmalade any more, so

Susan got to her feet. Cutler also rose and drew out her chair. Close to her now he looked younger. A faint odour of shaving soap still clung to him.

Cutler went to the table where he had left his hat and coat. They all began to trail from the room in that peculiarly aimless fashion of people who have time to kill. There was no thought in their minds that they might do anything but wait. The front door now stood open, with the sunlight streaming in on the tiled floor. Outside, parked neatly where Racey had first left his car, was the open sports model in which Cutler had arrived. Unobtrusively standing within the shadow of the wall, it was marked with his own kind of quiet and menacing efficiency.

As the others moved on, Louis pulled Susan aside abruptly. She felt, with astonishment, an awareness of his physical presence. The knowledge startled and shocked her, so that she listened without comment to his instructions. "See if you can get Cutler into the morning-room. I want to talk to the 'old man,' and he's better kept inside the house if we can manage that."

But Cutler was already at the door and was looking at them as if he had guessed Louis' words. "If I go through the garden and the orchard will that bring me to the field where I saw the hangar?" There was the same polite insistence in his voice.

Susan said swiftly: "Mr. Cutler . . ." But she didn't continue. It was pointless and stupid when they all knew that nothing would prevent him going where he wished to go. "I'll show you the way," she finished dully.

He smiled at her—that mild, pleasant smile with which he had first greeted them. He didn't triumph, but accepted calmly the fact of her submission. "Thank you," he said politely.

She stepped out before him, leading the way to the garden. He opened the gate for her, but as she passed through he halted her. The light pressure of his fingertips on her arm possessed a sense of urgency. He said: "Are you Louis Taite's wife?"

She felt a hot flush burning round her collar and on her cheeks. Her first impulse was one of annoyance, and she made a movement to break from his hold and walk away.

"Please don't," he said quickly. He loosened his grasp. "I'm not just being stupidly inquisitive."

"Then why ask?" she replied tartly. "Surely you don't have to put that in the official report?" She began to walk swiftly down the path through the tall grass.

He hurried after her, but there wasn't space to draw up beside her. He fell into step behind. Without looking at him, she said over her shoulder: "I dislike official inquiries, Mr. Cutler."

He caught up with her as they entered the orchard. "This isn't official."

She quickened her step. "I don't want to discuss it."

He stood still and called after her: "I think you'd better. If you don't give me some information I'll ask Louis, and that's going to be rather painful all round. And I mean really painful. You see, we used to know each other in 1940. He's forgotten me, of course."

She stopped and wheeled slowly.

"Look," he said, "I think we'd better begin all over again. I'm David Cutler and I used to be C.O. at Reading when Racey was stationed there. Am I making sense?"

"Yes, go on."

"I know Racey as well as one man ever knows another in the services. Louis used to blow in sometimes. I liked him, too, because there wasn't anything to choose between them in those days. After a while Racey was posted away, and I didn't hear anything more about them. Then in the V2 period Racey applied to come back. I heard then about what happened to Louis. It didn't surprise me much when he looked at me this morning as if he'd never seen me before."

"I see," Susan said thoughtfully. She began to walk very slowly down the path through the trees. After a minute she stopped and turned to him again. "I don't understand fully," she said. "I suppose you really are from the Customs?"

He nodded. "Yes, that's true enough. It isn't my usual job to go chasing about the country after people like Racey. I'm hoping for his sake that whatever he's got—if he has anything at all—is relatively unimportant. I happened to hear about this job and connected Racey's name and the fact that I remembered he lived here. I thought that if he was going to get into trouble, it had better come from me."

"What will you do if he has anything with him?"

"He'll have to be charged, of course, but I'll be able to dispense with a lot of ceremony about the thing. You needn't have dozens of police swarming over the house."

"And do you imagine Racey will thank you for that?"

"And why not?" He laughed, a deep, slow laugh. "Believe me, I know Racey well enough to know that. He's not the type whose price will make him buck at a little help from a friend when he needs it. The fact that I may have to charge him wouldn't worry him in the least."

They walked on in silence and halted finally at the gate into the field. David Cutler didn't go any farther, but stood there by the hedge, looking across the field towards the hangar. After some time he glanced sideways towards his companion, but she was staring back into the orchard. The bright morning sun caught the side of her head, and where it had seemed dark red before, it was now gold. She was pale, and her eyes held a thoughtful, almost preoccupied expression. He knew, instinctively, that she was not actively concerned with Racey's fate; an awareness of it hung in her mind as a kind of background to some bigger problem.

David said gently: "Do you mind now answering my first question?"

"About me?" She turned her face towards him. "Yes, you're right. In a sort of fashion I'm still Louis' wife."

He smiled briefly. For a second she saw a touch of sadness in it. "I remember giving Racey twenty-four hours' leave to go to your wedding."

"You remember that . . . after all this time?"

"One didn't easily forget Racey or the things he did. He sometimes talked about you, and I used to wonder which of them, if either, you'd marry. I was glad it was Louis."

She shrugged. "It didn't make much difference, did it? When the divorce comes through I'll be free of both of them."

He nodded. "Racey told me things came unstuck between you. You went back to America."

"Yes, that's right." Then she added crisply, "Does all this matter to you?"

"My dear lady, it didn't matter two hoots until I walked in this morning and saw you all sitting there in a picture of domesticity, and I didn't know whether you were the same wife, the ex-wife, or perhaps a new wife. It did even occur to me that you might be Racey's wife. I simply began to ask questions to avoid treading on people's corns afterwards."

"You're careful, aren't you?" Her tone was tinged with malice.

"That's what I like to think." He said it gently.

She knew then that she had been angry for some minutes and had refused to admit it. Now she was aware that she didn't want any more of his company, his impersonal politeness. She looked at him coldly and felt her annoyance growing because he could seem indifferent to it. "I'll have to go," she said curtly. "You can make your way back, I expect."

He began to say something as she turned away, but she didn't stop to listen. Her feet crunched noisily on the fallen leaves in the orchard, and through the foliage still on the trees, the sun shone down brilliantly. The cool green loveliness checked her mood of anger; she slowed her pace. Her anger now appeared foolish beside his calmness, and he would know as well as she herself that a sense of guilt had driven her away from him. Why was it, she wondered, that the thought of failure persisted within her, until every mention of her marriage seemed a direct reference to it? She halted out of sight of David Cutler. This, and the garden beyond, had been her favourite places at Hythebourne. During the long summer twilights she had lain here in the soft grass, listening to the grasshoppers, and the rise and fall of Louis' mother's voice in the garden beyond, as she and one of the gardeners had made their round of the flower-beds. Sometimes when he had leave, Louis had come here with her. There had been uneasy silences as the twilight had given way to the quiet dusk, their silences had possessed a companionable quality, but now they said nothing because suddenly there was nothing to say. He had been tender and kind to her during those months before Midge's birth, but it had been the kindness of a well-meaning stranger. They had suddenly lost the ability to communicate, so that not even their growing estrangement could be talked of. There had been nothing for her to put her finger on except that strange coldness, a new kind of formality which in the past had been torn aside by the passion of their love-making. She had thought about these things on those scented summer nights, and had wondered what he, lying on the grass beside her with his tall, lean body relaxed on the earth, thought about. Often, as they were there together, the bombers would come over, and the searchlights picked out the small clouds in the night sky. Then, it always seemed that he was glad they could go inside, could be relieved at last of their uneasy intimacy.

Susan felt an unfamiliar prickling at the back of her throat and behind her eyes, and wondered why, after these years, she should cry because Louis had not loved her in a way she had wanted. She hadn't shed any tears then, but at that time the rift had been too indefinite, the causes too obscure to permit the luxury of tears.

She dashed her hand across her eyes, and looked down impatiently at the traces of moisture. Quickly she started towards the garden.

II

THE FIRST sound of the plane was like an insect's tiny trumpet far in the distance. With each rise and fall of the light breeze the sound increased and diminished. For long minutes of tantalising uncertainty the household waited, but when the plane turned to circle back over Hythebourne there was no doubt that it was Racey.

As Susan hurried into the hall, Louis came down the stairs. Midge raced ahead of him, her face bright with anticipation, and without waiting for either, sped on out into the sunlight. She slipped quickly through the garden gate and down the path through the long grass. At the doorway Louis paused to wait for Susan.

"Have you seen Father?" he said. He wasn't looking at her, but searching the sky above for a sight of Racey's Proctor.

"I thought he was with you."

He glanced at her curiously. "No. I imagined you and Cutler and the Old Man were all over on the field."

She stood beside him for a second. Above she caught a swift glimpse of the reflection of the sun on the wing-tips.

"I saw him last with you," she said.

A sound behind caused them both to turn. The service-door stood open, and Sydney appeared, in shirt sleeves and apron, with the damp dish-towel still in his hands. He looked at Louis. "It's him, sir, isn't it?" The towel was twisted nervously in the thin, old fingers.

"Yes, Sydney. Do you want to come over?"

The other shook his head sadly. "Isn't anything I can do, sir. I'd rather not be there." Still shaking his head, he murmured something which neither could catch, and closed the door. They could hear his footsteps in the passage.

"Poor old chap," Louis said softly. "He'll take it badly. Of course, he worships Racey."

"He knows about it?"

" I should say he's known of it longer than I have. But Racey can't do any wrong in his eyes." He then caught her arm tightly. " Quickly, Susan. He's coming round."

The Proctor had passed over them and was now low against the outline of the trees in the distant fields. It was turning in a wide circle to come back towards the house. Louis started to run towards the garden, Susan following. There seemed little chance of keeping up with him, but unexpectedly, at the orchard gate, he stood and waited for her. When she drew level, he took her arm wordlessly and they ran on together. The smooth field lay before them, brilliant and lush in the sunlight. Across on the other side the hangar doors had been opened, and within their shadow stood David Cutler. They crossed the field towards him. He leaned idly against a wall, his cigarette sending languid smoke into the sun-warmed air. Looking at his relaxed grace, the nearness of the Proctor as it came in to land was quite unreal. As they approached he suddenly snapped to attention, dropping the cigarette and grinding it into the ground with his heel. He looked steadily at them ; but he leaned slightly forward, his weight balanced on his toes. Once again Susan was aware of his strength and confidence.

From behind the hangar Midge came towards them. She ran lightly, her whole face flushed with excitement which gave itself expression in an occasional skipping movement and a small laugh. Above the noise of the plane she called loudly : " I hate it when he bumps along. He always looks as if he's going to tip over." Then suddenly including David Cutler in the conversation she added : " But he never does. He's a very good flyer."

Cutler moved closer to them. His face carried for Susan a terrifying conviction of fear and his body was tense. He addressed Louis. " Where is your father ? "

" How should I know," Louis said rudely.

The other scanned the field anxiously. " My God, if he's . . ." He broke off, and turned to stare at the plane directly above their heads. It was landing, and at half the length of the field the undercarriage was almost on the ground.

Midge shrieked wildly: "Oh, look, look! He's down . . . no . . . up again. He's down! He's down!" She danced forward joyously.

The Proctor was moving across the field at a diminishing speed, slowing to take the turn and taxi back to the hangar. The dread in Susan's heart was almost suffocating; she glanced down and saw Louis' hands clench and unclench rapidly.

David Cutler's eyes followed her gaze. "Careful, Taite," he said in a low tone. "It won't do any good to warn him. You'll only get yourself hauled into this trouble."

At his words the small hope which had begun to swell within Susan faded. An indeterminable distance seemed to stretch between herself and the Proctor, which Racey had now, casually and confidently, begun to turn towards them. The moment the plane came to rest beside them, the moment he climbed down to greet David Cutler like a friend, would seem the beginning of the end of all that Racey's way of life represented. He had been foolish and wrong, but she didn't try to subdue the pity she felt.

At the other end of the strip the motor quietened and the small craft commenced its slow turn. David Cutler's shout ripped through her thoughts like a knife.

"Get back! Oh, my God . . . Get back! *Get clear!*"

From the cover of the hedge which had concealed him, Lionel Taite had emerged to begin his desperate dash to the Proctor. He ran blindly and uncertainly, all his frail strength pulled together in this gigantic effort to reach his son. With this single purpose before him he stumbled across the grass, his fixed objective the plane which appeared to have quietly come to rest close by. No thought troubled the old man of his son not seeing him, and he hurried onward with a feverish determination. The plane's slow turn was unexpected. Dimly he was aware of shouts, but that had been expected, and he took no notice.

A woman's scream split the air as the small group at the

end of the field saw him run directly towards the invisible, turning propeller.

Racey's contorted and agonised face did not halt him in his final spurt to reach the plane. The upwards swing of the blade caught him on the thigh the same second as Racey cut the engine.

There were no cries from the old man as Louis and Cutler raced towards him. He lay motionless on the ground beneath the plane, and above him the propeller was already becoming visible as the revolutions slackened in speed. Racey flung himself from the cockpit and was beside his father before the others reached him.

He bent over the still body, and his breath came in loud hoarse gasps, like half-strangled cries. "Oh, God," he said. " Oh, God."

Louis dropped on his knees and felt for the old man's heart. "He's still alive," he said. He touched the still body gently.

David Cutler, leaning over him, saw the bright blood soaking into the grass. The blood was on Racey's trembling hands, had stained the knees of Louis' trousers. The warm sun shone down on it, and in that swift moment—before he could bring himself to think of what must be done, with the sound of Susan's running footsteps coming closer and the child's farther away—the thought flashed through his mind that he hadn't expected the old man to have so much blood. He had seen blood before—had even seen a young airman cut in half with a propeller, but no one expected to see an old man die this way. He would very soon be dead—dead even before they could reach the house. Cutler wanted to do something to help him, but he didn't know how. This was the worst kind of bewilderment.

Angry because he was helpless, he turned sharply towards Susan. "For God's sake get the child out of here. Don't you know any better than to let her see this ?"

Midge's shrill piping screams had already begun. She had glimpsed the blood-soaked grass and the hideously torn thigh. The screams were like those of a hurt animal—

continuous, terrorised. Inarticulate, save for those strange half-human sounds, she gazed dry-eyed at the scene. She didn't turn away from the sight, but her clenched hands and her legs went rigid.

David guessed that she continued to stare because she had no power to do otherwise.

Susan turned swiftly and caught her up. The slight body was still rigid in her arms. She lay as if she had been frozen with terror. Her screams doubled in intensity. Susan caught her close and began to run.

Cutler dropped down beside Louis. He tore at the buttons of the old man's shirt. Life was leaving the quiet body rapidly. They were aware that Racey had stood up and slipped away from them. When Cutler looked up from his examination, Racey's hands were gripping the wing, and he was being sick, terribly sick. The sour smell rose on the breeze, the sounds of his retching were closer and louder than the child's screams.

Louis got to his feet. He glanced across at his brother; to Cutler, watching, his face giving no indication of his thoughts. " We've got to get him to the house," he said.

Racey rested his forehead against the wing. His face was deathly pale, but he had stopped retching. " I can't," he said hoarsely. " I can't touch him."

Cutler called to him. " I don't think there's much need to hurry." He had his fingers on the limp wrist. " We can't do anything for him. I think he's dead."

Racey looked up towards the speaker for the first time. Recognition showed dully in his eyes. " Oh . . . it's you," he said flatly. " Why are you here ? "

Cutler waved his hand in aggravated impatience. " You'd better go to the house and get some blankets," he said crisply. " We can't carry him like this."

Racey stared down at his father. His gaze was curiously impersonal. " Are you sure he's dead ? "

" No . . . I'm not sure," Cutler snapped.

" I killed him, didn't I ? " Racey asked.

Louis said loudly : " Shut up. Go and get some blankets."

His body rested limply against the wing. He seemed to make an effort to hold his head up. "But it wasn't my fault. He came straight at me. The propeller was turning and he didn't see it. He walked right into it." He looked, from one to the other in appeal. "That's right, isn't it?" His tone rose in a high, fevered pitch. "That's right, isn't it?"

"Pull yourself together, for God's sake," Louis shouted. "Go and get the blankets."

Racey stared at them for some moments and then wordlessly wheeled round and began to run towards the gate through which Susan had gone. The loose chin-strap of his helmet stood out stiffly from his neck as he ran.

Cutler gazed after him, and the muscles round his mouth tightened a trifle. He looked up at Louis and seemed about to say something but didn't begin. Then he bent over the old man once more. Louis dropped on his knees beside him.

There should be more dignity in death, Louis thought, as he stared down at the body of his father. A death like this was too swift for compassion, for pity. It was ugly and brutal, lacking in everything which the old man might have expected at the end of his life. When the young died violently they had the beauty of their youth to gild them, but when age was robbed of dignity death became grotesque. He remembered the time his mother had lain dying . . . the shaded room, the whisperings round the bed. He was firey with resentment as he looked at his father's face. The lips were blue and pain-drawn. He was thankful that the eyes had closed in unconsciousness and he didn't have to meet that dreadful death-stare. Then he, like David Cutler, looked down at the blood and the mutilated side. The agony must have been frightful during those two or three minutes while he lived. The breeze suddenly stirred the old man's scanty hair, and to Louis, the movement seemed irreverent. One expected the dead to lie still. He wished that his father's face might have worn any expression but that of surprise and shock. It was the kind of thing which wiped pity from your heart and, if you were like Racey, it made you sick when you looked at it.

He watched with faint astonishment as Cutler spread a handkerchief across the dead man's face. It was going to be difficult to start thinking of his father as being dead.

They began gently to straighten the old man's body from its lines of frenzied pain to stillness and dignity.

Midge's weight seemed to grow in Susan's arms. But more intolerable, as she hurried through the garden, was the burden of the thoughts she carried with her. They had broken with bewildering force about her at the moment when Cutler's stern order had compelled her to turn and face the terrorised child. To turn and suddenly face the accumulation of responsibility, to know with deadening certainty that the failure of her marriage was not the question of a relationship dying between herself and Louis, but the diverting of the life-stream which fed this child. Responsibility for failure rested deeply upon her now because Midge was overwhelmed in the kind of emotional crisis which demanded the aid of a mother, and Susan, touching the child for the first time in six years, holding the resisting body close to her, knew the sensation of impotence. Why should she, she asked, expect Midge to regard her in any light but that of a stranger who had appeared for a few hours, and who would surely disappear as quickly ? What permanance—but more important, what right of permanance—did she hold in the child's life ? And now, lacking even the skill to calm her, she was asking the charge of her from Louis, assuming the authority which for the first time she doubted her powers to administer.

How perilously close, she thought, one wandered towards the edge of self-destruction and never knew it. The feeling of guilt, repressed with firmness during each waking hour of these years, had at last found its release at the instant of the child's first scream. It tore at her now unmercifully, and its pain was like nothing she had ever known before. Useless to move with increased speed with Midge pressed in her arms, because it pursued with equal ease, hammering at her with the force of shattering blows. It was with strange relief that she heard Racey's footsteps behind her and turned to watch him coming.

Beside her he slowed.

"Keep her out of the way. She'll have to be quietened somehow." He began to run again.

She called after him. He glanced over his shoulder. "What is it?"

"How is he? . . . your father?"

"He's dead," he shouted. The words burst from him with violence. Then he ran on.

Susan pressed the child closer to her. The screams had not lessened; she uttered the cries as if the very sound would deny the reality of what she had seen. She did not clutch at Susan, but lay stiffly, dry-eyed still, and fingers clenced into her fists.

Susan bent over her. "Midge! Midge!" she said softly. The child didn't seem to hear. The dazed, terrorised expression was like a mask over her features. Her face had a sickly pallor. Looking at her, a new desperation seized Susan. She caught Midge more firmly, pressing her face in against her breast, and began to run. The child's muffled cries echoed faintly round the garden. The sounds brought a rush of memory upon Susan. The garden seemed to be peopled with all the distant voices of her past. Louis' mother speaking with her quiet accents, correcting, admonishing; Louis' own voice breaking with eagerness and passion on that summer night the first time she had come to Hythebourne. Midge's own cries came back to her, and the vision of the baby basket laid down on the path between beds of scented autumn flowers. Why should she remember now? she wondered. There was no time to remember. There was the terror in the child's face to think of—and the bewildered fear in Racey's.

At the garden gate she began to call Sydney. Her cries and the child's blended strangely. She stumbled across the gravel court, for the burden was growing heavy. Trembling, she stood in the hall and her shouts echoed over the house.

Sydney appeared on the stairs, Racey behind him. His arms were full of blankets, but when he saw Susan and the child, he passed them swiftly to Racey and ran down the remaining steps. " She's not hurt as well, Mrs. Taite ? Not Miss Charlotte ? " His tones quavered, begged her to deny it.

" No, Sydney. She's had a nasty shock. We'll have to get her to bed."

The old manservant looked away from her, looked in a bewildered fashion towards Racey. " What shall I do, sir ? You'll need help." He indicated the blankets.

Racey paused only to shake his head. " There's three of us. We won't need you, Sydney."

Sorrowfully the old manservant's gaze followed Racey as he sped out into the sunlight. Then, when the garden gate had banged behind him, he turned towards the terrified child.

" Hush, now, Miss Charlotte ! Sydney is here. He won't let anything happen to you." Deftly he took her from Susan's arms, cradling her with the ease of long experience. " Hush now . . . hush now." He jerked his head towards Susan, indicating that she was to precede him up the stairs.

She obeyed him because she had no will to do otherwise. The sight of him taking the child in his arms had brought to her a fresh recognition of the shadowy part she played in Midge's life. That his action had been instinctive and therefore unintentional, lessened it not at all. He had taken Midge from her simply because his years of service to the child had established first claim. Susan knew that she herself had abandoned all right to it. She leaned heavily on the banister, because suddenly the stairs were too steep. The walls seemed to sway forward with powerful menace. Her breath was coming shortly. At the landing she had a brief glimpse across the garden and orchard, caught once more the brilliant reflection of the sun on the shining surface of the Proctor. She was thankful that the trees hid from view the sight of the three men toiling around that still form, but the horror of what she had witnessed was none the less real. The bright green grass soaked with the bright blood—that was something one would not forget soon or easily. The warm beauty of the autumn day was destroyed, was false and harsh and jarring. Shivering, she made her way quickly along the passage towards Midge's bedroom.

Sydney laid the child on the bed with the tenderness of a woman. Mournfully he patted the rigid little limbs, murmuring to her in a voice weighted with his anxiety. He drew the coverlet over her gently, murmuring all the time. Midge had turned her face into the pillow, and her shrieks continued, muffled but still audible. Gradually, as Sydney mumbled his soothing phrases, the hand which Susan held in her own, began to grow limp. The cries dropped to a whimper, and gave place, at last, to real sobs. Gently, Susan turned her face round, and saw that her cheeks were now tear-streaked. Bending towards Sydney she whispered : " Get her a hot-water bottle and bring the dark blue bottle with the tablets which you'll find on the bureau in my room. Quickly ! "

While Sydney was absent Susan went on holding Midge's hand, sometimes stroking the thin, childish arm. The tears rolled unchecked down her face, but the terrifying rigidity had completely left her body. She sobbed quietly, head once more turned sideways into the pillow.

When Sydney returned, he helped her administer half of one of the tablets in the bottle. Together they wrapped more blankets about Midge.

" I'll stay with her," Susan said softly. " You'll be needed downstairs now."

He nodded. " What shall I do, Mrs. Taite ? Master Horace said . . ."

" Wait in the hall, Sydney. They must come soon. They'll tell you what needs to be done."

As the old man turned to go, she called again to him. " Sydney ! "

" Yes, Madame ? "

" I'd forgotten. . . . God, how stupid of me. You'll have

to telephone for the doctor immediately. I should have done it as soon as I came in."

Suddenly the manservant's face crumpled. The slightly impersonal mask of the well-trained servant slipped away; gone too, was the tenderness which he had shown towards Midge. Lines appeared darkly under the eyes and around his mouth. His features hardened in their expression of sadness and weary grief. "Will the doctor be any use, Mrs. Taite?" He uttered the words dully, as if his tongue was dry in his mouth.

She shook her head. "No, Sydney. He couldn't possibly have lived beyond the first minute or two—if even that long. But we must have the doctor at once." She paused, but the bewilderment and despair in Sydney's face forced her to find some words with which to attempt to comfort him. "He was old, you know. He couldn't have lived a great deal longer." She murmured, more softly: "It was so heroic—that last effort to save Racey. He was a very brave old man."

The other shook his head sorrowfully. "I am a year older than the master."

The pity she felt for him choked the words she wanted to say. She got to her feet swiftly, and crossed the room towards him. "Sydney, you mustn't grieve too much for him. We don't know what he thought when he died, but I'll swear that he was glad he was doing a service for Racey. Louis and Racey both—they'll need everything you've got now." Impulsively she caught at his hand and held it tightly. "If you go on as you've always done it's going to make it a lot easier for them."

He withdrew his hand slowly from hers. "Yes, that's what he would have wanted me to do. I'll remember that, Mrs. Taite." Some of his grim dignity returned to his face. He looked at her carefully, searchingly, and in that look Susan found the first traces of the kind of respect which he had never accorded to her previously. It was as if silently, they had formed a pact to guard the security of this house, to permit as few deviations from routine as possible, so that this morning's terrible events might come into their proper perspective against an ordered background. Sydney's expression of grief was not lightened, but when he left her with his light tread, she sensed that he had found some comfort.

She returned to the bedside and sat down, taking the child's hand once more in hers. Midge's eyelids flickered open for a second, but she turned drowsily on her side and settled more firmly into the pillows. Susan watched her face carefully, and then abruptly slipped on to her knees so that their two heads were close together. She wanted desperately to clutch the child to her, but it seemed futile. The time for that kind of demonstration was long past.

" Midge," she said in a low voice. " Midge."

It isn't often, she thought, watching the child's face settle into composure, that one single event can throw you back upon yourself, until every action is suddenly seen in a new aspect. And yet just that had happened in the instant when Cutler had reminded her of Midge's presence and she had turned helplessly to stare at her daughter. In a moment like that, she realised, you stopped being smug, stopped rationalising your own behaviour. You began to see how your life, nicely worked out to include, or not include, people like Midge, suddenly wasn't good enough. You wanted something better—you wanted to be trusted, and loved also, by this child. And then your own actions cut you off. Somehow you had to begin to retrace your tortuous way back to the time when that first decision had yet to be made. And it wasn't easy. All your whole life, carefully planned out, had never included or made allowances for events like the old man's death, and the sudden need for the child for guidance and comfort. You hadn't made allowances and you didn't know how to meet it. You had failed, would go on failing all along the line, and it simply hadn't occurred to you before. You were blind and selfish, and now, when you began at last to see, you were bewildered.

Her mind swung dizzily between emotions of fear and

despair, and all she could do was to cling tightly to Midge's
hand as if begging help and pardon. Now that her defences
against herself were so completely smashed she swirled
helplessly in the tide of condemnation, more helpless still
because she did not even begin to see a way back to self-
respect and integrity. It occurred to her, in those awful
moments, that perhaps she never would.

III

RACEY HELD his father's head, wrapped closely in a blanket,
during that stumbling journey to the house. Three of them
were too many, they walked with an unfamiliar, sidewards
gait, each holding stiffly to a part of the blanketed burden.
The sweat broke on Racey's brow as he regarded the two
who walked so awkwardly before him. He wanted to call
to them to stop, to gather his father's body in his own arms
and hurry on. It would take more than the courage he
possessed to press that blanket close to him, to feel against
his breast the stillness of tnat weight. When Louis had
tried to do this same thing, he had petulantly refused to
relinquish his share to his brother, the fear of betraying his
terror making him aggressive and loud-voiced. He was too
well aware of the glance of David Cutler when those
impatient, hot words had come pouring out, and he was
sick when he read the significance of it. There was sickness
in the pit of his stomach, and a dryness in his throat. He
wanted to clutch one of the trees as he passed and give
way to his sickness, even give way to the inward sobs
which had begun to rack him. The sweat broke more freely
under his armpits and on his brow. It ran into his eyes,
and he had to let it remain there, stinging and burning.

A nightmare of fear had closed about him from the
moment he had first glimpsed his father's strained, eager
face as he ran towards the plane. Since then he had struggled
but feebly with it, knowing that now, as in the past, there
was no release from it until he had burnt it out in drink
or talk or distraction of some kind. There was agony in the

thought that he was displaying his fear, but he was certain that something as monstrous as this could not be hidden. At the place where Louis' arms gripped the blanket the blood had begun to soak through. He saw it also on his own hands. His fear grew immeasurably. He tried to stop thinking, because thought could destroy all the slight composure he had drawn about him.

The sunlight beat down through the trees, making a lacy pattern upon the blanket. They had wrapped a grey army blanket about him. Racey could remember when the bombers had come in after raids the dead had been laid on stretchers, wrapped carefully in grey blankets. That memory had stayed with him vividly; it had become his own particular symbol for death and decay. This same symbol of death had invaded the security of Hythebourne. He had brought it with him, had shattered the gentle peace, had despoiled this bright day with its ugliness.

If only, he thought, he could get away from it for a little time—a few minutes even. If only these two, moving remorselessly towards the house, would grant him the saving space in which to fight with his fear and try to conquer it. But such an escape was unthinkable, because he was bound by a convention which did not recognise it. He gave a soft sigh, and Louis, hearing it, glanced back. Racey, knowing he had betrayed himself, did not meet his brother's gaze.

Louis turned back again, and in silence they continued their stumbling march towards the house.

In the doorway Sydney waited for them. He stood where the out-jutting stonework threw a deep shadow across his still, composed face. His thin figure was erect, but as the slow cortege approached, they saw him suddenly clutch the door-frame as his trembling hands sought a support for his body. He said nothing as they drew nearer, but even Racey, from the stupor of his agony, was roused to swift compassion for the suffering he saw in the manservant's face. Horror-stricken, Sydney gazed at the blanketed form, but still he uttered no sound. His lips were bluish and strained into a tight line. As he swayed and the sunlight caught his features at last, he seemed incredibly old and dried, as if he might crumble at a touch. But when they drew level he pulled his body erect once more, and gazed at Louis, waiting for his order.

" We'll take him into the study, Sydney."

Silently the manservant moved before them down the passage to a small dark room which contained Lionel's desk, crammed with untidy, and as Louis had often suspected, useless papers. A few straight-backed chairs stood about, and against the wall was the sofa where Lionel had rested during the afternoons. On this they laid him.

There was a long, painful pause of uncertainty then Sydney stepped forward and drew the blanket away from his master's face. None of the three younger men could see his features as he stood there gazing down, but he mumbled something hoarsely, far back in his throat. It might have been a prayer or a curse, and it carried all the old man's passion with it. He bent over his master with an unconcealed tenderness in his gesture ; he remained in that position for several minutes as if he were trying to understand the lines of pain and horror on the dead face. His lips began to move wordlessly as he stood there, but after a time he replaced the blanket gently and turned to face them.

He addressed Louis. " I've phoned Dr. Edwards, sir. I told him as best I could what . . . what had happened. He said he'd come immediately."

Louis nodded. " That's right, Sydney." And stirred by the sight of the manservant's suffering, he placed a hand tentatively on his arm. " He wasn't conscious more than a few seconds. He couldn't have felt much."

The manservant pulled away abruptly, his face unsoftened. He gazed round the three accusingly. " I know what I saw," he said in a low tone. " There's no one could look at his face and not know what he went through." Then he sighed softly and his aggression slipped away. " All my life I've served him—served him more easily than if he'd been my own brother." In a dazed fashion, as if the significance of the still form on the sofa had just struck him, he gazed at them.

A quiet sob broke in his throat and he turned to go. The three men parted before him as he stumbled from the room.

They stood about in awkward silence when he had gone. Racey, carefully keeping his eyes away from his father's body on the sofa, said: " Edwards should be here within the next few minutes. He'd only take a quarter of an hour from the village."

Cutler nodded, his fingers beginning to itch for the feel of a cigarette; he licked his lips, longing for the taste of the tobacco. " I need a cigarette," he said abruptly.

The two brothers gazed at him eagerly. His statement came in the nature of a release from their uneasy vigil. Released from the necessity of remaining, Racey said jerkily: " Come on. We can't stay here." He flung the door open, and the other two followed him into the passage.

He led the way into the dining-room, and Louis and Cutler stood by while he poured whisky into glasses hastily taken from a cabinet. He spilled a little, and when he moved the glasses round they left wet rings on the surface of the table.

Racey finished his drink in two gulps and returned to the table for more; with his replenished glass in his hand he faced Cutler. He seemed calmer, thought Louis, or else his struggle for composure was not so apparent. Racey said, a trifle sullenly: " I haven't seen you for a long time—not since I left the Command."

Cutler drew on his cigarette gratefully, determined that no one should detract from the luxury of this moment. He was not in a hurry to answer Racey's question—was even a little annoyed by the necessity. " No, that wasn't the last time. We ran into each other in a bar. Don't you remember that? It was . . . when? . . . You said you'd just got a job with Apsom Aircraft and you asked me what I was doing. Don't you remember?"

"Oh, yes," Racey said indifferently. He looked at his watch and frowned. "That doctor ought to be here. . . . What was it you were in? I've forgotten."

Cutler sipped at his drink. "Customs and Excise."

Louis leaned forward, watching his brother's face carefully as Cutler's words began to penetrate his clouded brain. He saw the first tremor of apprehension cross his features, but the drink and shock had deadened his impulses for he remained calm. Louis dismissed the possibility that Racey might be acting, because not even the hand which held the glass shook. Racey said thickly: "What are you doing here?"

A little flame of anger seemed to rip through Cutler's cool manner. "Can't you guess, you damned fool? Why do you think your father dashed out to the plane . . .? Why do you think he's lying in there now with his side ripped open? Why? Because he was trying to save you. He knew—everyone knew that I was going to search the plane."

Racey remained perfectly still, but the glass tipped dangerously in his hand. "What have you got on me?"

"What we'll have on you depends on what you've got in that plane," the other replied carefully.

Racey's face turned a dull red. "Who told you to come here? What makes you think you'll find anything?"

Faintly disgusted, Cutler answered carelessly: "We always find out. No one is ever quite clever enough."

"Useless lot of busybodies!" Racey snapped. "Pity you haven't got something to be more concerned about. And you . . . you of all people."

Cutler shook his head with weary contempt. "You don't think I've time to run round the country seeing to every trifling little job of petty smuggling, do you? You're damned lucky I did come. If I'd sent the regular man for this sort of thing, you'd have dozens of police milling round."

"Oh, for God's sake," Racey cried, wheeling round and taking up the decanter again. "What do I have to be grateful for?"

" Don't be such a bloody fool," Louis said.

Cutler's smooth firm brow furrowed with annoyance. " You'd better shut up, both of you. If the child hears you she'll start screaming again. God knows, things are chaotic enough without that." He pulled at his cigarette angrily, but neither of the two seemed to notice him any longer. Racey was leaning back against the sideboard, his elbows resting there, the drink in his left hand. Hundreds of times Cutler had seen him in that attitude, graceful, sullenly good-looking, hiding some sort of devilish fear and bitterness which occasionally broke loose, as it had this morning. Louis, hands in pockets, had gone to stand by the window, and for the first time, Cutler was aware of the change in him. His dark head, so much like his brother's, was bowed, slightly. His face was reflective in a way that Racey's never could be. It seemed at the same time, to be swept clear of emotion, as if the events of the morning had almost defeated him, and he struggled, in the sudden quietness, to regain strength. The sunlight shone in upon him. He raised his head to look upwards; it could have been, Cutler thought, a savage though unconscious gesture of resignation.

They stood in a silence broken only by the occasional clink of Racey's glass, until the sound of a car in the drive caused a little ripple of movement in all three. Racey's blank, sullen face turned towards the window with an unhappy little gesture.

Cutler said : " That's the doctor, I expect. Let's go out."

Louis nodded, and they left the room ; Racey came unwillingly, with slow steps. In the hall they waited while the young doctor parked his car, and then Louis went forward. Racey made to follow him, but Cutler laid his arm on him, holding him back.

Racey turned upon him quickly. " What the hell do you think you're doing ? "

Furiously irritated, Cutler motioned briefly towards Louis, who stood talking to the young man beside his car. " Someone's got to explain what's happened."

Racey made no reply, but angrily shook off the other's grasp.

From behind them in the service-passage Sydney had appeared, and the three stood and watched as Louis and the doctor approached. As they stepped into the hall, Racey opened his mouth to speak, then shut it again as quickly, falling back a little behind Cutler. At a nod from Louis, Sydney stepped ahead, and for the second time he was leading them down the passage towards Lionel's study.

They watched through the open door as the doctor made his examination. Racey kept up a restless pacing in the passage, coming to the door swiftly whenever the doctor turned to question Louis and listening carefully to what was said.

At last the doctor drew the blanket back into place, and they formed up again for their strange procession back to the dining-room. The doctor threw an interested and tolerant glance towards the decanter and glasses on the sideboard, and then began to shuffle with papers in his attaché-case. He was an erect, quick, young man, and Cutler knew that he had long ago sensed the odd situation, and played about now trying to find an opening.

He straightened and looked directly at Louis. "There'll have to be an inquest, of course."

From his lounging position against the sideboard, Racey jerked to attention. "What do you mean?" His eyes moved swiftly between the three.

The doctor shrugged patiently. "Your father didn't die of natural causes so there'll have to be an inquest. Purely routine."

Suddenly limp, Racey turned away.

"I'm sorry about this," the doctor went on. "I know it's unpleasant, but there's nothing I can do about it. It won't be anything much—about half an hour. The coroner is a very decent old chap. He'll get it through as quickly as possible."

Louis pulled out a chair and sat down. "We have known the coroner for a long time, Dr. Edwards," he said dully.

Then he looked up suddenly. "You haven't been in the district long enough, to know what good friends he and my father were. He won't like having to do this."

The other man shifted uneasily. "It takes time to know the business of everyone in a country district." He spoke stiffly, as if defending himself against criticism which had been piling up. "I'm sorry about the coroner. . . . I could speak to him about it. Perhaps he'd like someone else to take over."

Racey faced them again. "What does it matter who does it? Better old John Hayes than an outsider."

The doctor shifted his gaze uncomfortably to Louis. "Shall I leave the date for the coroner to arrange? Perhaps some day of next week?"

"No," Louis said. "That won't do. My wife will be asked to give evidence, and she's flying to New York on Thursday."

Racey moved impatiently. "Susan would wait."

"I'm not going to ask her to wait." Louis turned to the doctor. "I'll phone Colonel Hayes. We'll get this through to-morrow if that's possible."

"Then . . ." The doctor looked doubtful. "I suppose it could be done. I could get another doctor here this afternoon. We could have the report ready, I suppose, by this evening." He glanced about him, bewildered and half-appealing to them to remove the causes of his bewilderment.

But they gave him no help. As the silence continued he flushed darkly and angrily, leaning forward to make a note on the pad before him. In the stillness, the scraping of his coat-button against the table was hideous. When he had finished writing, he straightened and looked about him, resentful of the impersonal hostility which flowed between himself and the other men. Because he was a stranger, he had been made feel gauche and unimportant. He wanted them, in some way, to feel his authority, and didn't know how to achieve it. A sound at the end of the table caught his attention. Cutler had placed his finger-tips on the table and begun to drum them gently against the polished wood.

The sound irritated the doctor. He opened his mouth to speak, and annoyed, closed it again, when the other broke in before him.

"I'm afraid I've got something to do before we make any arrangements."

They all gazed at him. Apprehensive, Racey moved into the centre of the room, and Louis had shifted in his chair in order to see Cutler more easily.

He went on drumming. The sound grew maddening; perhaps he knew that, for he stopped abruptly, and the silence was deeper than before. "About the plane," he began. "I'll have to search that immediately. If there's anything there, we'll need to make other arrangements about the inquest." He paused and for the first time they knew him to be uncertain. He threaded his way through a maze of insinuation. "You understand, don't you? It might be rather difficult."

"Meaning," Racey said sullenly, "that you might need an armed guard on me?" Then he flared into anger. "What do you expect to find there—a crate of opium?"

A shadow of annoyance flickered across Cutler's face. He sketched an irritated gesture towards Racey. He walked to the door and opened it. "You can come with me if it would interest you—just as you please, of course."

Louis and Racey followed immediately. The doctor, left in the empty room, stared round in bewilderment, uncertain that the invitation had been extended to him. Then abruptly he got to his feet and went into the hall. The three men had already reached the garden gate; the confused murmur of their voices came to him faintly. With only a second's more hesitation he hurried to rejoin them.

IV

LOUIS HEARD the footsteps of the doctor behind and cursed inwardly. Without a word they allowed him to take his place at the end of the little column moving in single file through the long grass of the garden. Louis stared moodily at the back of Racey's neck, and he saw, suddenly, that beads of perspiration were standing out on it. As he watched, Racey brought his handkerchief up to wipe it. There was something hopeless and defiant about his action; it told him too fully that Racey expected trouble when Cutler examined the plane.

As he thought about it a fierce resentment broke over him. He stared at his brother in anger. Fool. . . . Bloody fool. All through he had behaved like a child who was blameless of nothing more than high spirits. Would nothing ever show him, he wondered, that the war was over, and with it the time for playing? All his life he'd played the fool, and let other people cover up or take the knocks for him . . . and he was doing it again. *He was doing it again.* Only this time no one had been able to cover up for him. There hadn't been any time, and now Racey's neck was wet with sweat and his hands were clenched, and he was walking into real trouble for the first time. Louis' anger left no room for pity. The old man had lain dead on the field, and Racey had been sick with fear for himself. It was that knowledge which twisted inside one like a knife, and didn't stop hurting no matter how one tried to forget it. Racey had been so sure that he was safe . . . he had been so sure of his own luck. His luck was always so good—hadn't he said that hundreds of times? He had believed in his luck, had trusted it like the movements of his own hands. It had failed so suddenly that he was left nothing to cling to, and as he sweated and stumbled on his way to the plane, Louis thought that he must be finding out for the first time in his life, what it felt like to be defeated.

They followed Cutler across the field. The young doctor had now drawn level with Louis, and in a low tone tried to question him. Impatiently Louis cut him off, and was immediately sorry. After all, he thought, the man wasn't to blame for wanting to understand the set-up, wanting to feel less of a fool than they had all made him seem. They had been unbearably rude to him. Louis wondered if it wasn't too late to make some amends; somehow these things were never forgotten and never got over. They rankled in the mind long after their importance had faded.

Near the plane the bright blood had dried a little on the grass, but there was a large, wet patch where the old man had lain. Louis didn't look at the propeller, but he knew the doctor's gaze had wandered to it. In the hedge a bird sang shrilly. Louis remembered it had sung like that while they had waited for Racey to return with the blankets. Suddenly, startled by their approach, it rose and flew out of sight. After that there was only the sound of light wind touching the trees in the orchard.

As Cutler got up to look into the cockpit, Louis realised that he was holding his breath. The three on the ground were silent as they watched closely. Cutler's head moved from side to side, and once he put his hand into the cockpit to touch something. He said nothing, and Racey moved impatiently about, shifting his weight from one foot to the other. At last Cutler glanced around, motioning Louis to come closer.

" Hold this, will you ? "

As he spoke he leaned into the cockpit and drew out a small wooden box. The tops of six bottles protruded from the straw packing. Louis placed it on the ground and straightened up immediately. But Cutler was already beside him. " That's all," he said curtly.

No one looked at Racey's face until Cutler, abruptly turning towards him said : " Was this all ? "

Racey shrugged, and his fear seemed to have slipped away from him. " If that's all you can find, then that must be all I brought."

Cutler said crisply : " One doesn't risk a smuggling charge in order to bring over a few bottles of brandy."

Racey was silkily smooth. " I suggest that whoever gave you your information had the facts rather mixed."

Cutler shrugged. " I don't for a moment believe that, Taite. It may just have happened that this time you were lucky. What went wrong? . . . Couldn't they get the stuff you wanted in Paris?"

Racey began fumbling in the pocket of his flying-jacket for a cigarette. He lit it carefully. Then he said: "What's the gaol sentence on half a dozen brandies?"

Cutler shrugged again. "I wonder how long it's going to take you to realise that I came down here—strictly outside my own job—to try to keep you out of gaol if it were possible. I don't think you realise how different this might have been. If I had caught you with what I imagine is your usual cargo you wouldn't have got off lightly." He half-turned, then glanced back towards Racey. "However, I'll have a poke round, just in case your manservant has taken it upon himself to risk moving the stuff." He paused, regarding the three before him. "You know, you're damned lucky I did come down. The regular man for this job would have the local police force out by this time pulling the place to pieces. In fact," he observed gently, "if I weren't so sure your father wouldn't have permitted you to use the house as a store, I might be tempted to do the same thing."

With that he left them. They stood in awkward silence while he began moving slowly along the hedges, stopping occasionally to thrust aside the foliage. It took him a long time to cover the whole field and to examine the hangar. The presence of the doctor prevented conversation between Louis and Racey. Twice in the interval Racey passed round his crumpled packet of cigarettes. Louis accepted gratefully, unaware until he took the first draw, of how badly he needed one. He stood, leaning against the body of the machine, with his eyes thoughtfully upon his brother. Racey had betrayed little or no emotion when Cutler had questioned him, but to anyone who knew him thoroughly, a small edge of his fear was still showing through. He was relieved, hopeful, but not quite certain. Louis would have given much to know if Sydney had removed the cargo, and if so, where he had hidden it. Racey's expression changed. Swiftly he returned to his old frame of mind; for him the old luck was still holding. Louis knew that, incredible as it was, he had almost hoped that Racey wouldn't escape. There ought to be a limit, he thought, to the number of things a man can get away with when he doesn't pay the price. Racey had never paid. It began to look as if he wasn't going to pay this time either. Under his breath Louis swore, and savagely tossed the cigarette butt to the ground.

He straightened as Cutler approached. He noticed that Racey's body jerked into rigid lines, and he began fumbling for yet another cigarette. On the grass under his feet were the half-smoked tips of the others. " Well ? " Racey said shortly, as Cutler drew near. " Find anything ? "

" Did you expect me to find something ? " Cutler laughed softly. " You're damned lucky. You'll get away with it this time. Don't be tempted again, though, because you'll be watched so closely you won't be able to go to bed in peace. They're not going to be very pleased when I send in my report—they don't like the bright boys being warned in time and getting away with it." He reached for a cigarette from the packet Racey held. " Do you mind . . . ? As I was saying—you'll be fined for the brandy, but that won't amount to much. And after this you'll have to be so well behaved you won't know yourself."

He accepted Louis' lighter gravely. " I heard the lunch bell when I was in the hangar. Shall we go over ? "

They followed him silently, almost meekly. His blond hair shone in the sunlight, and he moved before them in his assured, though mild fashion. Glad to escape from the presence of the two brothers, the doctor drew level with Cutler. They began to talk in low tones. The young man leaned eagerly towards the other ; he was talking, Louis supposed, about the accident, perhaps about the inquest. He talked rapidly, as if a restriction had suddenly been removed. The fact that Cutler was an onlooker in the tragedy, the same as himself, had brought them into sympathy. But Louis began to see, from the few words addressed to the doctor, from the fact that Cutler's eyes never once regarded his companion directly, that he himself did not welcome the young man's talk or overtures. Abruptly it was borne home upon Louis that Cutler was not an outsider—never had been. The slightly impatient tolerance of his attitude towards Racey was that of one who had known his faults completely and long ago forgiven them. Louis studied the back of that shining blond head carefully, until the touch of Racey's hand on his arm forced him to turn his eyes away unwillingly.

"That was a near thing," Racey said softly. His eyes were strangely bright.

"The day isn't over yet," Louis said testily. "Where's the stuff?"

The other shrugged. "You know as much as I do."

"Was it Sydney?" Louis said quickly.

"Don't see how it could be. He was there when the doctor arrived—he'd hardly have had time when we were in the dining-room."

"The cook then?"

"Useless!" His voice was contemptuous. "The woman would faint at the very suggestion of risk."

"Susan?" Louis uttered the name reluctantly.

"Could only have been Susan."

"But why should she?"

"Well, why not?" Racey was confident.

Louis glanced at his brother. "You're sure of yourself, aren't you?"

'I'm sure of Susan. She wouldn't let us down."

"She's got no particular reason to feel any sympathy for us . . . for you."

"She's got no particular reason for not feeling it either. I tell you Susan is a good scout. She'd help if she could."

Louis thrust his hand into his pockets. He walked a little way in silence. At last he raised his head. "Then Cutler knows." The figure in front had become menacing once again.

"He might have guessed, but he's not sure that I brought any stuff over. The best thing was that Susan left the case of brandy there—it looked as if the plane hadn't been cleared." He smiled a little with satisfaction. "That was damned clever."

Roused to resentment by his brother's tone, Louis asked impatiently: "The person who phoned me on Sunday—why didn't he get in touch with you in Paris? Why the hell did you bring anything at all?"

Racey looked at him in startled fashion. "You mean Stevens? Did he get in touch with you?"

"How else do you think I happened to be down here? Of course he got in touch with me. What I want to know is why he didn't contact you in Paris and stop you bringing any sort of a cargo. Lord knows, he had enough time."

Racey looked grave. "It's just one of those things—one of those stupid, impossible things which happen to throw the whole works out of gear. You see . . ." He continued uncertainly, "You see, I ran into a chap I knew years ago in a bar I always go to when I'm in Paris. We talked for a long time—I expect we drank too much—and with one thing and another I just didn't get along to the people who usually provide me with the stuff."

"Then what about the brandy? What about the stuff that's been cleared from the plane? Where did you get it?"

"Breedon got it for me," he replied. "It appears he does a little work in that line himself."

"My God!" Louis said simply. "My God!"

"What's the matter?"

"Nothing. Except that I'd like to know where it is you find all these people. Have you got one single acquaintance who is completely honest?"

"We've got to live," Racey said sullenly. "The bloody government doesn't provide jam any more with the bread and butter, so we've got to look for it ourselves."

"Depends on where you look for it." Then Louis shrugged, "However, it's your affair, not mine."

But Racey, hardly listening to him, was staring at the two ahead, and his forehead had gathered into a frown.

"Wonder how Cutler found out? And coming down himself was rather odd."

"Why?"

"Obviously the job's too small for him. He's one of these people who sit at a big desk all day and eager little men run round and try to please him. Lucky, though, that he's come, because once he's closed the case it stays closed."

And Louis, watching him, wondered if he consciously did not realise that there had always been people to do him services, just as Cutler had done. No matter how much they disapproved, no matter what Racey had done to be despised or condemned, there was always someone ready to help him. There was Cutler, and perhaps Susan to-day, and with equal certainty there would be someone else to-morrow.

"If only," Racey was saying, "if only I'd seen Cutler in time I'd have been able to get back over the Channel and dump it without any difficulty."

"The Old Man was trying to warn you," Louis said dully.

Racey stopped short. "Don't you think I know it!" His voice rose to a higher pitch. "Don't you think I know it! What do you think it felt like to see him coming towards me . . .? He was so bewildered when I turned . . . his face was screwed up in that way it goes when he's determined about something. Oh, God, he didn't even see the propeller. Didn't even see it. . . ."

Louis was silent, remembered the one cry which his father had uttered when the propeller struck him, and then the bright wet blood on the grass. Now for the first time he began to feel the pity he had denied to Racey. No matter how much he tried, this day wasn't ever to be forgotten. With them both, as with Susan and Cutler and Midge, would live the memory of that single, sharp cry, but Racey alone carried the vision of the Old Man's face—the confusion, the determination, and then the pain. No, he wasn't ever going to forget this day.

He touched his brother's arm in a slightly self-conscious

gesture of sympathy, and they walked on again. The sun was bright and hot. In the overgrown garden the smell of the damp grass drying was sharp and pleasant. Louis breathed it in fully; there was the smell of decay in the air as well, the smell of mounds of decaying, rotting leaves hidden in the grass. Never before had the desolation of this scene, familiar to him in the years since his mother's death, struck home so forcibly. For the first time the neglect and indifference seemed a breaking of faith. Some of the earliest things he could remember belonged to this garden—the low clatter of tea-cups and voices on drowsy summer Sunday afternoons, and the beloved silence when he had played in the garden alone. There was silence here now, a sad, heavy quiet which hung like a visible apathy between the high stone walls.

For Racey the smell of the mouldering leaves brought no fresh despair. Every living part of Hythebourne had crumbled when they had stepped across the doorstep with his father's body. There remained only the shell, the outward form of a house, and this broken bit of garden. The sooner it was closed the better; it was wearisome and futile to pretend that living could go on any more within it. 'I shall never come back again,' he told himself. 'Other people will have it, but I won't need to see how they will change it, how they will try to make it come to life again. It's dead now . . . it's dead.'

Involuntarily, at the garden gate they paused. The sun shone on the warm stone of the house, making it beautiful in a way that neither could deny. Suddenly anger rose in Racey as he gazed at it, because, in spite of him, in spite of what had happened that morning, it was living and vital still. He gave a sharp little sigh, and then walked on, lest Louis should suspect what was passing through his brain.

V

THEY ALL made an incredible effort to achieve normality during lunch, and now and then, to their surprise, it seemed to succeed. It appeared callous and unfeeling to sit down, to eat well, even hungrily, the soup and fish which Sydney placed before them, but there was nothing else they could have done. It became slightly shocking to remember that the cook, after the first few paralysing moments of trying to assimilate the news, had returned to the stove, and the lunch was served as usual, though twenty minutes late. Not death itself, Susan thought, could stop the routine. They would go on having meals at the same times, going to bed, getting up again even when, with the old man's going, the very reason for the routine seemed to have disappeared.

At the times when Sydney was not present, they talked a little, tried to recall the telegrams to be sent, the phone calls to be made. Having been upstairs to look at the sleeping Midge, and writing a prescription for more tablets, the doctor had gone, leaving them in a new intimacy with Cutler. It was now impossible to believe that he had drunk coffee with them that morning as a stranger. He sat talking with them as if he had been familiar with Hythebourne all his life, and it was he who removed much of the strain from the atmosphere, kept their eyes away from the chair where Lionel had sat, kept Racey talking, even, during those sickening moments when Sydney placed a plate at the vacant head of the table, and hastily removed it, uttering small, distressed sounds. Susan was relieved to finish, and rise.

Louis moved to open the door, and as she passed through he nodded slightly in the direction of the drawing-room. She made pretence of not seeing him, because, inevitable as it was that they would need to talk together, she was not yet prepared to face it. Those moments at Midge's side, the terrible period of self-revelation, had left her in unaccustomed bewilderment, a sensation that she had lost herself and was, in this state, too vulnerable, too open to the wounds of every chance word. Later she must make herself face the consequences of her acts, must face any accusation which might be read into whatever Louis should have to say, but for a little time longer she needed to be alone.

" Susan ? "

She turned. " What is it ? "

" Could I have a word with you ? " He spoke very gently, almost humbly.

The very gentleness seemed a threat. " Could you leave it a little, Louis ? I . . ."

He took a step towards her as Cutler and Racey reached the doorway. " I'm sorry about it, Susan, but this is important."

She saw Cutler glance from one to the other. He waited as did Racey, for her reply. Her lips moved stiffly. " Give me a few minutes. I've got to put a call through to London."

To be alone now seemed the most desirable thing on earth, but she was beginning to see that it must be sacrificed to the greater need—which was the need for Louis and herself to talk together and at peace.

She turned and walked quickly towards the dark, stuffy cupboard at the end of the hall which served as a telephone cubicle.

All the time while she waited for the call to go through she breathed urgent little prayers that Paul would be at the hotel. He had promised to be there when she returned, but that would not have been before five o'clock. ' God, let him be there,' she whispered. The sound echoed faintly round the dark walls. Her hand holding the receiver grew moist ; outside she could hear footsteps in the passage, and the low murmur of voices. Then they faded, and presently there was the sound of a door closing gently. The sounds about her increased the urgency of her need for Paul. Life at Hythebourne was stirring again after the first numbness, soon it would sweep on, and without Paul she would be caught up in the flow. Once more she whispered : ' Let him be there.' Back in her childhood she could remember this sort of invocation breathed softly at night when the light had been put out and the room was quite ᴄaɪᴍ. She couldn't recall whether she'd always got what she'd asked for.

The hotel answered, and she gave them Paul's name and room number. Half a minute later the operator was back to tell her there was no reply. Susan ran her tongue over lips which were now stiff and dry. "Will you kindly page him?"

There was the long tense wait; the pips sounded in her ear and she had a second extension of time. She wasn't hopeful any more, she was merely waiting to hear that he had not been found. Then faintly, from a long distance, she heard his voice.

"Paul?"

"Susan!" He seemed wonderfully near now, almost as if he had been able to reach out and touch her. She was warmed by the contact.

"Paul, it's urgent. Don't interrupt, because I've got a lot to tell you, and there isn't much time." She told him as quickly as possible, leaving out all reference to Cutler and the smuggled brandy. The relief of telling began to flow over her. She felt some of her tiredness receding. He listened in silence until she had finished.

"What are you going to do, Susan?"

"I have to stay. I can't leave when things are so uncertain."

"Is it quite necessary?" There was a hint of tightness in his voice.

"Paul, there isn't anything else to do. You understand? There's Midge to see to, and . . ."

He cut her short. "Yes, I know." She could hear a faint sound that might have been his fingers drumming against the receiver. Then he said: "I'm coming down. I'll get a car and come down. Right away."

She closed her eyes, and clung to the little shelf for support. "Yes, Paul. Do that." Her voice sounded strange.

"How do I get there?"

She told him as well as she could.

" I'll be there before dinner," he said. " Wait for me,
and don't let anyone start pushing you around." Then he
rang off.

Susan held the receiver in her hand, staring foolishly at
it until rapid footsteps in the passage jerked her back to
reality. She dropped it back into its cradle, and turned and
pushed open the door. Cutler stood outside.

He smiled faintly. " Hope I didn't make you cut off ? "

" No," she said stiffly. " I was finished." She made to
walk past him, but he called her back.

" Mrs. Taite ! "

" Yes ? "

He paused awkwardly. " I wanted to talk to you."

She said crisply : " I think everyone wants to talk to me.
Is there something in particular you wanted to say ? "

He nodded towards the telephone. " I'm going to phone
through to London now. They'll have to know all the
details. Of course, I'll have to tell them I've drawn a
blank."

" What has this got to do with me ? "

" From now on it will have nothing to do with you.
Once I make my report, the thing is closed—finished. You
understand ? "

" You mean—" she regarded him calmly—" you mean
that you have sufficient authority that if you say the case
is closed, it stays closed ? "

He nodded. " Exactly. Now what I wanted to ask you
—merely as a matter of interest, of course, because I
haven't a shred of proof—is whether you got to the plane
before we did. Either your brother-in-law has been very
lucky, or someone cleared it for him. I'd like to know
which."

She looked at him, and felt her liking for him increasing.
There was such simplicity in his demands. He had told her
exactly what was in his mind, and expected the same from
her. Had he been anyone else, someone less astute, she
would have suspected him of incredible naïveté. But he
wasn't naïve, he was just honest in rather a strange way.

"I couldn't tell you that," she said gently. "Either you'd suspect me of lying, or you'd be duty bound to search the whole farm. I shouldn't like either of those things to happen."

"Are you afraid of my ordering a search?"

She shook her head. "Mr. Cutler, I'm flying back to America on Thursday. I'll never see Hythebourne again or any of the Taites. That part of my life is finished, and it doesn't mean a tupenny damn to me any longer. Does that answer your question?"

He nodded, smiling quietly in his own peculiar fashion. "I expect it does. As well as I'll ever be answered." He shrugged and said: "It's a pity."

"What's a pity?"

"About all you people here. You're all in trouble . . . the Old Man, the inquest . . . and Racey will have to face a charge for that brandy. There's a hell of a lot of ways I could help if I were allowed to without stepping out of line about my job. But you won't be helped, will you? I know I'm a stranger in a certain sense, but I've known Racey a long time, and after what happened this morning ceremony doesn't hold water any longer."

"You mustn't count me among them, Mr. Cutler. I've already told you I don't belong here. If you're asking me to help, it isn't any use, because, in the first place they really don't want me here any more than you, and in the second place, no matter how much of a friend you've been to Racey, in his mind you're still wearing a badge which reads 'Customs & Excise.' And he doesn't like it."

He shrugged. "Oh, well, I don't suppose it matters very much. These things all pass."

"Yes, they all pass, and it's just as well for us that they do."

But as she walked back along the passage she was denying the words she had used. Until this afternoon she had believed the sentiments she had expressed to Cutler, but it occurred to her that perhaps she had heard herself voice them for the last time, and that they had only received utterance from force of habit. It was true, probably, that she never would see Hythebourne again, but the fact was no longer something to be taken calmly. She knew that all through her life she would remember this day, and that when she had told Cutler she no longer cared what became of Hythebourne, of Louis, of Racey, she had not spoken the truth. What had been truth just a few hours ago was now hideously reversed, and her mind, turning back upon itself in confusion would seek peace and tranquillity for a long time before, if ever, it was achieved.

Louis was waiting for her by the open door of the drawing-room. She was too weary to make further objection when he asked her to come inside. There were tired lines in his own face which troubled her: she saw her own weariness reflected there. Racey leaned against the mantlepiece. He still wore his flying-jacket: his hair had fallen uncombed across his forehead. He straightened when she entered, and watched her carefully when Louis pushed forward a chair and she sank into it.

Louis bent over her slightly. "Susan, was it you? Did you go and take the stuff from the plane?"

She passed a hand across her eyes. With the sun still shining on the ragged lawn outside, the room seemed chill. She said in a low voice: "Of course I took it. Who else did you think?"

Racey stepped forward. "What did I tell you, Louis? I knew it was Susan."

Louis said gravely: "You took a risk Susan. I suppose you realise how seriously you might have been involved?"

The thought that he had considered her danger warmed her. "Yes, I knew."

"Then why . . .?" Louis leaned closer. "Why did you do it?"

She wondered why they didn't accept the fact as accomplished and leave it. But it was not their way—it was not Louis' way to slip out of the situation with a graceful thank-you. She got to her feet. "Why did I do it?" she repeated. " Why does anyone do those things? It just occurred to me that I might be able to pull it off."

" How? " Louis asked quickly.

" Down the back staircase. . . . I saw you come through the garden. I guessed Cutler would stay with you until the doctor arrived." She finished dully. " It wasn't difficult."

They made way for her as she went and stood against the table, her back towards them. The chance which she had seized and used, apparently for no other reason than that it was there to be used, seemed to them amazing, and they stared at her in silence. Racey said at last : " Where have you hidden it? "

She turned and faced them. " I've stuffed all the packages down the fox earths in the bank of the east field . . . at the top end."

" You remembered," Racey said. " After all this time? "

She looked at him, wondering if he knew what it was like to remember too vividly, too painfully. Certain irrelevent details one remembered with astonishing sharpness—how she had once seen a fox go to earth in the bank, and had been glad, secretly and guiltily glad that she hadn't got to watch it hunted. She said to him : " One doesn't forget these things."

Neither of them spoke, they gazed at her, subdued, wary. She picked up again. " But don't imagine that Cutler is finished. He knows that if the plane was cleared, it was I who did it." She folded her hands before her. " I did . . . what I did, on an impulse. I don't regret it." She looked at Racey. " But please," she said, " don't go near the bank. Don't go near it until Cutler has left," She glanced about her, for the room seemed to have grown colder as she talked. " I think," she said faintly, " I'll go upstairs."

They let her go without protest until Racey, stirring quickly as if to make up for lost time, hurried after her. " Susan, I haven't said . . . it was damned decent of you to . . ."

His belief that she required only a few words of thanks hurt her. She said: "I merely did what anyone would have done, given the chance—what your father tried to do." She saw him wince, but her own misery seemed as great as his so she added: "But next time you do something like this, make sure the cargo is worth it. I expected something a little more valuable—lace, perfume, cartons of cigarettes—that's hardly your kind of stuff. What is it? —are you growing more foolish or less daring?"

Stung to anger, he replied too swiftly. "I didn't ask you to do it, Susan."

"But you haven't," she said quietly, "said that I shouldn't have done it." And then she left them.

She noticed, as she crossed the hall, that the door of the telephone cubicle was still closed. Very faintly she could hear the sound of Cutler's voice. When she began to climb the stairs a strange weakness attacked her knees—something born of her tiredness and the chill she had felt in the room downstairs. It was difficult to continue; she leaned heavily on the banister. Then, as she reached the landing, she remembered about Paul. Louis would have to be told that he was coming. It seemed an interminable journey to return to the drawing-room. She was conscious only of her weariness and the need for quiet. With infinite effort she turned and prepared to retrace her steps.

From the hall below Louis' voice reached her. "Is there something I can get for you, Susan?" He said it gently.

He stood at the foot of the staircase, watching her. "Louis?" she questioned. Her voice was a half-whisper. "Will you come here?"

He came quickly, taking the stairs two at a time. She still held the banister tightly. "What is it, Susan?"

She seemed to be fighting a mist of fatigue. It became terribly important to say these words clearly before she was too tired to utter them. "I've phoned Paul. He says he's coming down. He'll be here before dinner."

Louis made no protest. He did not even ask why. "I'll

tell Sydney," was all he said. "He'll fix a room." Then he added: "Cutler's staying also."

"Why?" She hated the feeling of panic which mounted at the mention of Cutler's name.

"The inquest," Louis said. "He'll have to give evidence."

"When is it?"

"As soon as possible. To-morrow, I hope."

To-morrow. After to-morrow she could leave Hythebourne. It would be all over then, all past. 'These things all pass,' Cutler had said. But she was too weary to think about it any more. "Yes," she murmured faintly. "To-morrow." She made to turn and continue her way up the stairs.

The pressure of Louis' hand on her arm arrested her. "Susan, you're ill."

"No." She shook her head. "Just tired. I don't know why I'm so tired. It seems so long since this morning."

He didn't wait any longer. She felt his arm under her shoulder, his other hand still clutching her forearm. The stairs were easier now; the polished wooden steps with the straight red carpet in the centre had lost that tendency to slip together before her eyes so that she didn't know where to put her feet. They reached her bedroom at last, and she clung to the foot of the bed, watching dully while he flung aside the cover. It was his hands which loosened her shoes, and his hands unbuttoning her jacket, and his fingers brushing her skin as he drew off her blouse. She stood wearily and her skirt fell in a loose pile about her feet. The soft comfort of the pillow closed about her as she lay down. From somewhere he brought another eiderdown, its warmth began to drive out the chill. Vaguely she sensed that he was moving round the room, touching things here and there. He opened and closed the hanging cupboard. She distinguished the sound of the curtains being drawn, and a deeper blackness closed in on her. It was delicious to lie in this warmth and peace, shut away from noise and disturbance.

For a long time there was unbroken quiet, yet it carried with it no sensation of being alone. Her eyelids flickered open, and she saw him, standing above her with his gaze directed at her face. He murmured something softly—she couldn't catch the words—then he bent and kissed her. The shock of his action made her lips stiff against his; he straightened immediately, and a moment later she heard the door closing gently.

V

SUSAN PLACED the tray by the bedside and looked down at Midge. The sounds of her entry had wakened the child, and now she lay watching with uncertain eyes. She seemed alone and lonely as she lay there, with her half-mistrustful gaze directed upon each of Susan's movements. She was frighteningly unreachable.

"I thought you'd better have some early supper, Midge," she said carefully. "You slept all through lunch and tea."

"I don't think I feel hungry," she answered, but she glanced towards the tray with interest.

"Perhaps a little milk? I've made you some sandwiches. You might be able to manage one."

The child looked thoughtful. "Was I sick?" she said.

Susan recognised the look of expectancy upon her face. "Yes. Yes, you were sick."

"Do I look sick or well now?"

Susan spent an unnecessary length of time over the answer, and the gravity of the decision seemed to satisfy the child's desire for importance. "I don't think you look very well."

Midge raised herself upon one elbow, and Susan saw her strive to assume a look of languor. "I'll have a small sandwich, please."

Susan selected one and watched her while she commenced to eat it. She began slowly at first, her gaze occasionally sliding to Susan's direction, but as hunger and her interest in the food asserted itself, she seemed less conscious of the other's presence. At last, forgetting her pose, she ate hungrily, and even motioned towards the glass in Susan's hand.

Fearful of distracting her attention, Susan didn't talk to her while she ate, but before the milk was finished she persuaded her to take one of the tablets which the doctor had left. She swallowed it without protest, declined the fruit on the tray, and slipped silently down between the bedclothes.

One thin shoulder still protruded. Susan's hand moved to cover it gently. The skin, where the childish, high-necked nightdress had unfastened, was incredibly silken. But she was too pale. Her hair was in tumbled disorder, Susan longed to comb it, but feared Midge's reaction.

Suddenly she turned her face towards the wall. Susan gazed at her in alarm, placing one hand tentatively on her shoulders. " Midge, what is it ? Tell me, baby."

" It's grandfather," she said sternly, and her voice was harsh in her effort to hold back the tears.

Susan slipped on to her knees and bent closer. " I know, darling, I know."

" But he's dead, isn't he ? " The words ended in a note of anguish, but still she did not cry.

What could one do, Susan thought, but kneel here, aghast and astonished at the sternness and the will behind the child's discipline. It was a projection of the old man himself, that she could grieve so tearlessly for him.

" Yes, dearest, he's dead." She struggled for words to direct towards the small, resisting back. " All old people have to die, Midge. They get very tired of living—and then, I expect he missed your grandmother very much."

She despised the poverty of the words and phrases when another woman would have had the right to take her child in her arms and comfort her in the only way possible.

" But I didn't think," Midge protested, " that he'd die and leave me."

" But he only left you when he was sure there was someone else to take care of you."

Midge flung herself round in a sudden excess of doubt. "Who?"

Susan's heart seemed to shrink within her as she realised the child's complete ignorance of everything which was taking place. She had no idea of the reason for Susan's presence, and not even any curiosity about it.

"There's myself, Midge," she said gently. "I want to have my share of looking after you now. I want to take you back to America with me."

She didn't seem to comprehend at first, because she lay absolutely still and said nothing. And then, Susan, watching her carefully, saw her wide eyes blink uncertainly, and their look of bewilderment increased. Until that morning she had been almightily secure within her world, dominating her grandfather, and through him, the whole of Hythebourne. And now, although not quite understanding what had happened, and unsure in what way his death would bring about change, in her childish fashion she had begun to have a premonition of change. It filled her with fear. Large, slow tears started in her eyes.

"But I don't want to go to America. I just want Grandfather back."

As passionately as she dared, Susan drew Midge to her, cradling her head against her breast and arm. She didn't sob or cry wildly, but the slow welling of tears under her eyelids was continuous and unrestrained. There was nothing more than passive acceptance, Susan felt, in her attitude towards her, the same as she might have given to any servant who tried to comfort her.

Despair and the full seriousness of the situation broke over her, but she went on holding the child, murmuring to her softly. Her arm grew stiff under the weight, but at last the tears no longer slid softly down Midge's cheeks. With the warmth of the sun gone, a little wind blew coldly through the open window. She drew the blankets gently over the child. Her breathings grew deeper, and she didn't stir.

In the passage she met Sydney. "I've just been with

Miss Charlotte, Sydney. She's asleep now, so I'd leave the tray if I were you. We don't want to risk waking her."

He nodded slowly. " Very good, Mrs. Taite." And then, " It's a mercy she can be got to sleep. I was afraid. . . . They were very much attached to each other, you know, Madam. He adored her, and she him. Poor little mite, she'll miss him."

" I know," she said slowly. " You'll all miss him, Sydney."

He lifted his shoulders slightly in a gesture of half-resignation. " I haven't much time left myself, Mrs. Taite. We are both old men. But I'm glad it was he who went first. I'm so used to his ways : he wouldn't have found anyone to suit him so well."

He seemed to find some comfort in the thought, but as she listened to his footsteps when he moved away they were tired and uncertain. Since the terrible happenings of the morning his body seemed to have shrunken and grown more withered. Round his mouth she had seen lines unnoticed before. The spirit of the manservant seemed to have faded with his master's—he was already himself half on the way to death. The hours of the night when he was alone and freed from distraction would be bitter for him, she thought. The shock and realisation would come fully then, and there would be no one to help him. Knowing this, she was glad for the child's sake that she had forced Midge to take the sleeping tablet, because for her, at least, the dark hours would be undisturbed by thought or memory of the old man.

Back in her room she began to dress in the half-light of the autumn twilight. The sun had gone down behind the distant fields and hedges and the sky was that peculiar blue-green. Susan paused to notice how the dusk had gathered into the blackish mass of the trees, and how the sky was more deeply blue around them than elsewhere. There were soft bird cries, and, as a chorus, came the persistent calling of the rooks who nested in the trees by the dovecot. A chill little breeze was stirring, occasionally whipping the curtains to motion.

She completed her dressing slowly, unwilling to go downstairs, and take up the routine once more. Much would have happened during the hours she had lain here ; telephone calls, messages sent and received, the inquest and funeral arranged. If only Paul would come soon, she thought ; if there were no need to face Louis once again with the memory of that light kiss brushed across her lips to stand between herself and the defence she had built against him.

Cutler would be there too, smooth, calm, polite, watching Paul with interested eyes. And Racey. She prayed that Racey would have lost his mood of depression and self-accusation. She would come upstairs early, because Racey might start to drink, might want her presence to help him forget what had taken place this morning. But perhaps they would leave her alone with Paul for a little time ; surely they must know how badly she would need the kind of support he was able to give her. But they had a strange way of not understanding her, or perhaps understanding too well.

She switched on the light. Its strength immediately nullified the pale colours of the twilight sky. She walked to the mirror and examined her face more critically. With careful and deft strokes of her hands she applied the cosmetics which lined the bureau top, thinking that Paul's arrival gave a new zest to the performance. As she drew the stopper from the perfume bottle, the strangeness of the situation, involving herself, Paul and Louis, came home to her with desperate force. Thoughtfully she leaned closer to the mirror. She would see Paul and Louis side by side ; for almost two days they would be there constantly together, contrasted and compared. This peculiar circumstance had arisen unbidden. She wondered had Paul immediately seen the chance for what it was worth, and seized upon it. He could be ruthless and infinitely calculating. And above all, he wanted to be sure. Susan's eyes narrowed. Paul would have risked much in order to be sure—sure about Louis, and sure about her.

She replaced the stopper unhurriedly, although the sight of the rooks rising into the darkening sky above the dovecot told her that a car was approaching, and it was probably Paul's.

There was no one in the hall when she went down. Sydney had lit the fire, and dozing before it was Midge's puppy. On the table was a small scattering of yellow telegram envelopes, some of them unopened. It was beginning, she thought. All through the next day their stream would continue, and soon after would come the flowers. Death became not just a happening but an occasion. But for to-night, at least, there would be peace. How still the house was. No sounds from the bedrooms, not even running water; no voices. The quiet, fire-lit hall had a waiting atmosphere, and the noise of Paul's car on the gravel outside was like a harsh fanfare.

She switched on the porch light, and flung the door open. It had grown much darker; Paul's figure, as he got out of the car, was scarcely distinguishable. Only his familiar, friendly voice calling across to her was reassurance.

"Susan?" His soft, short greeting was mingled with inquiry, and she knew that for him as well as herself there had been moments of fear and doubt during these past hours.

She came towards him swiftly in the darkness, heedless of the chill wind striking through her thin dress. He took her in his arms immediately, not kissing her, but just holding her body close to him as one might have done with a child. He sought to do nothing more than reassure her. The warmth from his own body flowed through her. She said in a low tone: "I'm glad you've come."

He released her gently, turning to get the baggage from the car. She saw, with surprise, that one of the suitcases was her own.

"I've brought some extra things for you," he said. "I had an idea that it was considered proper to wear black at

163

an inquest. I didn't know whether you'd stay for the funeral."

Paul had always thought of things like that. It was a strange mixture of kindness and efficiency. It was the gift which made it possible for him to control a newspaper syndicate and remain human. Never once had he lost sight of the practical side of the situation, and there had never been a problem which he hadn't met and solved with this curious simplicity of his. He would enter the house, she knew, and at once the alertness of his face, his firm, lean body would make all the rest of them appear degenerate. The furnishings would seem shabbier, more worn, simply because he was among them. He would be polite, but there was no mistaking the fact that Paul would never have lived in a house like Hythebourne. Things of beauty he loved and cherished, but their age was no virtue in his eyes. That Hythebourne was beautiful in places, she knew he would agree. Its lofty, chill rooms, the ancient plumbing, the leaky roof were things which he couldn't tolerate. She felt a faint stirring of apprehension as his footsteps crunched into the gravel behind her. In the porch he drew level and they stepped together into the hall.

He put the bags down and made for the fire immediately. The puppy stirred sleepily. He bent over and touched the soft flaps of its ears with exquisite gentleness. Then he straightened and looked about him.

" This is really Old England, isn't it, Susan ? " he said caustically. He pointed to the stone floor beyond the rug. " The original foundations, I'll bet. Been here since Norman the Conqueror. Any ghosts ? "

" I never saw any," she said faintly.

He caught her arm and drew her closer to him. " Did you hate being here, Sue ? "

" I was unhappy here."

He nodded. " Not quite the same thing, is it ? Louis' mother . . . she was alive then, wasn't she ? "

" Yes. She didn't like me . . . but, no . . . perhaps that's wrong. We didn't like each other."

"You've been thinking about all that, haven't you?" His gaze wandered over the hall once more. "This house has a lot of memories, hasn't it, Sue?"

She defended herself. "Memories? Yes." She looked at him steadily. "This was where Midge was born. That alone brings memories."

"Yes," he murmured. "Yes."

Silence fell between them. Not a peaceful silence; the air was alive with their separate thoughts. From the library came the sound of a clock striking seven. Susan glanced towards the closed door. In there Lionel's body was laid out. She would not go in there, she knew, not even before the funeral. That was the kind of courage she had never possessed, the kind of courage which seemed unnecessary. She had seen him when he had lain either dying or dead in the field, and she didn't want to see him now, flowers about him, his face stiffened with death. She wished that the funeral was over. His living presence seemed still to hang over the house, and would do so, she thought, while his body remained there. How lonely was death; how suddenly and finally it had cut him off from his beloved and time-worn routine. For the first time a personal sorrow began to tinge her thoughts of his death. They might have known each other better, they might have shared things a little more in the days when she was here. She might even have shared her homesickness with him, and the small things about Hythebourne which had given her pleasure. But she had never once told him of these things. They had remained strangers, each untouched by the other. Because he was dead he made the past bitter. There had been no effort on either side to come closer. They had failed each other, and with his death the failure seemed to now rest solely with her.

Wildly, in an excess of self-accusation, she turned to Paul. "Come into the drawing-room. There's so much you've got to be told about . . . all the things I couldn't say on the phone."

The drawing-room fire was bright. She spread her hands

before it thoughtfully, feeling his presence behind her like some sheltering cloak. " Paul," she began slowly, " I don't think you'll understand completely what I'm going to say. . . . You won't understand my part in it. Perhaps it's just as well you came down to Hythebourne. While you're here you might be able to see how this life gets into your bones, how you react in a particular way, just because you're here, and not anywhere else."

" Susan, what are you trying to tell me ? " In spite of his care the anxiety came spilling into his voice. He was aware, quite well aware, that much more had happened here than she had told him on the phone. The house had much more about it than the atmosphere of death. Death was comparatively simple because it suggested an action completed ; here there was an air of expectancy, as if something further was to happen. It was almost the urgency of fear.

He moved close to Susan. She leaned back against him gratefully, and he slipped his arm about her body. In a low tone, still gazing into the fire, she began to tell him the events since Louis' arrival the night before, of Cutler's early visit that morning, the suspense of waiting for Racey's return, and the final tragedy of the old man's death. As she described the happenings afterwards her voice wavered uncertainly.

" I didn't know what to do, Paul. I wasn't sure, no more than anyone else, that Racey had actually brought anything back from France. Then, on the other hand, if he had, there would have been the devil to pay. You just don't know how it felt. I was there alone. . . . I saw Cutler come back with Louis and Racey . . . what else could I have done except go and satisfy myself that there was nothing in the plane."

He said quietly : " But you went believing that you would find a cargo there. You meant to take the risk, didn't you ? "

" There was practically no risk. The opportunity was there. I simply took it."

" It wasn't simple at all, Susan. Did you remember that

if Cutler had caught you with the stuff you wouldn't have been allowed to go back to America until the case was heard?" He paused a little. "And did you remember that people go to gaol for smuggling?"

"Yes," she said. "I remembered all that."

"And still you took the risk?"

She twisted in his arms suddenly, facing him. "I had to, Paul. Don't you see that? Back here at Hythebourne I was one with them again. I was part of the whole set-up. It didn't matter what I felt about Racey . . . or Louis. Nothing mattered except that I had to do what would be best for all of us."

"For all of us," he repeated softly. "You didn't want to stand apart from them, did you?"

"It didn't seem possible not to help."

"Have you explained this to Racey—to Louis? Did they ask you why you did it?"

She didn't answer his question, but said: "When I'd done it I almost wished I hadn't. I didn't want to have to explain to them. I didn't want them to try to thank me." She sighed. "You see, Paul, it's gone on for so long. I've been the one who's in the wrong because I walked out on Louis and Midge. They've got used to thinking of me in that way, and I didn't want to give them—or myself—the shock of stepping out of character."

"Sue," he said gravely, "when you say 'them' are you sure you don't mean 'Louis'?"

She shook her head slowly. "I don't know, Paul. At one time it might have meant the same thing. But they're so different now. I haven't got used to the difference. I'm not really sure which of them I think about."

"Sue, what troubles you so much about this place and these people? What you risked for them sounds crazy to me. But if it was what you thought you ought to do, then it's all right."

She looked at him, knowing fully that he didn't understand. He was struggling against the tide of those months she had spent here, trying desperately to be one with her, refusing to be left behind. But it was useless for him to struggle. At Hythebourne he was out of place; he was not part of the pattern. Even with the feel of his body firm under her arms he was not quite real. She gazed at him in an abstracted fashion; his features seemed to have retreated behind a mist, they were blurred and uncertain.

He saw the look, saw its vagueness and saw how her eyes had fallen upon him with the startled gaze of one who sees a stranger. Her body was in his arms but her mind had gone wandering off on some nameless track. He couldn't follow her; it was exactly as if she had closed a door upon him gently.

Long after Paul had said good night, Susan lay awake in the darkness. The house was full of the sounds that are magnified by the very quietness—the rushes of wind against the panes, the soft creak of ancient timber. She looked at her bedside clock and saw that it was almost midnight. The hours had passed slowly since his arrival. Dinner progressed badly. They hadn't known how to behave. Cutler, Paul and herself stood outside the tragedy. Unwilling to blunder in speech, they suffered torments of embarrassment in their silences. Conversation had begun in fits and starts and lapsed again. There ought to be rules for how one should behave on this precise occasion, Susan thought; their gauche sentences were strung out in a seedy row. The poverty of her own inventiveness appalled her. In the darkness her face grew hot at the memory of how she had failed.

Louis had not been present at dinner. Cutler explained that the Coroner had phoned him, and he had gone off immediately. As Cutler talked, Racey entered with sullen grace. He had shown no surprise at the sight of Paul, briefly acknowledged the introduction, and sat down. After passing the decanter round, he had noisily splashed water into his own glass. Glancing at him, Susan had seen his face flushed with impatience and bad temper. Paul had eyed him curiously, and treated him with grave courtesy, which seemed to aggravate his passion further. He had scarcely spoken at all, and after dinner had excused himself from joining them in the drawing-room.

Involuntarily their eyes had followed him as he mounted the stairs, his hunched shoulders indicating the sort of torment they could only guess at. Hurriedly, as if ashamed of prying too deeply, they had turned away, and gone into the drawing-room. But Racey's restlessness had infected each of them in turn. Released now of his presence and free to talk, they found they no longer desired it. Words were stilted and harsh. A little fluttering sigh of relief broke through the two men's composure as Susan rose and said good night.

Now she lay here in the quiet room, sighing for the sleep which evaded her. The wind rose in fitful gusts, moaning in the chimneys. And down along the weedy drive she caught the first sound of Louis' car. For a long time she lay still, straining for his footsteps. They came at last, up the stairs and past her door. Then he paused and turned back again. He waited a long time beside the door; she heard his hand tentatively finger the knob. At last he turned it, and the one far-away light in the passage outlined his body. Unmoving, she gazed at him while he leaned forward, trying to pierce the darkness around the bed. She didn't speak, nor did he, but suddenly she sensed that he knew she was awake. The seconds moved on slowly, and still they didn't speak. The thin chime of a china clock in one of the bedrooms broke in. A ripple of movement passed through his body. Abruptly he closed the door, and the light was gone.

TUESDAY

I

THE MORNING was soft and mild; yesterday's sun again made bright patches on the polished floor, timidly touched the silver on the table, lost itself among the faded folds of the curtains. The room was as usual; the table laid as it was always laid for breakfast at Hythebourne. In the orderly array of cutlery there was precision, but not peace. A sense of impending events made the atmosphere restless and alive. One caught it all over the house—when one stood to listen to the silence, just as Susan stood now, within the deep door-frame of the dining-room.

Louis stood listening also, and looking at her. Her face matched the silence, he thought. Serene when one first glanced at it, but ready, in a second, to become full of meaning and animation. Her skin was so pale above the black she wore, but the colour of her hair was unsubdued. She might look confident and untouchable as she stood there, in a spot where the sun had not reached, but there was a hint of weariness about her. He wished she would stir or speak, anything to break that lifeless pose. She merely stood there, head thrown back, her body braced against the dark wood behind her in an attitude of listening.

"Susan?" He moved away from the window.

She started and turned in his direction. "It's you," she said. The words reached him in a breathless rush. Her composure wavered and trembled.

"You're down early," he said. "Didn't you sleep?"

"Sleep?" she repeated. It seemed to take her a long time to fasten her mind on an answer. "Oh, yes, fairly well. But one always seemes to wake early in strange houses."

" Hythebourne is not strange to you, Susan."

" How can one say that ? " she murmured. He had to strain towards her to hear the words. " I never came off my period of probation here, did I ? " She spoke softly, as if to herself, as if it mattered little whether or not he heard. Not looking at him she walked forward, catching the back of one of the chairs and leaning against it heavily. He saw how tightly her hands gripped, but her face gave no indication of strain, but reflectiveness. " I never thought I should come back here, Louis. I don't have happy memories of this place."

Catching up with her mood, he said softly : " He is dead now . . . they are both dead."

" They are not my memories, Louis, although they are part of them. There's so many mistakes I made, and it's difficult to face them again. If it had been your father and mother alone who had made my time here unhappy I could have got over that—but they weren't everything. Just part of a whole."

He said eagerly, too eagerly : " We both made mistakes, Susan."

She shook her head, and her air of intimate reflectiveness dropped away from her. She frowned. " I didn't come here to discuss our mistakes. It's all much too late."

" I hoped that we might be able to talk things over . . . it doesn't seem right that you should leave without my knowing how—where our lives went wrong."

" Why should I talk over something about which I've long ago made up my mind ? Why should I confuse myself with old issues ? That's all over and done with. Why should I go back ? "

" Are you in love with Paul Berkman ? "

Unhesitatingly she answered : " Yes."

" Then there is no danger for you in telling me why our marriage failed. You're going to marry him—nothing you tell me is going to alter that. Why are you afraid ? "

Her tone was firm. " I'm not afraid."

" Regret then ? "

" Regret ? Why not ? One always regrets one's mistakes."

" Enough to want to rectify them ? "

Her lips tightened. " Why go on, Louis ? This sort of thing gets us nowhere."

Her fingers beat an impatient little rhythm on the chair as she waited for his reply. He thought, watching her, how swiftly she woke to anger, how much more life-like she was now than when she had stood in the doorway a few minutes before. Still gripping the chair she leaned a little forward so that her face came into the shaft of sunlight. How extraordinary her hair was, seen like this. Her lips, closed tightly, were still large and full. Without wanting to, he began to take in each detail he saw—her beautifully proportioned body fitting and carrying the black suit in a way few women achieve. And the white blouse tight to her throat seemed to throw the redness of her hair and the suit into dark contrast. His eyes slipped down to her hands, still now, and patient—as serene and quiet as when he had looked at them with the fingers curved round the stem of the glass on that first day. She was so much the product of her environment, he thought. Behind her serenity were the traces of that cultivated efficiency of the newspaper world, the world of little time and no second chances. How much, he wondered, did she love Paul Berkman, and how much was he still her boss—the man who ran the show ? They had worked together, and that counted for much between a man and a woman. If they had learned to respect each other's abilities they could easily have mistaken that for love. But there wasn't time to learn all these things. There wasn't any time at all. A few more hours here at Hythebourne, and then she was gone. She would bear away with her all the things he wished to know, all her undiscovered qualities, all the fascination of the way she turned her head, and her still hands. He wished that she might stay—just a little longer. But what use was it to taste of these things, and then to see them slip away? One might drink, but the glass was drained in the end, before one's thirst was gone. Why struggle against it? Let her go before the need for her becomes too real. She stood there, her body and face alert as if for flight, and she didn't belong with him. She was not of his world. She had left it long ago, and it was not in his power to call her back. He remembered how he had stood in the darkened doorway of her room last night, gazing towards the too-silent blackness of the bed. There had been no sound of her breathing, yet he knew she lay awake, as tense as he. It had seemed for one individual second their minds had come into contact, had bridged the gap for a swift moment, and then the union was broken; they were slipping away from each other back to their separate identities. But the moment had held no reality. It was not logical, not sane for him to imagine that she might wish for a better understanding. Why should she? For that matter, why should he wish it when he had no guarantee that it would be all for their good?

"You're right, Susan," he said. "This gets us nowhere."

She relaxed. Her grip on the chair rail grew lighter, and in her face he saw the lessening of tension, and the death of her small hope. There had been hope there, he knew, but its significance was worthless. Why did she, he wondered, continue to hold out her hand and withdraw it just as swiftly; why did she tantalise him with a half-promise she never fulfilled? Irritation began to mount within him. He tried to hold it down, knowing that sanity would desert him if he allowed this anger to grow. He looked at her, so cool, and serene, the calmness settling back upon her features, and he longed, just once, to lean across and strike her—do anything that might shake her from that too secure position. But was it worth the effort? Was anything worth troubling about except to get all this weary business finished? One could be a fool too long.

He turned away from her. He went to the sideboard and began to fill his plate with the steaming bacon and tomatoes which Sydney had left. He wasn't hungry but it was something to break that long spell of silence which had fastened upon them, something prosaic and ordinary to break his mood. From behind him there was no sound. She hadn't moved, he knew.

" Can I help you to some of this ? " The inquiry was formal. He hadn't wanted it to sound like that, but in her presence he was stiff, and his tongue was awkward. He wondered if she sensed any of this, if she understood how disconcerting her coolness became. And perhaps she thought him a bore, someone insensitive to the finer shades of her actions. And perhaps, worse than this, she didn't care one way or another.

His hands grew clumsy. He dropped bacon fat on the polished wood of the sideboard.

She didn't reply immediately, but came round to his side. " I think I'll have cereals."

He watched, fascinated, the smooth movements of her hands as she went through the motions of filling her plate from the cardboard packet. She stopped abruptly as she became aware of his concentrated stare—stopped and turned to look at him. There was wonderment and questioning in her gaze, and the kind of softness her eyes had not held before. " Louis . . ." she said. Then the words were halted, as if something forbade their utterance. He wanted desperately to hear what she was going to say. He leaned closer eagerly. But she said nothing because they had both caught the sounds of someone crossing the hall. Louis straightened and stepped back from her.

Paul came to the doorway and stood there looking at them. His gaze lingered on Susan with intimate familiarity, as he might have examined a well-beloved painting. When at last he turned to Louis his look was critical, but not unjust. His eyes flicked over the other in the way that those who worked for him had come to recognise. Susan saw it, and remembered, back through the four years which separated these two occasions, that he had looked at her with just this expression the first day she had managed to get into his office and had asked him for a job. This was the side of Paul Berkman that people who met him only once remembered, the tough unimpressionable pressman, the business man who handled the company's shares and wrote the leaders for his morning syndicate with astonishing brilliance and sureness of touch.

But they hadn't spoken, and Susan realised as yet they had no cause to. Hurriedly she murmured: "Louis, this . . ." But then, quickly, watching Paul's face, she reversed the order. "Paul, I want you to meet Louis. Paul Berkman."

Paul came forward and took Louis' hand with his controlled politeness. There was no reason why they should be cordial, and she was glad when neither attempted it.

Paul said carefully: "Sorry I didn't have the opportunity to ask your permission before coming down. I figured Susan might like me here, so I came."

"Susan has been a great help to us all," Louis answered. "Naturally she could ask whom she pleased."

Susan turned quickly and began to fumble with the plates. "Are you eating, Paul? There's bacon and tomatoes in the dish."

She knew it was absurd to talk like this, but it served the purpose, for Louis went to his place at the table and sat down. The situation became almost normal.

Paul said: "I'll have coffee, thanks."

She concentrated on the task of pouring, too fully aware of his eyes upon her. When she turned to hand him the cup he gave her one of those rare and unexpected smiles which broke across his face in an incongruous, charming fashion. She returned it warmly and then, curiously elated, she took her place beside Louis. Because Paul was present there was no longer any difficulty in speaking to Louis. Once more the impersonal screen had dropped between them; they talked as if those few seconds before Paul's entry had never existed. "Louis," she said clearly, "I'm planning not to be here for the funeral."

He glanced up quickly from his plate. "Yes. I didn't expect that you would want to stay."

"When will it be?" Paul asked.

"To-morrow. In the morning. Racey and I hope to get up to Town by evening." He paused awkwardly, looking from one to the other. "There'll be some things we'll need to discuss."

Susan spoke quickly. "Our plane reservation is for Thursday morning."

Louis looked directly across at Paul. "That makes things a little difficult. We'll have to see the solicitors about Susan taking Midge. There's always dozens of papers to sign and it's better if she can do them on the spot."

"There's an evening plane on Thursday," Paul said. "We'll take that."

In those words it was all settled. Susan began to feel the efficient way it would go forward. Such plans left no time for indecision, no time to trace back events in one's mind and re-assess values. This increasing desire to probe behind the change in Louis tantalised her, yet she hesitated to move on to a further analysis of him because greater knowledge might serve only to confuse her without clarifying the issues. With a sickening kind of regret she knew that years ago a little more humility in her approach to him might have wiped away even the possibility of such a scene as this. And yet, wasn't it equally right to think that this, her second and more mature choice, was the better. Judged from almost every angle it was—that is, every angle but a few.

She caught Louis' attention. "I'd like to take Midge up to London with me to-morrow. I wouldn't like. . . . I don't think it's wise for her to stay for the funeral."

He gave her a reflective look, and one of half-surprise. "I'd be very glad if you'd do that, Susan. I think she needs to get away from all this."

"How does she take it—the kid?" Paul asked. His tone was gentle, as if sympathy towards the child had been instinctive.

"It's hard on a child of that age," Louis said slowly. "The part of her mind which remembers seeing her grandfather hit by the plane is still terrified, but she just doesn't seem to realise that he's gone. I think, unconsciously, she's expecting him to come back. If she's taken away from here and given a few distractions we might avoid a reactionary shock." He prodded disinterestedly at the bacon, now resting in lumps of congealed fat on the plate. " Poor kid," he added in a tone so low they hardly caught the words. " They adored each other."

In those last few words the tragedy became personal. It was the break up of the unity between the child and the old man, a dissolving of a partnership. Midge had become symbolic of the finality of death. Because she remained she became of greater stature in their minds, grew in importance far beyond anything she had ever before attained. Susan found herself glancing towards Paul in a gesture of helplessness, but for once he remained silent. There was no relief from her own thoughts. She gazed down at the untouched cereals in her plate. The milk had soaked through. They lay in a sodden, wet mound. She began to eat them ; they had no flavour. Then she put down her spoon and spoke to Louis.

" What's to be done with Midge to-day ? She can't be taken to the inquest." She thought, as she uttered the words, how sharply they must have fallen on her hearers.

Louis said quietly, a trifle absently : " I stopped off at the Blake's on the way home last night. They're having her over. She went about half an hour ago."

" Before breakfast ? "

" I thought it was better," he replied patiently, " if she were well away before she gets caught up in any of the fuss of our leaving. There are four young Blakes—if she's kept busy over there she won't be so miserable, poor mite."

Wretchedly Susan gazed down at her plate. The child had been looked after but through no foresight of her own. Without looking across at Paul she knew the expression his face would wear. He would be wondering where, in this reflective man at the table with him, was the Louis of her descriptions. Humiliation made her cheeks burn. The child, who should normally have been her charge, had been too adequately cared for, and if she and Louis had been fighting a battle he would have won on this round. But he didn't seem to care about it—to be aware even of her discomfort. Paul would see it, she thought. He missed nothing that was relevant. Each happening since their arrival he had seen and interpreted in his own fashion. He couldn't, nor did she believe he would even if it were possible, stop this forward rush of events. She wondered if perhaps he welcomed this opportunity, with them all assembled here at Hythebourne, to weigh up the relationship between herself and Louis. But at this point, bewilderment touched the scene, and not even Paul could place his accurate finger on the exact bond which existed. For they were different persons, and if there was any bond at all, it was tentative and wary, ready to dissolve before it gained any real permanence.

Cutler entered, and the strain broke before the force of his quiet and adroit handling of a situation which he sensed rather than had evidence of.

"Good morning." He looked towards Susan, but his remark included the other two. "I'm afraid I'm very late. I meant to be reasonably early. We'll be leaving soon." His briskness brought the desired impersonal note into the conversation. Susan listened silently. A faint nagging worry about Racey's absence began to gnaw at her.

"If my brother rides with you, Cutler, on the way back, my car will be free for Colonel Hayes and his wife," Louis said.

"Is it usual in England," Paul remarked silkily, "to have the coroner and his wife to lunch after the inquest?"

Louis took a long time to turn and fix his gaze on the other. "Colonel Hayes," he said, "was my father's greatest friend. It isn't going to be any less painful for him to conduct this than for us to go through with it."

"I'm sorry," Paul said. His tone hadn't softened. "I had forgotten, after all these years away from England, that county people always know each other. It's the sort of blunder one has constantly to be forgiving Americans for. Isn't it, Susan ? "

She was again identified with him as the one outside this circle, outside even the formalities which the old man's death had brought about. Now her refusal to remain for the funeral seemed churlish. An outsider who was aggressively determined to stay outside. She stirred uneasily but didn't say anything. Cutler handed her a cup of coffee, and gave her the distraction of finding the sugar, and stirring the dark-coloured liquid slowly.

They finished breakfast in a desultory fashion. No one talked, save to inquire about the day's arrangements. There was general relief when Susan excused herself, and they were free to go.

Upstairs, Susan went immediately to Racey's door and knocked. " Come in," he called.

He stared at her as she entered. He was standing before a low bureau, his tie dangled from one listless hand. Her eyes flickered over the untidy litter of his shaving gear, and when she looked back at his face she saw that he had cut himself, and had dabbed ineffectually with a handkerchief to stop the flow of blood.

" What brings you, Witch ? " He turned back to the mirror.

Uncertainly she said : " I wondered if you were up."

He shrugged. " Charming of you to be concerned. But this happens to be one of those days when you have to get up, no matter how much you wish the night would go on for ever."

She pushed the door behind her. It closed with a crash. " What is there to be afraid of ? "

" Try it yourself and see." He spoke very quietly.

The words dug into her. They were the sharpened points of his fear. Very quickly, so that the sound would stem the rise of her own doubts, she said : " Nothing is going to happen. Nothing can happen. Cutler is satisfied."

He flung the blood-stained handkerchief away from him with a low curse. " Blast it to hell ! " He swung towards her furiously. "God, can't any of you see? Does no one understand that it would have been better for me if I *had* been caught with the stuff. How do you think it feels to have killed your own father, and then pay a miserable fine for the few bottles of brandy they found. How do you think it feels? Tell me that!"

Unwillingly she said: "I think it would feel like hell."

He laughed hoarsely. The contraction of his skin broke the congealing blood round the cut, and a thin red stream began to move slowly down his face. He brushed at it carelessly with his fingers. "If they'd send me to gaol it would be some way of paying off."

"It wouldn't help. You know that."

He extended his smeared fingers towards her in a gesture of appeal. "Look, Susan. I'm going to get off scot free—absolutely scot free. It's the last thing in the world I want, and if I weren't such a bloody coward I'd tell them about the rest of the stuff, and take what's coming to me."

She leaned back against the door. Racey said nothing more, and the room was very still. She saw the crumpled bed, the pyjamas he had tossed to the floor. His words were echoing back in her brain; the astonishing discovery in them made her reel. Here was Racey telling her that his fear was not of death but of life. Unsuspectingly she had touched the source of his stupendous courage and daring. Long ago, during the raids, the laughter in his light blue eyes had masked a fear more sickening and hideous than her own. She tried to swing away from the thought, but it kept coming back. He had always been afraid, and his fear of showing it was worse than any other kind. She wanted to go away and think about this astounding fact. Already it was beginning to have bearing upon Louis, but in a way she couldn't as yet properly define.

She said gently: "Could you use a drink?"

"No," he answered dully. "I couldn't leave it at one drink. I'd get so tight I couldn't stand up straight at the inquest." He added with emphasis: "Drunk. Disgustingly drunk."

She said nothing and her silence seemed to irritate him, for he burst out at last. "For God's sake, Susan, don't stand there with your ' holier than thou ' expression. You ought to think yourself damned lucky that I am such a coward. If I burst the whole works wide open I wouldn't be clever enough to keep your part of it hidden. It pays, sometimes, to be on the right side of a coward."

He turned back to the bureau, tilting the glass so that she could no longer see the reflection of his face. The quiet shut down on them again. She opened the door and slipped through noiselessly.

II

THE WHOLE scene was bright in the sunlight. On the mellowed red roofs of the village cottages, the moss made its own distinctive patterns in green. The cluster of shops, with their shuttered windows, leaned together crazily, clung to each other for dubious support. In the warmth and peace of the deserted roadway two dogs rolled together in disinterested play. Then one of them started up uncertainly for a point at the end of the village street. His shadow, trailing like a half-discarded cloak, gave him a curiously bedraggled aspect.

Susan watched him out of sight, watched him as he turned in by the end of the stone wall of the churchyard. Then her gaze slipped back along the street. Close to her, the huddle of parked cars gave an unfamiliar importance to the squat, fat little village. In the open doorway of the post office a solitary woman stood, her eyes fixed greedily upon the building which was the library as well as the local hall. But save for her presence there was no sign of life. Then, far down at the end of the street, she caught a faint movement. The dog was returning, his shadow before him now. He seemed to be trying to catch up with it.

"Paul," she said at last, "have you got a cigarette?"

Silently he found and lit one for her. She leaned back against the warm leather of the car seat. In the sunlight the smoke was blue. " How long have they been in ? " she demanded.

He looked at his watch. " Twenty-five minutes."

" Isn't that a long time ? Surely they must be wanting me soon ? "

Paul said lazily : " You won't find a country coroner willing to hurry himself. They only get an inquest once in every ten years."

" Oh, blast them ! Racey's nerve will go to bits if they keep him waiting about."

He placed a hand on her own, lying motionless on the seat beside him. " Take it easy, Sue."

She jerked her body stiffly to attention. " Paul," she said, " have you thought how badly this would go with me if Racey lets slip about the rest of his cargo ? Have you thought what will happen to me ? "

He nodded, his lids drooping lazily. " Sure. I've thought about all that, and I still say take it easy. A guy doesn't crack up on a thing like this."

She continued to gaze at him, mistrustful of his reassurance. " The doctor will tell."

" Yes, he'll tell. But what the hell does that matter ? Cutler knows no more than he does, and between them, all they've got is a couple of bottles of brandy. So long as Racey keeps his mouth shut your part in this business finishes here."

" But can we trust Racey not to break down ? " She could feel the eyes of the woman in the post office upon her, and she spoke sharply.

He answered dryly. " You can always trust a man to save his own skin."

His hand closed about hers more tightly, and under its pressure she felt her irritation fading. She shut her eyes and tried not to remember what the village looked like, how its cheerful colour was in some way a vague threat, the threat of respectability and smugness towards herself and people like her. She opened her eyes quickly and the red roofs seemed to leap at her with powerful accusation.

She flattened her body against the seat as if to escape it.

Paul turned to her wonderingly. But his unspoken words were cut by the sudden sound of laughter which curved out sharply into the silent street.

"What are they laughing at?" she demanded abruptly. "There's nothing to laugh about."

"They always find something to laugh about," he said. "Even when a man's going to be hanged they find something funny to laugh about."

The laughter, so sure and confident, roused her fear. It was a fear of those few moments when she would stand before the thin and grey-faced coroner in the dusty hall, and hear herself telling about what had happened at Hythebourne. A sickness which had lain in her stomach now seemed to rise and fill her whole body, until even her arms were weak with it. It became difficult to keep her eyes open.

"Paul?"

"Sue?"

"I wonder why I care so much about all this? Why do I care what happens to them?"

He didn't reply, but through the hand still holding hers she sensed the stiffness of his body. She turned to him and saw that he looked tired, his face and jaw tensed, and that his tanned skin was stretched tightly across the bones.

She persisted. "Do you know why?"

Suddenly he withdrew his hand from hers, and brought the other down hard upon the catch of the door. It swung open, and as he stepped out he said: "You're the only person who knows that, Sue. Figure it out for yourself." Then he began to walk away.

She watched him go. He vanished unhurriedly through the door of the hall where the policeman stood. Without him her sense of insecurity grew. It mounted like the unbidden rise of tears to her eyes, something she was powerless to check or prevent. In the long hours since yesterday morning the sense of true proportion had gradually deserted her, so that now, with Paul gone from her side, he seemed to lose his identity and become merely a symbol of the life that she had chosen, placed cruelly in contrast to the symbol which was Louis. In his presence the disunity of her thoughts were collected and pieced together again, the disintregated personality and background were once more the familiar whole. But he brought with him no abiding sense of safety. He was like a puppet in a nightmare, nodding and smiling, and waiting all the time for the decision which every passing minute seemed to make more inevitable. She admitted to herself at last that this tight sickness in her stomach wasn't only a fear of standing before the coroner in that tiny, crowded space, but a much larger fear that the whole structure of her planning might be threatened, might finally topple and collapse. Her palms grew sticky with sweat ; she placed them against her thighs, feeling through the thickness of her skirt their uncomfortable heat.

Then faintly she heard her name being called. It started inside the little building, and the policeman outside began to echo it. It was a supreme effort to turn and gaze in his direction. The mist before her eyes strangely distorted the thick, blue-clad figure, so that he seemed to sway weirdly. With a numbing sensation of fatigue making it almost impossible for her to stir, she at last caught sight of Paul coming towards her rapidly. He opened the door and took her arm gently.

" O.K., Sue. They're ready for you."

She asked, with stiffening lips : " What's happened ? How far have they got ?."

He guided her steps with infinite care across the uneven street. " The doctor, Louis and Cutler have said their piece. You just tell them exactly what you saw and leave it at that."

She gripped his arm more tightly. The policeman watched them with interest, had even half-raised his arm to hurry them on, but she held Paul back. " How much do they know about Cutler coming down here ? Do they know he was sent ? "

Without changing his expression, he nodded. " Not even

a gentleman's agreement can get round a thing like that."

"Then," she said dully, "they all know about Racey."

"They know as much as Cutler will tell them, and that's very little."

They began to move on again across the rough stones with the sunlight beating down upon them. The two dogs parted before them, and stood staring in a curiously detached fashion. Just before they reached the policeman Paul said in a low voice: "The coroner isn't a gossip. Remember that—it helps."

She nodded, a number of questions forming in her head, but there wasn't time to ask them. In the doorway he released his hold, and she stood alone.

Inside the small room was packed and airless. The restless, seeking faces of the crowd turned upon her as she entered. Her name had already run round the room in a swift whisper when Colonel Hayes had called it, and now they were silent again. Among them she saw some she recognised and could not put names to. They watched her with the intentness of curiosity which needed to be satisfied. They craned forward on those uncomfortable, backless benches, the shopkeepers and the people they served, to catch every detail of her appearance. Paul walked behind her in the front of the improvised court, and already she sensed the note of inquiry spreading through them. The bare, worn boards rang loudly under their footsteps. Colonel Hayes was seated behind the librarians' desk. Someone had placed a jam jar of blazing yellow chrysanthemums on it. Their unselfconscious beauty became incongruous in that crowded, dusty room.

Someone gave her a Bible, and she swore to tell the truth. She hadn't remembered about that. The panic began to rise again. The scene before her grew blurred. Only vaguely did she distinguish the faces of Paul, of Louis, of David Cutler together on a long bench at the front. Racey was beside his brother, but he kept his eyes down. She glanced towards the Colonel; he gave her a brief nod of recognition, at the same time calling for silence.

" You are Mrs. Louis Taite ? "

It seemed ridiculous to answer such a question from a man she had talked with dozens of times before at Hythebourne. She answered that she was.

It didn't continue in this way. He dropped the impersonal formula immediately, and asked her, in his quiet, restrained voice, to tell what had happened since her arrival at Hythebourne on Sunday.

She went through the details quickly. When she told of Louis' arrival in the evening, the coroner interrupted.

" Why, Mrs. Taite, did your husband not drive down with you and his brother ? "

She drew in a breath sharply. " We hadn't planned to come down together. He made up his mind that he wanted to see me, and so followed us down."

" What was the reason for this ? "

" I am flying back to New York on Thursday. There was a lot we had to discuss before then. There was very little time." He paused, and a fraction of his uncertainty and discomfort was apparent to that eager audience. Then he laid down the pen he had held and said clearly : " Is it correct, Mrs. Taite, that your husband instigated divorce proccedings against you some time ago ? "

" Yes."

" And it was this he wished to discuss with you when he came down on Sunday evening ? "

" Yes."

" I see," he said. Then he rapped loudly on the desk to still the murmur which had crept among the benches. " Please go on, Mrs. Taite."

There were no more interruptions. He allowed her to go forward with the events of Monday morning, passing over her description of Cutler's arrival without comment. It amazed her how easily the details of the accident came, but how clear each one remained in her mind. So clear that she almost felt she must tell how green the grass had been in the morning sunlight, how the wing-tips had flashed, and how bright and red the old man's blood had been.

"What did you do when you saw that the deceased had been injured . . . when you saw him fall to the ground?"

"I had no opportunity to do anything. I ran to him, naturally, but Mr. Cutler told me to take my daughter away. She had seen the accident and was terrified."

"Of course," he said quietly, "of course."

"She was hysterical," Susan said. "I took her back to the house and put her to bed. When I finally got her quietened, and asleep, I came downstairs again. By that time the doctor had arrived."

"Ah, yes," he said. Then looking directly at her: "Just one more question, Mrs. Taite. In your opinion could Horace Taite have done anything to avoid injuring his father? Was there any possible chance that the accident could have been avoided?"

She said firmly: "No. Absolutely not. He turned the plane in the normal way to taxi back to the hangar. I doubt that he had time to even recognise his father before it happened."

He nodded. "Thank you, Mrs. Taite. That will be all."

The hum of talk broke out again. The packed benches seemed to sway with their load of humanity; that breathless kind of murmuring which she had noticed before crept round them. She paused uncertainly upon the cleared space in front of the coroner's desk. The room became just a bewildering mass of faces, but even in her confusion she was aware of the naïve, careless splendour of the brazen flowers in their homely vase. She wanted to take them with her, out into the sunshine, and see them against the background of the sky. At that moment Paul stood up. His body rose like a familiar landmark above alien country. She turned towards him with a gesture of relief. As they walked down the narrow passage between the benches, the coroner's voice broke into the medley of sound.

"Horace Taite, please."

Without turning her head Susan was aware that Racey had risen slowly and had come to take his place before the coroner's table. As she stood in the sunlight on the steps she could hear his low voice repeating the oath, and, indistinctly the first question of the coroner.

Paul placed his hand under her elbow. " You don't want to listen, Sue. He won't have anything fresh to say."

She hesitated for just a second. " I wanted to hear him."

But he swung her suddenly to face him. " It's not helping anyone if you do that. Racey doesn't want to see you standing here."

She acknowledged it with a nod of her head, and once more allowed herself to be led forward. The woman, still leaning in the doorway of the post office, displayed her quick interest in her body, which straightened as they came into sight. Her curious eyes followed their progress to the car. When they were inside, she relaxed and resumed her former position.

Susan counted off the separate minutes of their wait. Paul's hand rested lightly on her thigh, and under the drawn-back sleeve, she could see his watch. The minute hand was moving on with maddening, impersonal deliberation. Spellbound she gazed at it, saying nothing, until the first sounds of movement within the hall caused Paul's hand to tighten about her. She looked up and saw that the steps were sprinkled with people. They spread fan-like across the village street, their voices swelling and rising to a discordant chorus. Then at last their unity broke, and they began to move off, some to walk slowly along the street, others to come directly towards parked cars. There was the sound of departure in the air now; the slamming of doors, the good-byes tossed carelessly to acquaintances. Susan stared straight ahead, dimly aware that Paul's grip hadn't slackened, that he understood in some way, that if she turned her head, if she moved only a fraction, it would bring a crowd of half-strangers avalanching upon her, claiming her after the six years' absence. The rigid set of her head grew painful, but she didn't relax it until the final farewells had been called, and the last car had drawn slowly from its position and moved unhurriedly up the village street and out of sight.

It seemed an endless time before they came into sight,

but she looked at last and saw them all gathered upon the steps, Louis, Racey, the doctor standing at a short distance from them; Cutler walking with the colonel, and the colonel's wife already half-way to the car. Paul reached swiftly across her and lowered the window. The woman's voice came clearly to them.

Her tones were crisp, as though she repudiated any suggestion of uncertainty in her approach. "Susan, my dear, how are you?" Her faded eyes ran quickly over the younger woman. "Not looking as fit as you used to. A little pale. Someone should fatten you up."

Susan's stiff lips managed a reply. "Mrs. Hayes, may I present Paul Berkman?"

Across Susan they shook hands. Sadie Hayes' greeting came promptly and confidently, while her brisk and frank stare took in Paul. Afterwards, when Susan had time to reflect upon it, she remembered how smooth Paul's voice had been, how he had lulled the woman into a sense of intimacy, had pierced that frank brightness to disclose the curiosity which lay beneath. Half-satisfied she withdrew to Louis' car where her husband was already seated. Paul leaning from the window on the other side had signalled to Cutler. He came immediately.

"Is everything all right?"

The other nodded. "Accidental death. Just routine, you know."

Susan, glancing about the little circle made by the three remaining cars, knew that there was nothing routine in it. It was a sharp and savage change which would presently bring the established pattern of life at Hythebourne to a complete stop. Her eyes came to rest on Racey, already seated in Cutler's car. He had lit a cigarette, but he wasn't smoking it.

"And Racey?"

Cutler shook his head. "Took it rather badly. It's natural, I suppose."

He moved away then to shake hands with the doctor, whose car had crept out of line from the others. The young man turned to give a vague salute in their direction, and then the small black car started off alone. It left them with nothing more to be done but to go back to Hythebourne. Louis started off first, and Susan found that they were sandwiched in this tiny convoy. It gave her the unpleasant sensation of being watched, and overlooked. She wanted to forget about Sadie Hayes in front, about Racey's huddled figure behind, but it wasn't possible.

Lunch at Hythebourne immediately assumed importance. Both women kept their hats on, and Sydney wore the second of his black coats. The wine he produced was dusty from the cellar, and Susan guessed that it had lain there for a long time, waiting for some occasion like this. Louis had taken his father's seat at the head of the table, and each was conscious of trying not to notice it. He sat uneasily there, and his conversation with Sadie Hayes was abstracted and desultory; she seemed dissatisfied with it, turning often to Cutler on her left to relieve the long silence.

To Susan, when she had entered the room, Louis had gravely indicated the seat opposite his at the other end of the table. She had wanted to refuse, but at once she had felt the lifted eyebrows, and the waiting silence which had fallen on the group, and she had dropped into it wordlessly. As she glanced along the table she found Paul's eyes upon her. He smiled that curiously familiar and detached smile which told her nothing of his thoughts. He shrugged his shoulders, an odd mixture of gravity and amusement, and gave his attention to Colonel Hayes who sat beside him. Susan watched Sadie Hayes settle to unabashed enjoyment of her food, establishing at once that she knew very well it was no occasion for light meal-time talk and that one might as well give up pretence. Gradually they adopted her attitude. There was frank relief in all their faces when the meal ended, and they trailed off to the drawing-room for coffee.

Paul found a seat over by the window. He sat there alone, almost cut off from the rest of them by the curtains which hung to the ground. For some minutes, as he waited for

Sydney to serve the coffee, he gazed at the scene of tangled and overgrown lawn in the sunlight. The talk behind him gradually lessened until he seemed no longer to hear it. His eyes rested on the fantastic structure of the stone dovecote, and his thoughts were upon the look he had seen come over Susan's face as she had taken her place at the table opposite Louis. As if doubting the truth of what he remembered, he drew his eyes away from the sunlit view, and turned to where she was seated. Her body, in the black suit, and her red hair, were magnificently outlined against the pale wall. She sat silently and uprightly upon a small gilt chair, and as he watched she leaned forward in response to something Cutler had said to her. Then Sydney came to him with the small coffee cup, and when he moved away, Susan was rigid once more. She held her coffee carefully, but listlessly in her hand, and the perfect stillness of her face and body would have been wonderful had they not contained so much menace for him. His eyes moved from her to Louis. Louis lay wearily in an armchair. A tight frown knitted up his forehead, and the lines of his face, like Racey's, were sharp with fatigue. Paul's gaze was taken by the hand which held the coffee-cup and the fingers in which a cigarette rested. They were fine well-bred hands, but they lacked the effeminate quality which he had trained himself to notice and recognise. The hands wrung an unwilling respect from him, the face became strong and not merely handsome. Suddenly the eyes jerked open, as if Louis had become aware of an added current in the room, and following his glance Paul saw that Susan was looking directly at him.

Across the intervening space they gazed at each other in a kind of fascinated wonder. With her body still held rigidly, she had leaned slightly forward, and the cup swayed dangerously in her hand. Her lips had fallen a little apart, and the stern cast was gone from her white face. She looked as if she might rise and go forward towards Louis, might even touch him to assure herself of the reality of his presence. It was a look of awakening, a look of incredulity and dawning apprehension.

The danger of it was very close to Paul. His impulse was to cry out, to rush to her and block from her vision the sight of Louis in his chair, to do anything to break the deadliness of that gaze. With conscious effort he forced himself to turn his eyes away from her and stare out across the bright wilderness of the lawn.

III

THEY ALL stood in the hall to see Racey drive off with Colonel and Sadie Hayes. Surprisingly he had offered to take them home, and they, not very willingly, had accepted. Sadie Hayes' strong, lined face was screwed up in her determination to find something to say to Racey; the Colonel sat in the back, heedless of his wife and Racey alike.

When the sound of the engine had ceased they were thrown into one of those pauses from which there seems no escape. Louis, obviously the one to break it, made no attempt to do anything. He stood, hands in pockets and his eyes on the ground, apparently careless of their presence. It was the silence of people who, having shared a common experience and emotion, cannot any longer fit themselves to the conventional pattern of casual behaviour. They each were waiting for something to happen, and nothing did.

In the end it was Cutler who showed them the way. He spoke, and Susan glanced at him in surprise. He interpreted her look, and knew it was because in those moments of silence she had been aware only of the two men who stood beside her. He felt a new pity for her bewilderment.

" Would it be any help if I went to get Midge ? " he said slowly. " It's almost three o'clock."

Louis jerked his head up. " She's expecting me. I'd better go." He looked at Susan.

She didn't say anything, just stood returning his gaze. He was forced to speak again.

" Would you like to come ? Midge would be pleased to see you."

In sudden alarm she took a step away from him. Instantly

she felt Paul behind her. "Yes, Sue. The kid would like to see you."

She half-turned to him, but there was no hint in his face that the words had any further meaning. She looked from one to the other, and they both watched her with curious intentness.

"Yes," she said finally, and began to walk towards the car. Louis followed her more slowly. He slammed the door behind him, and as the car swung round the gravel court Susan saw that Cutler had disappeared and Paul was alone in the doorway. There was a terrible solitariness about the way he stood there, and courage in the smile he gave her as they passed between the two high walls and moved off down the drive.

When they reached the road she said: "We could have walked. It isn't half the distance across the fields." She knew it was a foolish remark, but was conscious only of the need to say something and leave behind the memory of Paul standing alone.

Louis took a long time to answer, almost as if he understood that she didn't need one. "You're tired," he said at last. "You've had enough to-day." There was little solicitude in his voice. It was just a plain statement of fact, and she accepted it that way. She sank back against the seat, fixing her eyes on the road, curving away before them between green hedges. There was a sense of confinement, of being utterly alone with Louis and being forced to face this problem, while the rest of the world waited outside these barriers of foliage. The urgent need to break free of whatever bound her in this prison of confusion caused her to turn to him sharply.

"I must talk to you about Midge."

"Yes," he said heavily.

"I've asked you before. I want to take her back. You know that."

"Yes."

"Then you've decided?"

"I told you," he said gently, "that you've got to decide

that yourself. You've seen her now, you've seen the life she's used to. The rest is up to you."

She said defensively: "And what if she stays? What will become of her when Hythebourne is sold?"

"It's time she went to school."

"School? Yes, for eight or nine months of the year. What are you going to do with her for the rest of the time?"

"There's room for her at Carlton Mews with me."

She looked across at him quickly. He felt the purpose in her gaze, and turned to meet her eyes briefly. "Louis, I must ask you," she said. "Do you intend to marry when the divorce is through?"

He experienced the irritation of being questioned when there was no definite answer to give her. He wanted to shake her off, to refuse a reply, but it was anger against himself, not Susan, for this indecision, which troubled him. To commit himself to words was to go further than he wished, make tangible what had merely existed as an idea.

"Probably," he admitted, "I shall marry. It's someone I've known for a long time. Her name is Elizabeth Duncan."

The few sentences contained finality, as if he had politely bade her good-bye and closed the door. For perhaps the first time she came to realise that after she was gone his life would continue, and would change and expand. He would not always remain as she saw him now. The thought was painful. It rendered her insignificant, an incident in his life which he would presently pass over and be done with. There was some unknown person called Elizabeth, and it was she who was now important.

His words sang through her brain like a mournful little tune and the truth of them was inescapable, like something she had known for a very long time, and refused to admit. She looked down at her hands, spread emptily in her lap, then suddenly back at his face again. He caught her glance, and without warning drew the car to the side of the road and stopped it.

He swung sideways in the seat. "I want to talk to you,

Susan, but it isn't any good if you're not going to be honest."

" What is it you want to know ? "

" I want to know everything that is your life. I want to know what it is you're taking Midge to."

She hesitated. " That's not easy, Louis. That's six years you want condensed into a few minutes."

" Try, Susan. It's very important. Start with Paul, if that will make it easier."

" No. . . . Everything started reshaping when I got back to New York with only the experience of a few years on a small-town paper in Maine, and driving a few politicians round London. The beginning was pretty tough, but I found a job which eventually led me to Paul. He was the start of the big-time stuff."

" Yes ? "

" I had a job as a sub on one of his women's magazines. And then, from God knows where, he discovered that I knew things about fashion and clothes. He took a risk and gave me the job of fashion editor. He worked me like a slave until I'd proved to everybody that he was right."

His eyebrows lifted. " He could find the time to discover these things about you ? "

" Paul," she said reflectively, " is one of those rare phenomena who know their own business from the bottom rung. In the middle of a political campaign he has time to notice that a story in one of his small magazines isn't up to scratch. If you know your job he pays you well. If you make mistakes you go. There's no half-way with him."

" And he has money ? " As he asked the question he frowned.

" He probably has more money than he'll ever know how to spend."

Louis sat perfectly still for some minutes, and then said : " What about Midge ? Does he want her ? "

" He wants what I want, and that includes Midge."

" What will you do with her ? "

"She'll go to school."

"And you'll keep your job?"

"Yes."

When he made no comment, she turned to him. "You think that's wrong?"

"Nothing's ever wrong, Susan, that we ourselves don't make it so. If you've got a good reason for keeping on your job, then obviously it's right for you."

"I've got every reason. Newspapers are Paul's whole life. If I'm going to share it, I've got to share every part of it."

"Yes ... yes, I see that. But what about Midge? How does she fit in with all this when she's not at school?"

"I spend every summer in Maine. That would be Hythebourne all over again for her."

"Not quite," he said, in a tone so low that she hardly caught the words.

With that fragment sinking deeper as they sat in silence, she once more experienced the feeling that she was committed to something of which she didn't know the limit, nor of which she could even guess the price to be paid. The tantalising uncertainty of Louis' thoughts pressed against her. Had he, any more than herself, any real solution? Or did he merely hint and point obliquely at something which didn't exist at all?

Then in a sudden, overreaching desire for honesty, one of the series of small climaxes to which the emotional strain of the past two days had brought her, she turned and laid a hand on his arm. She placed it there with confidence in his interpretation of her action. "Louis ... I wanted to say to you ..." Her eagerness made her over-anxious.

Calmly he helped her over the difficulty. "What is it, Susan?"

"Simply I wanted to say that I'm sorry."

"Sorry?"

"About everything."

"You mean about Father's death—and Racey?"

"Not just that. About my part in things—every single

thing that's gone wrong. I'm damned sorry we made a mess of our marriage in the beginning, and sorry that I hadn't got the guts to hang on a little longer and see what way our lives worked out. And Midge—that's my fault too. No kid of seven should be like Midge, but she can't help it, poor mite. I guess even a mother with a few wrong ideas is better than none at all."

He stopped her. "Why do you say these things? Surely you must know the blame lies with both of us? It's not yours to take on wholly."

She said, more slowly: "I've told you this because I came over here believing the blame wasn't mine at all. I thought I'd taken the only course open to me—and that it was morally better to end a marriage than let it disintegrate into a sordid wrangle. I've begun to see that because you arrive at one particular solution to a problem, it isn't necessarily the right or the best one."

"There were many things," she added, "that I might have done. I should have stayed on because of Midge—and when you came from France . . . after the crash . . . I should have been here to help in whatever way I could. I lacked so much faith—faith in both of us, and hope that we might eventually have come to understand each other."

He said nothing, so she went on. "I imagined, when I came, that I should get custody of Midge, and assume the responsibility of looking after her with rather less trouble than I'd take over a new section of the magazine. And now I'm not sure."

"Of what?"

"I'm very unsure," she answered, "that I've any right whatever to Midge. I've earned no right to her regard or affection—I don't even know how to talk to her. She's my child and yet she's not, because I've done nothing to produce the person that she is."

He said seriously: "What do you want to do?"

She turned to him fully. "Will you trust me with her, Louis? I don't know how well or how badly I'll do the job, but I'm just asking you for the chance to try."

He made a movement to start the engine. "If you're certain you want her in that way, then you must take her."

IV

CUTLER TURNED thoughtful eyes upon the group round the fire. Susan, a little apart from the others, her face in profile; Midge half asleep, had squeezed her small body into the chair where Louis sat; Paul and Racey were at opposite ends of the sofa, and they alone had broken the silence in the last fifteen minutes. Racey, a glass of brandy before him, was trying to talk about riding, and wasn't succeeding very well. Susan looked as if she didn't hear them, and for the first time, Cutler felt a prickling of irritation as he observed her air of calm, expectancy.

What were they waiting for, he wondered, when the hours between now and Thursday were so few, so limited ? The child, lying pressed against her father, was the point of their problem, but they did nothing to work towards a solution. There was such danger in waiting too long, waiting until the cycle of events took charge, and the decision was out of one's hands. He looked at Paul, looked at the lean, controlled features, and wished that he would take command, would allow his careful efficiency to be exerted. And then, continuing his stare, he suddenly knew that Paul would make no move while they were here at Hythebourne. To-morrow, back in London, he would be different. Cutler was sure of that. Paul would win in the end, because he alone of any of them would have the determination to force a decision. And Susan would go with him because she was afraid to stay behind.

Racey put his glass heavily on the table beside him. The sound roused the child, who stirred in Louis' arms. He bent close to her face. "It's long past bedtime, Midge. You've been asleep."

Racey got to his feet quickly. "Let me take her up." He looked round the group, but no one spoke until Susan, rising slowly, said : "I'll take her, Racey."

Suddenly restless she went to take Midge from Louis : " She's too heavy for you. I'll carry her up."

Susan said quietly, and her voice betrayed her weariness : " Yes, if you'd like to." Then as they got to their feet, she looked from Louis to Paul, and finally at Cutler. " Good night."

Paul moved across to open the door. First Susan, and then Racey, with Midge in his arms, left the room. Following Racey, Paul himself slipped through, and closed the door behind him. He was gone before Louis and Cutler could be aware of his action. There was only the diminishing sound of their footsteps in the hall and on the stairs.

In the suddenly emptied room they were left in unexpected intimacy, the first time they had been alone together during the two days.

Abruptly, and without asking, Louis rose and refilled the other's glass. Watching his action, Cutler thought of the confiscated case of brandy which had been sent off to London yesterday afternoon, and wondered if Louis was thinking of that also. When Louis sat down he watched the other carefully for a few moments before he spoke.

He was uneasy. " Would you . . . is it possible for you to stay for the funeral to-morrow morning ? " Before Cutler framed a reply, he went on: "I think it helps my brother to have you here."

Cutler raised surprised eyebrows. " I wasn't aware of it. I rather thought I would have the opposite effect. I'm not exactly here on a friendly visit."

" There's another reason," Louis said, fingering the stem of his glass. " The whole district will be at the funeral. They know about you . . . and they know by this time that you were Racey's C.O. If you're at the funeral it's going to make something like a few bottles of brandy unimportant."

Cutler looked at him thoughtfully. " Does that still matter to you ? Surely, once the house is sold, these people will no longer be your concern ? "

Louis shifted in his seat. " I don't think I'm prepared to

199

face that question yet. Somehow, no matter how much I want Hythebourne off my hands, I still can't quite see us without it. It's like a tooth that's been aching, and when it's gone you don't feel much relief, just a sense of surprise and loss." He drained his glass and got to his feet. "So there you have it."

Cutler finished his drink in silence. He watched Louis put the guard round the fire, and plunged the room into semi-darkness as the lights over the mantel were extinguished. They walked together to the door, but there Cutler halted him.

"I've wanted to ask you . . ."

Louis nodded, cutting him short. "Yes, I know. I've been waiting for you to ask. You want to know whether I've remembered you."

His nervous fingers coiled around the door-knob. "I remembered you," he said reflectively. "It was when you started to yell . . . before the plane hit the Old Man."

For the first time Louis saw confusion on the other's face. "I'm sorry," Cutler said. "Why didn't you tell me to mind my own bloody business ? "

"It doesn't matter," he answered awkwardly. "I'm glad you asked—it gets it over with." He paused, as if uncertain, then picked up again with a fierce rush. "The bits slip back into place pretty slowly, you know. I wanted to mention it to you . . . but I kept putting it off. It always makes me feel such a damned fool."

He put up his hand and flicked the switches of the remaining lights. The act was final, and discouraged comment. When he glanced at Cutler again, his expression was blank, as if nothing of their conversation had ever existed.

"I told Sydney I'd lock up to-night," Louis said. "He looked worn out." He started down the corridor towards the service-door. With his hand on it he paused and finally turned back. "Oh . . . good night."

"Good night," Cutler said. He watched as the swing-door closed silently behind the other.

V

SUSAN WOKE at that hour of the night when the darkness and silence made it seem as if it could never be morning again. A sense of aloneness pressed about her closely, and at the same time she was acutely aware of the shared intimacy of the quiet house. She almost forgot, in those first seconds of waking, that the last six years had ever been—almost as if she were back to that period when a sudden awakening at night was accompanied by the sound of planes overhead, and how one had always lain waiting for their swifter return back across the channel.

And now, with a movement more instinctive than reasonable, she got out of bed and felt for her dressing-gown and slippers. The darkness in the passage was close and heavy, and even against the lighter square of the window, the trees in the wreck of the lawn below threw solid black shadows. She found her way up the stairs to Midge's room, and then immediately knew the reason for her coming. The child's sobs were faintly heard through the door, and they were muffled as if breathed tightly into a pillow.

She opened the door, and there was a swift stirring in the bed. " Midge, don't be frightened." Her voice was hoarse and scratching in the darkness.

The small body was warm and unresisting as she caught Midge up in her arms, and during the journey back down the stairs she felt the dampness of the child's cheeks against her shoulder. In her own room she felt her way back carefully to the bed, and when they were settled together, she could sense the guarded neutrality in the figure lying close to her. Then as the slow minutes passed, and Midge's first surprise was spent, there came the gradually expanding confidence and trust. When at last the child was asleep, Susan pressed her face gently against the tumbled hair and slept also.

WEDNESDAY

I

DEATH WAS inescapably present that morning. Early, even before breakfast, it was there in the abrupt little snatches of talk on the stairs, the flowers which had arrived yesterday and whose perfume escaped to fill the hall whenever the library door was opened. It was present in the sharp little sentences tossed between the people who moved about the house, the orders which no one troubled to obey, or were too preoccupied to hear. There was a stirring and a movement through the rooms, and a sensation of haste, as if they had all suddenly realised that there was no more time.

They all met round the breakfast table, self-conscious about their dark clothes, and trying not to notice that the others were the same. Only the child, Midge, had no dark dress, and she alone was completely natural. Her clear, high voice kept cutting into their murmured sentences, her piping words often penetrated the thin layer of their conventional behaviour. She dominated the room that morning as she sat with her back to the windows, and her hair reddened by the sunlight. She alone had animation and vitality, untroubled by thoughts of the formalities of the morning. By contrast she made them all palid and expressionless.

It was only when she was gone that they were able to talk freely. They became less of a group contrasted darkly against her vivacity ; they emerged more into their separate personalities. When the door had closed behind her, Louis set down his coffee-cup and faced them.

" Susan, have you any idea what you'll do with Midge to-day ? "

She said stiffly, holding her cup with fingers which had grown weak with anger : " I don't think we need worry about that. I'll manage to amuse her."

" I wasn't worried," Louis said. He swept his hair back from his forehead in a gesture which dismissed the suggestion. He glanced at her in a puzzled fashion. She knew that he wondered at her petulance, and she was ashamed of it.

He chose his next words with care. " Then could you bring her back to Carlton Mews about six ? Racey and I should be there about that time."

Before she could answer, Paul said quietly : " Do you think you could keep to-morrow morning free ? There are things to be gone over, and Susan and I are leaving by the night plane." His voice, though low and controlled, carried a hint of impatience, as if he were welcoming this return to London and his own world of authority.

Louis' face darkened. " Yes, naturally."

They had thrown the politely worded sentences at each other like missiles, and for a moment the hostility which had lain quietly between them seemed ready to stir and rise. Susan glanced from one to the other, and apprehension made her powerless to move or speak. She wanted to stand up and wasn't able.

The sound of Cutler's chair scraping across the polished floor released the tension as if he had visibly cut through it. He looked at his watch. His polite unawareness of the near-scene was a triumph of convention and well-bred indifference, Susan thought. He might have been speeding them on a pleasure jaunt as he spoke.

" You ought to hurry, you know," he said, looking across at Susan and Paul. " It won't be very good if the child gets caught up in the . . ." His smooth flow of ready words broke, and he didn't finish.

" Don't fuss," Racey said. He got to his feet slowly. " Midge is the only one who has any idea of how to behave sensibly. One has to be adult before one gets upset by wreaths and telegrams and platitudes." His face was shadowed darkly, as if he hadn't slept. He set his chair in place before the table and added: "There's plenty of time. Service isn't until eleven."

They stared at him, and no one spoke. He was angrily conscious of their eyes upon him as he moved towards the door, and there, beside Cutler he halted and turned back to them. "It's a pity you're not staying to hear the will read this afternoon, Susan." He leaned against the door-frame, hands in pockets. "Not that I imagine Father has remembered you, but there's just a chance, you know, that you might have been left a few mortgages." Then he addressed Paul. "It's all we've got left in England these days, you know—mortgages, overdrafts and the dollar-gap." He wheeled lazily and walked away.

They listened in silence to his footsteps in the hall and later to the sound of a door opening and closing, and knew that he had gone into the library where his father's body lay.

Louis stood up. He kept his eyes on the table, but his words were for each of them.

"You'll have to overlook that," he said. "Only that I know it's not true, I'd say he's tight and has some excuse."

"Oh, what the hell!" Paul said impatiently. "We all know what the guy has been through. He doesn't need an excuse." He pushed his chair aside quickly. The gesture was an angry dismissal of Louis' words.

Too soon the bags were ready and brought down. Outside in the sunshine Sydney stacked them neatly into Paul's car. His body was old, Susan thought, as she regarded his bent back, and the last two days had strained his fading vitality beyond recovery. To-night he would be alone at Hythebourne. She had meant to ask Louis about him, what would happen to him when Hythebourne was sold, but as with so many other things, there hadn't been time. What had she gained, she wondered, by these days here; little but a heap of vague impressions to be sorted out in security on the other side of the Atlantic. So many questions formed and few answered; a train of thought begun and not completed—and never could be. These ideas ran swiftly through her brain in the moments while she stood watching Sydney pack in the bags, and the light wind brought the smell of the dew-damp grass and the mouldering leaves from the over-grown garden to her. Slowly she turned and walked inside.

In the hall, Louis, Paul and Cutler waited. As she entered Susan saw them fix their eyes on the stairs and upon Midge, who came down rapidly holding the high banister awkwardly. Louis started a movement in her direction, but the expression on the child's face halted him. She reached the bottom and stood quite still, staring at the library door.

Louis sought the right words. " Come, Midge. It's time to go."

She answered him clearly. " I'll say good-bye to Grandfather."

He made a gesture as if to detain her, and then his hand dropped helplessly to his side. Midge walked with her light, child's step towards the door, opening it and slipping through soundlessly. They stood motionless and waiting. Susan could feel the sweat start on her palms and she knew that they had expected her to go with the child. She had possessed the strength neither to prevent Midge doing what she wanted, nor to enter the room with her. The fear of what was inside ran through her body like a white-hot pain. She could not control or subdue it. The knowledge of her cowardice was bitter, but she felt with certainty that had she followed Midge she would have been forced to turn away in fear and repulsion from the sight of the old man. The minutes passed with deadly slowness ; Sydney finished with the bags ; he came to stand in the doorway, close to Susan. He joined the tableau they had formed, his eyes fixed, as theirs were, on the library door.

When it opened at last, Racey appeared, holding Midge by the hand. There was no sign of distress in her face ; it was composed and grave. She broke from Racey's clasp and came quickly towards Louis. He put out his hand and caught her small one into it. They walked out to the car that way.

Before she turned to follow them, Susan glanced again towards Racey. He stood, his hand on the door, regarding the small group. The tight weariness on his face was unlightened. "Watch her, Susan," he said, looking towards Midge. "She'll be all right—if she doesn't break completely." He added, then, indifferently, "See you this evening."

They placed Midge in the front seat of the car between them.

She busied herself trying to make her thin, straight legs reach the floor. As Paul started the engine Louis came round to the open window. They regarded each other without interest.

Louis passed him a slip of paper through the window. "I'm phoning through to my solicitors this morning. Will it be all right if I say you'll be along this afternoon? They're in Clifford's Inn. Susan is anxious to have Midge as soon as possible, and if you hurry them they should have some papers ready to sign in the morning." He looked, then, across at her, but she was staring straight ahead. He stepped back from the car. "We can discuss it this evening."

Paul nodded briefly, slipping the folded paper into his wallet. "I'll see these people immediately after lunch."

Midge twisted in the seat to gaze after her as the car moved in a circle round the gravel court. Cutler and Racey had come to stand beside Sydney in the porch. Louis was alone in the centre of the sunlit space. As the car swept down between the high walls which bordered the garden on both sides, Louis lifted his arm to wave. Midge responded wildly, and as they passed the dovecote, only the roof of the house could be seen. Then she slumped limply back in her first position. Watching, Susan saw a flicker of emotion cross her pale face, and when the car reached the road, the first tears stood out on her lashes.

Reaching out swiftly, Susan caught her into her arms, and the child's sobs broke harshly.

They reached London shortly before noon. The sun had grown hotter; in among the traffic the air was heavy and stale with exhaust fumes. On Vauxhall Bridge Susan leaned forward for the brief glimpse of the river down towards Lambeth and Westminster. The tide was low; on the flat, exposed mudbanks, small craft lay on their sides. Close at hand the mud was like wet cement, thick and dark grey; the embankment rose steeply above it. Down the thin channel of dark water left by the tide, a police launch moved smoothly. As she watched it it turned in a neat circle and headed back towards the sloping green-edged embankment of Battersea Park. The graceful sweep of steel on Chelsea Bridge was like an edging of black lace against the hot noon sky. The river, the embankments, the buildings stretching upwards were many tones of grey; against the grey mudbanks the gulls were startlingly white. As far as she could see to both sides, the red buses, flowing in even streams across the bridges, were the only objects of solid colour.

Midge, lying against her, dozed fitfully. Dust had caked faintly on her damp cheeks. The fit of weeping had exhausted her; she lay still and limply, her sticky and chocolate-stained hands folded on the short, crumpled skirt. Some of her brown hair had escaped from the long plaits and fell untidily in a fringe about her face. Absently, Susan looped one strand behind her ear.

"She's going to look like you, Sue," Paul said, not glancing at either of them.

"She has their eyes."

He halted behind a bus. "She has Louis' and Racey's expression, but she's much more your child than his."

"I think," Susan said evenly, "one can always see in children the characteristics one wants to see."

"Meaning what?"

"Children are such individuals. They are just so much

themselves, and whom they happen to resemble is incidental."

Watching the traffic, he didn't reply. They continued in silence all the way to the hotel. Paul drew into the entrance, and Susan began to wake Midge gently. Sleepy and dazed the child slid out of the car, stretched cramped limbs gingerly.

With the car emptied of their bags, Paul drove off to the garage, and Susan took Midge's hot hand in her own. Waiting for the lift, the child pressed close to her, not saying anything or moving, but keeping her eyes fixed on the scene before her. In the lift she held her breath, and turned to gaze backwards as the doors closed silently behind her.

In the bedroom she stood perfectly still beside the dressing-table while Susan tipped the bell-boy, and when he had gone, her light blue eyes flashed about her expectantly. The grave, pointed little face, puckered in an unfamiliar expression of wonder and curiosity. She drew one shoe slowly across the carpet, examining the track it left in the pile. Her sticky hand had left a mark on the dark wood of the dressing-table. Seeing this she searched for her handkerchief and began to rub at it furiously.

Susan said uncertainly : " I shouldn't worry about it, Midge. There's a person who comes round specially to do that sort of thing."

She drew her hand away quickly. " Sydney said I wasn't to give any trouble."

Susan sank down on the bed. " But that's not trouble, Midge. The woman doesn't mind . . ." And seeing the child's face cloud with bewilderment, she added quickly : " But if you'd like to do it, then I'm sure she'd be very pleased to have you help."

Midge nodded, and produced the handkerchief again. Wetting a corner of it in her mouth, she began once more to rub at the spot.

Unwilling to watch her any longer, Susan went into the bathroom. The water was cool on her wrists ; she splashed more on her face. After a few minutes, she was aware of Midge standing in the doorway. " You'd like to come and wash, wouldn't you ? "

The child nodded and came forward. She stood at the basin, completely absorbed in her washing operations. Susan saw that she was efficient and careful, replacing the soap on the tray, the towel in its place on the rack.

When she was finished, she said : " Can I look out of the window ? "

" Of course. I'll open it for you."

She remained there, her back towards the room, while Susan unpacked the bags which had come from Hythebourne. The formality of shyness had attacked both of them. Susan longed to break through it, and feared Midge's indignation and fierce reserve. The awareness of each other, and of the silence, was acute ; the slight noises of the bags, the closing of the cupboard doors, were intensely magnified. Glancing carefully at her, Susan saw that she seemed to have lost interest in the traffic moving below, and now stared straight ahead across the tops of the trees. She leaned forward a little farther and then said : " What's that place over there, a big one ? "

Moving a little closer, Susan followed her line of vision. " That's the Hyde Park Hotel."

" It looks exactly like a castle. All towers and things." She raised her face towards Susan's. " Do they have castles in America ? "

" No. I don't think so."

" Why not ? "

" I don't think they've ever needed them," she replied simply. " The castles in England were built before America was discovered. When everyone got over there, they decided they didn't want any more castles."

" Well, how did they fight their battles ? "

" They had different kinds of battles then. The castles weren't much use. There wasn't anyone like King Arthur then."

" That wouldn't matter much. King Arthur was a bit

of an old fool." She added swiftly: "But it's funny, that!"

"What's funny?"

"Having no castles."

Susan smiled. "One gets used to it," she said. "But we have a lot of tall buildings."

"Taller than this one?"

"Yes, much taller."

"Why do they build them so tall?"

"Because there are so many people, and they have to find a place for all of them."

Midge shrugged elaborately. "I shouldn't like it. The lift makes me feel funny." She stopped speaking because her eyes had fallen on a table near the window. On it lay a pile of sketches from the Paris salons. "What are they for?"

"When I was in Paris I had to write about them for an American magazine. I went to the dress shows and then sent cables and pictures back to New York so that everyone would know what the newest styles were like."

Midge nodded absently, moving to the table to thumb through the sketches. She looked at each carefully, but said nothing. Susan turned to the dressing-table and began to comb her hair. The child continued her absorbed study, occasionally turning back to view one a second time. She finished at last and laid them down, stacking them into a neat pile. She said to Susan: "Does anyone ever wear clothes like those?"

"Yes, of course, Midge. Quite a lot of people—those who can afford them."

"Do they cost much money?"

"Yes, a great deal."

"Does everyone know they cost a lot of money? Is it easy to tell?"

Susan laid down the comb. "Yes, pretty easy, Midge. One sees the cloth they're made of, the way they're cut, and how they fit—it isn't difficult to tell."

Midge came close to the dressing-table; stared into the

mirror at Susan. "When I have a lot of money I'm going to wear clothes like that, so that everyone will know just how rich I am."

Susan twisted on the stool. "Beautiful clothes, Midge, should never be worn just so that everyone will know they cost a lot of money. The people who make the clothes are artists, and when they create a beautiful dress it's to make a woman look beautiful and to make her happy. It's not just money."

"I don't know," the child said uncertainly. "I'll have to think about it." She fingered the edge of the table, then added: "I don't look very nice right now, do I?" She glanced into the mirror. "Perhaps I'd better do my hair."

"Shall I do it for you?"

"Can you do plaits?"

"Yes, I think so."

She stood quite still as Susan began combing the brown-red hair, only occasionally shifting from one leg to the other. When it was finished she watched as Susan took a hat from the cupboard and put it on. "Are we going out?"

"We're going to have lunch downstairs. Paul will be waiting for us."

"Does everyone wear a hat?"

"Not everyone." She looked round at the child. "Would you rather I didn't wear this because you haven't got one?"

"No," she replied carelessly. "Keep it on. I like it."

Together they left the room. In the lift as the descending motion caught Midge, she clutched Susan's hand, and closed her eyes.

II

LUNCH OVER, the afternoon faced them emptily. Paul left for Clifford's Inn, and Susan knew he would spend the remaining hours between one news-agency office and another and half the editors on the Street, always one of his correspondents with him. While they smoked cigarettes, rode in taxis, waited for lifts, the policies, the shaping, the attitudes of the articles which would be cabled across the Atlantic for the next year, would be thrashed out. He might buy or sell, casually, but not without thought, the rights to feature stories, and back in New York his editors would curse what they termed interference. But his touch was sound, and in the end they accepted what he had found for them.

Susan's eyes followed his quick progress across the foyer, saw him pause impatiently on the steps while a taxi drew in from the stream of traffic. In a second he was inside, and before the glass doors swung open again to admit the next arrival, it was out of sight. His going was like the withdrawal of a force which held her steady; bewilderment and confusion threatened whenever he was away. With a mild sense of panic she gazed about the foyer, and the renewed sensation that time and events moved past her with impersonal speed, and she was alone in the centre of movement, did nothing to reassure her.

She looked down at Midge. " What would you like to do this afternoon ? "

Naturally enough, the child shook her head. " I don't know."

Susan found the echo of her own uncertainty in the reply. Timidly she took Midge's hand ; they moved towards the glass doors and out into the sunshine. Here the noises of the traffic seemed to hammer down upon them. Midge hand clutched Susan's fingers in a painfully tight grip. Across the road in the Park half a dozen dogs from the Mayfair flats had come to be exercised, their owners striving with polite determination to keep them separate. She pointed towards them, but Midge shook her head. Susan sensed that she was afraid of the traffic, so they began walking in the direction of Marble Arch, Susan finding things to talk about until the child's tension relaxed a trifle. At North Row she stopped, fascinated by the barrow-boys, gazing with startled eyes at the silver wrapped fruit, and the long skirt of imitation grass which surrounded the barrow. A light, gritty wind touched it, and it rose and fell with agitated grace.

" 'Ere y'are, Miss. Two bob a box. Best quality "— thrusting a packet of dates towards Midge.

She shrank back, trembling, and Susan hurried her on. They waited by the traffic lights to cross Oxford Street. Midge gazed upwards in confusion as the people crowded about her, blocking her line of vision. She stumbled and almost tripped in the excitement of that moment when the amber changes to green and the crowd spills into the road, with its hurrying, pushing movement. At the Corner House, the lunch-time rush was over. The women, fortified with spaghetti on toast, the orchestra's version of *The Merry Widow*, and a good cup of tea, had long ago sailed forth, children hanging to shopping bags, to find bargains. The sunshine seemed to have brought them out in overwhelming numbers; they jostled each other, eager and shrewd eyes seeking reductions, and dresses that would wash. The street stretched away before them, tightly crowded, noisy, the shoppers reflected darkly in the plate-glass, the men selling nylons and watching for the police, the vendors with trays filled with oddments which squeaked, jumped or danced on strings for which they asked fantastic prices. Susan was wearied at the sight of it. She looked at her watch and then down at Midge. The child gazed at her expectantly. She raised her hand and a taxi drew into the kerb. She bundled Midge in before her.

" Wigmore Hall, please."

They rumbled round into Portman Square, and at the lights sailed past the waiting traffic from Baker Street. Midge stared round the dark interior of the cab, wriggled over to see her face in the mirror. When they stopped suddenly at lights farther down, she lost her precarious perch on the edge of the shiny leather seat, and fell forward into a heap on the mat. A nervous little laugh escaped her ; after that she held the handle of the door.

At Wigmore Hall Susan studied the posters and saw that

the afternoon offered chamber music—Haydn and Brahms. She looked doubtfully at Midge. "Do you think you'd like to hear a concert?"

"Yes." She replied unhesitatingly, although the words could have meant very little to her.

Susan bought the tickets: Midge stood on her toes and tried to see into the box-office. "If you don't like it we can come out in the interval," Susan said.

Midge said nothing, but followed eagerly and with strange assurance as the attendant led them forward to their seats; nor did she break her silence during the time while they waited, but sat up with grave attention when a light patter of applause marked the quiet appearance of the musicians.

The sensation of numbed inactivity which the past days had produced remained stubbornly with Susan for long minutes after the first bars of the Schubert C Minor quintet had reached out into the listening darkness of the auditorium. Note followed note, and they were solitary sounds, unrelated to a whole. Then the lyric strain rang through with a sweetness which touched her at last, cut through to the source of the bitterness and self-questioning of which the child beside her was the embodiment. The music vagabonded along, poetry and pure song moving it forward in sweeps and gushes, vast and bold in reach. Listening now, she found the harmonies trembling sometimes on the edge of disaster, but where they fell down, it was merely a leap down the hill into banks of flowers. The restless pushing sea of it flowed about them both, and the child, small face sharp with attention, gave a sigh which might have been ecstasy or fear. The full realisation of the music, the sweetness and the light, were terrible for Susan, hitting impersonal blows at the built-up forces of her prejudice and pain. The power of it, expanding, reaching an arc, having its end in its beginning, found no parallel in her own life, but never before had she felt this barrenness, this need for it. The last movement swept on to its ordained climax, reaching it by the intuition of lyrical genius rather than by the processes of reasoning, but in her it awoke no response but that of her own torturingly unsatisfied desire for completion. It ended, and its sweetness lingered in painful contrast to her doubts.

They returned unwillingly from the refuge, facing each other doubtfully, only to find that in some way the music had crashed through the high barriers which kept them apart. Midge, not understanding, only vaguely aware that somehow there was now ease and confidence to replace their restraint, turned towards Susan, her eyes wide with excitement and pleasure.

" Did you enjoy it, Midge ? "

The child placed her hand on her stomach. " I felt funny here. It screws me up inside."

Looking at her, Susan knew that she herself could stand no more of it. Her fingers stabbed the programme. The Brahms F minor. She was too familiar with it, too familiar with the twilight greys of the slow movement, the grave threading through the melody, like all the regrets and the sorrows she had ever experienced. And then the finale, when the song twists about, growing suddenly agitated and restless. Too well she remembered the reflective strain which seems to halt the movement towards the conclusion, and then, abruptly finding the pattern, the melody is passionately sure and true. It rushes on to its end, and doesn't wait for her, and she is left clutching at a solution which is not her own.

She touched Midge lightly. " Are you tired ? Would you mind if we left now ? "

Midge said immediately : " No, I don't mind." She began putting on her tight little gloves carefully.

There was a gentle warmth in the sun when they emerged on to the street. Together they examined the windows of *The Times Book Club*, and then crossed to gaze at *Debenhams*. Midge objected to the models because they had no faces. She followed Susan dutifully past the side windows of *Marshalls*, until, on the corner of Oxford Street, she tugged suddenly at Susan's hand and drew her back.

" Isn't that a beautiful hat ! " she said.

Susan's eyes followed her pointing finger. The window
was small, and showed half a dozen dresses of the kind
Midge should have worn. The hat rested with a row of
four others, on a stand. The child's fascinated gaze had
fallen on it and remained there, lovingly gloating over each
detail of its buttercup velour, the rich velvet ribbons which
trimmed it. It was a foolish hat, smugly conscious of the
fabulous price ticket which stood inconspicuously by it.
For a child, its richness was absurd ; no young face could
have carried its ostentation.

Susan looked down at Midge. " Would you like a hat ? "

" Yes, please. I'd like that one."

Susan said uneasily. " Isn't it rather too old for you ?
Perhaps one of the others . . ."

But the little face flushed with longing. " I'd like that
one, please."

" Well . . . come inside. There might be one there you'd
like more."

But in the end they bought it. After Midge had impatiently rejected all the others, they got it from the window
for her. Triumphantly she took it from the saleswoman's
hands, put it on herself, and faced the framed mirror
delightedly. It was quite wrong for her. The colour made
her face pale, her hair faded ; the tight green coat became
tighter and shorter, and her thick country shoes were
incongruous. But she saw only the hat, the hat with its
bold beauty, and it satisfied her newly awakened craving
to feel this small piece of luxury under her fingers, to touch
the velvet caressingly, and to know that it was hers. She
saw none of the inconsistencies of her costume ; the hat
alone mattered.

She wore it proudly and too consciously. As they ate
tea together in the restaurant, her head was never still,
turning from side to side, until she was sure that nothing
else within sight could touch the splendour and magnificence
of the hat. And in Bond Street, her eyes, quicker than
Susan's, saw every mirror, and in shop windows, as they

216

passed, she thrilled to each reflection of herself. The happiness on her face was a light which touched every corner of it.

III

THE SUN had long ago left the courtyard of Carlton Mews when Susan and Midge arrived there. One could sense the dusk gathering about the housetops and in the trees in the gardens beyond. The pale lamplight scarcely reached into the corners where shadows lay thickly. Their footsteps echoed back from the stone walls, and Midge touched Susan's hand timidly. As they climbed the stone ramp together, a light from one of the windows suddenly sprang out into the darkness; they drew into its friendly shelter. Then, as abruptly, the curtains were drawn, and they were left in the darkness again.

Louis answered Susan's ring. He looked tired as he stood in the doorway. Greetings were difficult between them, neither knew how much or how little to say. It was strange, she reflected, that they both understood the other's embarrassment, and were childishly unable to speak the first words. He closed the door behind them. A sense of peace and homecoming swiftly overcame her. Then down the red-carpeted hall she gazed towards the open door of the sitting-room. The sound of voices came to her—Racey's and Cutler's. They brought the present back too sharply—they were the practical factors in this meeting, the barrier which never left Louis and herself free to reach out towards each other's thoughts. They had discovered no means of communication in these days together, and now the chance had gone forever. But what else could she expect, Susan wondered, when she had cut through his every effort to know her? How much words had held them back; they had lived through their hours in a private little hell of uncertainty and the relief of speech was denied them. The deadlock which existed between them was one of her own making. Seldom is one forced to face the results of one's obstinacy as forcibly as the situation was presented to her. All her instincts were around in her own defence, and they were sadly insufficient.

And he appealed finally to her as she stretched to take her coat. "Susan, do you think you could spare time to see me later this evening, or perhaps to-morrow morning? I think we ought to talk?"

He asked it without force, without stress. The right to hope had almost left him. She wanted to touch him, to take his hand in hers and let him understand that his hopelessness was more painful than any blow, wanted to let him see that if he suffered, she suffered also. She said, with an uncertainty she knew he sensed: "I think it's all right if you come along to the hotel later this evening. I'll let you know when Paul arrives."

And because she didn't want him to look into her face any more, she caught Midge's hand quickly and walked with her down the passage to the sitting-room.

The two men rose as they entered. Racey, cigarette in hand, stared at Midge. "Good Lord! Where did you get the trick hat, Spider?"

The child seated herself carefully on the sofa. "Mummy bought it for me," she said with dignity.

It was the first time she had called Susan by any name. There was an instant awareness of it in the room. Susan could feel Louis behind her, could feel the unconscious hesitation in his step. And then quickly, too quickly, he said: "Drink, Susan?"

"Please. Gin and French."

Her seat faced Racey's, but when she spoke it was to all of them. "How . . . how did things go to-day?"

"They were about as lousy as they could be." He ashed his cigarette with a movement which betrayed his furious irritation.

Cutler shifted uncomfortably. Over his smooth features there passed a look of bewilderment and slight fatigue, as if all day he had suffered Racey's bad humour and was prepared to do it no longer. He answered Susan as if

Racey had never spoken. " They went off quite well . . . as well as those things ever do."

" Yes," Racey said, picking up his glass again, " everyone was very tactful. Not even the vicar mentioned accidents, and no one whispered the word ' brandy.' But it was in their minds, make no mistake about that."

" Perhaps you're mistaken." Louis brought Susan her glass. He carried his own in his other hand. " We do—all of us—have this extraordinary idea that our lives are important to other people, our sufferings matter to them. But they don't, not a bit. We hear that Jones has gone bankrupt and his wife's run away with another man. Do we think about it ? Of course we don't. We say : ' Poor Jones,' and then we close our doors and forget about him. It means no more, no less."

" It's a pity," Cutler said, talking to no one in particular, " that this century has no interest any longer in the affairs of its neighbour. We none of us can afford it, none of us dare to do it. We are interested in people only in so far as they touch ourselves."

" Then," Susan said slowly, " carried to its maximum, that attitude turns life into a meaningless pattern. It becomes nothing more than turning a page of a book, a shout in the street."

" That's God, that's life, that's eternity or oblivion." Racey drained his glass. " I read that in *Ulysses*. A shout in the street—the beginning and end of everything."

" It was," Louis said, getting to his feet and taking his brother's glass, " an interesting, if too personal example of the beginning and end of things this afternoon. We agreed, Racey and I and Father's solicitor, that Hythebourne should be put on the market as soon as the stuff can be cleared out of it."

A little silence greeted his statement. Susan, glancing at Midge, saw that she had taken off her hat. She held it now in both hands, completely absorbed in fingering the velour and the trimmings. She had heard nothing of the past conversation.

Susan, uncertain because she wondered how much right to comment they would allow her, said: "Is it quite necessary—I mean, is there no chance of hanging on to it?"

"Why?" Racey asked her.

Louis handed him the refilled glass. "The beginning and end of things, Susan. It was important to make a decision, and we've made it. We're going to end it. Hythebourne will no longer absorb our time or our energies, as well as our ill-spared money. In that way we gain. And also, in the same deal we lose, because we no longer have anything upon which to hang our affections or our loyalties. We are cutting ourselves off from our past, the good as well as the bad."

He sat down. "Why should I," he said, "burden myself further with anything so demanding as Hythebourne. At best it could be only tolerably well-paying, at worst, a millstone round my neck. I'm suddenly tired of giving my thought, my time, my ambitions, to something which when I die, Midge here may very well regard as worthless."

"Amen to that," Racey murmured. "The world crumbles round us and we hasten to free ourselves from our encumbrances. Our children inherit nothing, not even responsibilities." He lifted his glass. "Here's to the brave new world."

"I will show you fear in a handful of dust," said Cutler unexpectedly.

They all turned and looked at him, all except Midge. His polite controlled face was just as before, as if he had not spoken. But he had exposed them, and they were afraid to look at each other.

Suddenly Midge slipped off her chair, holding the hat carefully. She glanced across at Louis. "Can I go into your room, Daddy?"

"Why, Midge?"

"I'd like to try my hat on in front of the big mirror."

She went, but her going only produced a renewal of the tension. They had all said too much, too much to withdraw to their old ground of impersonal behaviour. Cutler was regretting his words. To try to escape from the situation he had created, he went and refilled his glass. And then, when they were beginning to feel that the silence would never be broken again, the door-bell rang.

Louis went at once to open it. Through the open door Susan caught the tones of Paul's voice. She turned her eyes expectantly towards the door. Some of her helplessness left her with his coming. Why, she wondered, did she always require his presence to bolster up a failing determination?

When Paul stood among them he brought the contacts of another world with him. His greetings were quiet, though not stiff, but somehow his vitality contrived to make them all appear as dummies, moving to a conventional pattern, sitting still and watching life go by on the other side of a glass sheet, and seeing themselves in a distorting mirror. 'What does he see us as?' Susan wondered. 'Does he see us as pallid, indecisive creatures, allowing him to do our thinking for us—too lethargic to stir or move?' Among them all there was an awareness of the conversation before Paul entered the room. They looked at him now and saw that he was not of the kind who could stand aside and see their age and achievements rocket into dust. He would interfere—perhaps disastrously—but he would not stand aside. And so with Hythebourne. Paul would have taken up the farm again with energy and made it pay, or else he would have sold it without sentiment. To his mind it would have been as simple as that.

As he accepted the drink which Louis gave him and sat down, Cutler rose to go. They all recognised the movement for what it was—a tactful withdrawal to allow them to discuss the news Paul had brought from Clifford's Inn.

He shook hands with them as politely and impersonally as if he had met them half an hour ago, as if the days and the happenings at Hythebourne had never existed. His words meant nothing to Susan, but somehow as he held her hand she fancied that his tone held a hint of disappointment, just a trace of regret and warning. Louis and Racey went with him to the door.

Paul smiled across at her. "Now that," he said, nodding towards the open door, "is what I call a true Englishman. They do have emotions, I'm told—the basic ones—but you'd have to live on a desert island with one of them to find that out. That guy, Cutler—if the ceiling fell in on him this moment he'd murmur faint apologies for causing you the inconvenience of dying."

"They can't be turning you sour, Paul—not yet."

"I've spent the afternoon talking to one specimen after the other. Good guys, all of them. Solid stuff—you could trust them with everything you'd got in the world. But hell! they won't make up their minds! They'll write, they'll get in touch with you, they say, and all I want to know is what use that will be when I'm on the other side of the Atlantic? I've been doing nothing but asking the same questions, put the same propositions as I did last Saturday, and only one guy in six had any sort of a definite answer for me. It's enough . . ."

He broke off because Louis and Racey had returned. Louis took a seat and his own unfinished drink; Racey remained standing, leaning against the mantelpiece.

Louis looked towards Paul. "You've seen the solicitors?"

"Yes," Paul said briskly. "Everything's O.K. They'll send the papers round to the hotel in the morning for Susan to sign."

"That's quick," Louis murmured without any conviction.

"You and Susan," said Racey, "aren't the only people in the world who've ever had a divorce. They're more or less used to getting things fixed about the custody of children."

They took no notice of the remark, or tried to. Susan said, wrinkling up her forehead: "About Midge. Will we have to wait for the whole thing to come through before she can come over to New York? She should start school . . . it ought to be as soon as possible."

"I've asked about that," Paul said. "As long as Louis is willing, she can come to you as soon as she gets a visa.

There's some sort of court order to be got, but it's merely routine."

Routine. The word hammered into Susan's brain. The end of a marriage had passed into the sphere of that word. People and their relations to each other then, after all, could become names and numbers on pieces of paper. She said to Louis : " You'll arrange that, will you . . . about the visa ? "

" Yes, of course," he said stiffly. " As soon as possible." She wanted to believe he had spoke this way because he also felt the humiliation of what they were doing.

Then the telephone rang. Racey stood upright. " I'll get it," he said. " I'm expecting a call here."

But he was gone only a minute. " It's for you," he said, putting his head round the door and looking at Louis. " Elizabeth."

Louis went to take the call, and after that Susan heard nothing of the conversation which went on between Paul and Racey. She even had a confused impression that she herself contributed to it, but no memory of what she had said remained. All her thoughts and attention were focused on Louis' answers, and the fact that he was talking to Elizabeth. She could hear nothing, only the tones of his voice, but her imagination formed the sentences they would speak to each other. She wondered why it mattered to her, and searching her mind, could find no true answer. Her questioning always led up blind alleys and returned to the central point of her doubt. For the first time, while she sat half-listening, to the talk of Paul and Racey did she dare face it completely, and ask herself the question. Six years ago, had Louis been the person she now knew him to be, would she have left him to go back to New York ?

She considered it while the talk flowed around her, and the cigarette smoke grew thicker. How completely futile to have started upon this train of thought when it was all much too late. There was nothing to be done about it, not now. But even so, she wondered how she could have come to miss so much about Louis. How could she have overlooked the patience and calm of him, the way he had come through these last days, less well equipped, by the fact of his loss of memory, to deal with the situation than any others. And they had left it all to him—Racey, herself —they had done nothing. And now, without protest, he was keeping the child here, inconvenient and unsuitable as it was. It was a heroic sort of gesture, one which made her mean and small by comparison. But somehow, she didn't think he himself was making that comparison. He had been generous beyond belief, and somehow, it was harder to bear than anything else. Why was it, she wondered that you always wished those you wounded were unworthy of better treatment ?

But now she heard the tiny bell as the receiver went down, the thought of Elizabeth thrust itself up once more. Well, Elizabeth would have him now, and even had she wanted to there was nothing to be done. Strange to think that she was years too late—strange that one could be as late as all that.

By the time he reached the door she was standing. " Louis, we must go now."

His eyebrows shot up. " Already ? " Impossible to tell if it were merely a polite inquiry.

" Yes . . . I'm rather tired. Midge and I have been to a concert. It tired me more than I thought."

Racey laughed, a little unpleasantly. " A concert and a hat in one afternoon. You must have got on well together."

She flushed, and was angrily aware of it. " I think she enjoyed it."

Then Louis said unexpectedly : " You've made her very happy. It's difficult for men to realise that things like hats can make a difference to kids—kids like Midge, that is."

She liked him for saying that, but once again his generosity was a reproach.

He held her coat for her. " Is it possible for me to see you later on ? " he asked in a low voice. " I think we should talk, and to-morrow will be rushed for you. I could come to the hotel later."

Paul had caught the tone but not the words. He was looking at her and frowning slightly. "Not to-night," she said quickly.

He said nothing more, and the chill of her refusal was like the cold air which wrapped about them when the door was closed and she and Paul stood together in the dim light of the Mews.

IV

THEY WALKED back to the hotel in companionable silence. Strange, Susan thought, how precious to her was that quality of Paul's—to leave her alone when he knew she needed it. As they climbed the slight slope in Haymarket, he slipped his arm through hers; his action was kindly rather than intrusive. It was a source of satisfaction to her that they could still respect the privacy of each other.

And over dinner he did her talking for her. There was never a silence between them, but yet she need make no effort to stimulate conversation. The problems which immediately concerned her he did not touch upon, until suddenly, laying down his knife and fork he said: "I must be crazy, Sue. I did something this afternoon I thought I'd never bring myself round to."

She raised her head. "What did you do?"

"I bought a story from Louis' agent to serialise in *Mercury*."

"I didn't know he'd written one," she said. She spoke slowly, trying to get the meaning of his words clear.

"It was offered to me on Saturday, and I passed it on to Jacobs in the London office to read. He's dead keen on it."

"Is it good?"

"It's away ahead of anything else I've seen over here. It comes out in the spring on this side, and Doubleday's will probably do it in New York."

"Tell me about it?" It suddenly was imperative that she should learn this new aspect of him.

"War book. Rather naturally, I suppose. Think half of

it's his own story. It's one of these rare things which make you wonder can he possibly do it again, or has he put everything he's got into this one job. In any case, it's good—damned good."

She pointed out calmly : " But you didn't have to buy it. You could have left it alone. Not you, Paul."

" Look, Sue, the book's good. Far too good for any petty act on my part to keep down. If I hadn't taken it some other magazine would, so I'm not exactly playing Boy Scouts."

" Yes . . . I see that," she said. And then, " Does Louis know about it yet ? "

" Not yet. I've told his agent to keep it under his hat until we've gone."

All through the meal she thought about it, thought about it even when she heard her own voice answering Paul. How much about Louis still remained unknown to her, how much further would she have to go until she found all of him ? Riding up in the lift he spoke of it again.

" Was Louis writing when you were here ? "

She shook her head. " If he was he never told me of it." Unwillingly she admitted the possibility. " Of course, he knew quite a bit about it—English at Cambridge, and then the job with his publishing firm—but he never talked of writing. Somehow . . ." Reluctantly she made herself tell him the truth. " We never seemed to talk of things like that . . . never made plans about what we should do after the war. We never thought beyond the week after next."

They stepped out of the lift. The doors closed softly behind them. " Perhaps," she said slowly, " that's one reason why I left him. We never gave ourselves a future."

As she turned the key in the lock, they could hear the sharp ring of the phone. She hurried towards it and picked it up. It was Louis.

" Susan, you won't think again about my coming round ? I wouldn't keep you long."

She hesitated, and in that moment's silence, aware of

Paul standing by the still open door, aware of Louis waiting for her answer, she knew she had no more strength to face the conflict which would begin anew, even though it might be confined wholly to her own mind and emotions. She was infinitely weary. It was saner at this moment to allow Paul to hold her in his arms and blot out every other image, then to take up the problems again with Louis.

"I'm sorry," she said. "Not to-night."

As she turned from the phone Paul was beside her. Strange she thought, as he kissed her, how intimately, how completely he knew the point where her strength broke and gave way to dangerous weakness.

THURSDAY

I

SUSAN LAY with her eyes closed, struggling to shut away encroaching wakefulness. Through the drawn curtains the light had begun to make itself felt in the room; when her eyelids flickered open for a second, the furniture stood out sharply dark from the surrounding brownish wash of light. Below, the noises of the traffic grew until they were no longer a stream of single sounds but a continuous heavy drone. For a long time she had lain like this, on the edge of sleep, hearing the thin ticking of the clock, and wakefulness advanced steadily. Her mind was running forward unwillingly to the necessities of the day. Sometime, when at last it was over, when all the things had been got through, she would be taking the plane and leaving England. Her thoughts would go no further than this; to this point they returned again and again, and the hours lying heavily between were covered in a kind of obscuring mist. Out of this mist, advancing and conquering all else, was the knowledge that after to-night she need be afraid no longer. And then suddenly the thought, unbidden, 'Afraid of what?' sprang itself upon her. She attempted no answer, but clutching the sheet, her body twisted in terrible apprehension.

But the day broke upon her too abruptly, with no warning other than a knock when the maid entered with the breakfast tray, and then a little later, Paul.

There was no time for preparation, but he didn't seem to see that anything was wrong, or if he saw it, wisely made no comment. Already dressed, he sat beside her on the bed, and was charming and gay in the way he could be when he wished. She found herself laughing at something he had said, and the simple assurance that everything was all right entered her mind again. Responding to an impulse she put out her hand and touched his own.

He stopped talking. Into his face came the surprised expression which one sometimes sees in the eyes of an animal when it is unexpectedly caressed. He said slowly : " What is it, Susan ? "

She edged back into the pillows. " Nothing . . . I just wanted to do that."

" Yes." Their swift reunion went unmarked by words, only a simple gesture of friendliness. Controlled and unemotional, it was like Paul himself. He went on talking, but her happiness was very great, the kind of brightness inside her which made the beginning of the day an excitement. How far, she thought, they had strayed along their different paths in these last days. But somehow it was right that they should come together again before their adventure ended ; she wanted to re-affirm her faith and trust, have him know this happiness. The urge was unbearable. She thrust aside the loaded breakfast tray and moved close to him.

" Paul ? "

His reply was spoken in a low tone. With one arm he pressed her body tightly against his ; his free hand lost itself in her loosened hair. " Sue ? "

" You understand . . . these last days ? " It was imperative that he understand, but yet how to put into words what had merely been an idea, the merest shadow of doubt.

" Sue, don't worry. I knew." Her head was forward on his shoulder, and suddenly he bent down and brushed the skin behind her ear with his lips.

" You knew ? You knew it would be like this ? "

His fingers, fan-like, spread themselves through her hair. He pulled it high, and slowly let it slip down. It fell about her shoulders. " Only a fool is never afraid, Sue. I knew you would doubt. I knew you'd be afraid."

" I'm not afraid any more." It was true. A new freedom

flowed through her body in sweet, secret gushes. Her heart and flesh and senses seemed to ache with the sheer happiness of being here with him, of being held in this long embrace of love with no intrusive thought separating them.

He looked down at her face against his shoulder. "You're sure? You're coming with me to-night?"

There was hardly need to say it. "Of course I'm coming."

He felt the weight of her body against his and through her nightgown, its warmth. One forearm, thrown round his neck loosely, was near his face. Upon it he could see the faint golden hairs. There was the smell of health and vitality about her, one had caught immediately the knowledge of the immense vigour and frank sensuality which could spring to the surface in a second. Down the smooth flowing line of her arm a few tiny brown spots marked a trail. He knew a fierce longing to run his lips along that flesh, to put his teeth gently into its whiteness. She stirred in his arms. The red hair on her shoulders slipped aside, and her throat and neck were swept clear of it. Staring past her he could see the place on the pillows where her head had lain. Extraordinary the pleasure he gained in merely knowing how she slept with a hand thrown across the sheets, and how, in the morning, the blankets always trailed on the floor.

At the back of his mind he framed a curse when the phone rang beside her. She let it ring twice again before she loosened the hold round his neck and stretched out to pick it up. Back again, and close to him, he could hear the conversation. She said absently: "Hallo." He caught the precise English tones, and then listened carefully. The solicitors in Clifford's Inn had sent their chief clerk round with the papers. Was Mrs. Taite free to sign them?

She hesitated, raising inquiring eyebrows towards him. He gestured in the direction of the sitting-room. She nodded. "Would you come up to Mr. Berkman's suite, please? I'll be with you as soon as possible."

She replaced the receiver as Paul rose. "Perhaps," he said, "I'd better go in there. Will you be long?"

" Fifteen minutes. Too long ? "

He began feeling for his cigarette case. " I'll read through what you're going to sign. Save you some time." She watched him while he lit the cigarette. The tightness which had shadowed his features appeared to have lifted. The cheekbones were prominent in his lean, handsome face, but around the mouth the habitual lines of concentration were relaxed and calm. While he drew on the cigarette for the first time he seemed to smile. Abruptly he took the cigarette out of his mouth and bent and kissed her.

" Hurry, darling. I'm never sure how long I'm going to hold out in conversation with an Englishman."

When he was gone she flung the bedclothes aside. In the bathroom she stepped out of her nightgown, reflectively watching the water gush into the bath. To-morrow she would be in New York, back in her own apartment. Nice to be back amongst one's own things again. And then the office with the pile of accumulated mail waiting for her, and too many people on the phone. It quickened her senses a little. New York in the fall was a wonder of which she'd never grown tired, never been too hurried to notice. The exhilaration of the thought carried her through dressing, went with her as she opened the door to Paul's suite and a thinnish man in a raincoat rose to greet her.

" Good morning," she said.

He shifted his Homburg from one hand to the other. " Good morning, madam."

It unnerved her more than familiarity would have done. She crossed quickly to where Paul had spread the papers on the table. He drew a chair up for her, and settled himself on the arm. She could feel one of his hands lightly on her shoulder.

" Everything looks O.K., Susan. Just sign where they've marked."

She flicked through the papers, saw her own name, Louis', Midge's, and signed quickly. On formal papers they were transferring the child from one to the other, and it struck her as an action so cold-blooded that she shivered slightly as she watched the clerk bend over to add his own name. His hands were swift with the blotting paper, and with a sense of shock she realised that there was nothing more. Midge's whole future was affected by this action and there was nothing whatever to indicate it. When they had gone the application for custody would move along the normal channels, speeded, if possible, by pressure from the solicitors, and this frail-looking, white-haired man was packing away the stiff-edged papers with the knowledge that routine was once more in motion. Did he ever stop, she wondered, to consider the people concerned; did he, for example, know the feeling of guilt which possessed her, the certainty that she was separating the child from her background without any real conviction that she could ever replace it?

Perhaps, having spent his life among such situations, she thought, the clerk was capable of divining this, and at the same moment wishing she would hurry and give him time to get a cup of coffee before going back to Clifford's Inn.

As she watched him fumble with the straps of the document case the phone rang. Paul answered it. " For you, Susan. It's Racey."

" Racey ? " She hurried to the phone. " Hallo."

" Susan ? I'd like to see you for a few minutes."

" Where are you ? "

" Downstairs."

" Hold on a moment." She covered the mouthpiece and spoke to Paul. " Are you using this room ? Could I tell Racey to come up here."

He looked at his watch. " There's a woman coming soon to take letters." His brows wrinkled. " I wanted to get through some work before lunch."

" Doesn't matter." She spoke to Racey again. " Ask them to bring you up to my room. I'll be waiting there."

" O.K. See you then." He rang off.

They accompanied the clerk to the lift, he all the time talking about the weather. It occurred to Susan then that she hadn't had time to look from the window, and apart from her own particular area of grey sky, seen from the bed, she couldn't tell whether or not it had been raining. The clerk seemed to know about it though.

The maid had taken possession when Susan got back to her room. The bed had been made, and from the bathroom came the sound of water. The woman looked up from wiping the bath as she entered.

" Good morning," Susan said.

" Good morning, madam."

" I'm afraid I kept you back—staying in bed so long." She gestured towards the bath. " Do you think you'll be long ? I've got someone coming to see me."

The woman smiled pleasantly. " I can leave the dusting till afterwards, madam, if you'd like the room free now."

" Thank you," Susan said. " That would be a big help."

Racey's knock sounded on the open door as she turned. " Oh, Racey. Come in."

" Good morning, Sue."

The maid gathered together her cloths, and Racey stepped aside to allow her to pass. As she went she closed the door.

" Come and sit down," Susan said. " Over here by the window. Cigarette ? " She waited for him to come and take his place in the chair opposite her own.

He didn't speak while he took the cigarette, found his lighter, and lit one for both of them. Then he sat down. " What time does the plane go ? "

She knew he wasn't interested in the plane, but she answered patiently : " I'm not sure. About ten or eleven, I think. Paul will know."

He looked amused. " Paul settles everything for you, doesn't he ? "

She shrugged. " Why not ? Why should both of us trouble about things when there's only need for one ? "

" Fair enough, I suppose. Is your job like that ? "

" Like what ? "

" Paul making the decisions, you carrying them out."

She flushed. " He owns the magazine. He doesn't run it as well."

" So he does let you do some work ? "

She beat down her anger. " No one in that sort of business gets money for jam, Racey. I worked damned hard to get the job, and now I work even harder to keep it."

He raised impersonal eyebrows. " I don't see either of you doing much work in London."

" I don't have any work to do in London. As for Paul . . . how can you say what he's done ? You don't know."

" Oh, yes," he said wearily. " I can guess. He's just about turned Fleet Street upside down. He's clever, isn't he ? "

" He's been a correspondent in most of the capitals in Europe. He knows his job."

" Same thing, Sue. Same thing."

She didn't bother to reply, and he didn't seem to notice the silence. She played nervously with the cigarette, then said : " Racey ? "

He glanced at her in surprise, almost as if he had forgotten her presence. " Yes ? "

" You didn't come here to talk about Paul. What is it ? "

" Oh, to hell with it." Savagely he stubbed out the cigarette, and got to his feet. He stood by the window, back towards her, hands in his pockets.

" I came to thank you," he said coldly.

" Thank me ? "

He swung round. " In the name of Heaven don't play the innocent now. I'm not in the mood to take it."

" You mean the stuff you brought back from France."

" What else ? "

She said stiffly : " I didn't expect your thanks. I expect it even less when it's such an effort for you to express it."

He pulled his hands out of his pockets. " Oh, come off it, Susan. How can I be expected to say anything and mean it when you're sitting there like a bloody Sphinx, with your mind thousands of miles away." He leaned back against the window. " It's hard enough for any man to thank a woman for a favour, but it's twice as difficult when she's not even paying attention." He spoke roughly. "What are you thinking of?"

It was easier to be honest. "New York. I'm thinking, Racey, how good it will be to get back there, back to all the things and people I know and understand."

"You look," he said sourly, "as if you're about to enter into the Holy of Holies."

"Perhaps I am. I wouldn't expect you to understand."

"Understand? I think I do—a little."

She said softly: "I don't think so. How could you ever know what it means to be going home to a fresh beginning. This business"—she gestured vaguely—"is all through. You see, Racey, I'm much more of an American than you think. I *like* the way things are there, and I want to go back to them."

He had turned sideways and was staring down at the traffic. "Big words, Susan. Are you sure you mean them?"

"I don't understand."

Still he didn't look at her. "Down at Hythebourne," he said, "you belonged. It didn't matter whether you were American or Chinese, you still belonged there. To save me, or to spare Louis—we don't question the motives now —you ran a terrific risk. You were as cool and sure about that as if you'd planned it all along, and knowing at the same time that if it was discovered you were in for a hell of a lot of trouble. No stranger would have done that. Whether you deny it or not, you'd certainly chucked your hand in with us then. You still belong there, Susan. Part of you always will."

"Is this," she asked, "supposed to make any difference to my going back to New York?"

"None whatever. What I didn't want you to do was go back with the idea that you could shake us like dust out of your mind for ever. Even with the New York labels on your luggage, the nylons and Paris clothes—even your American habit of pushing straight through a business and getting it done with, you're very much English. You're

235

even more English now than you were last time. That's why you helped us at Hythebourne, and that's why, when Midge is a young woman and visits this country, she won't be wholly American either."

She said uncertainly : " Racey, would you mind . . . ? "

He came towards her. " Sorry, Witch. I've let you down rather hard."

She found herself saying : " It doesn't matter," and both of them knew it was untrue.

He stood above her, but they didn't look at each other. " Well, Witch . . . thanks for everything. Be seeing you sometime."

After he was gone she sat smoking a cigarette and thinking about what he had said until the maid returned with her pile of dusters. Then she went and sat quietly in the sitting-room where Paul was dictating letters to a prim woman of thirty-five. The sound of his voice, monotonously reciting the standard phrases, interspersed here and there with a crisp word from the woman, was the refuge behind which she sunk her thoughts.

II

PALE SUNLIGHT washed down the buildings when Susan walked back to the hotel. Her mind was still crossed by the currents of conversation which had taken place between Paul and the New York editor with whom they had lunched. A stout, hard little man, who grew red in the face when he climbed the stairs, he was familiar to her as the type of person who inhabited her own particular nitch of existence. They were all of a type, the newspaper men, the editors, the correspondents. She knew them thoroughly, and wanted no other companions, no other kind of life. It was satisfaction to know how deeply with Paul she shared the hurry, the push, the immense and unending excitement of the press world. Her own job lying on the fringe of it, it still gave her admittance to the spell-binding circle. It was a world she could cut adrift only with pain and regret. And then she wondered, as she turned into Curzon Street, why the thought of leaving it should have entered her head at all.

As she turned from the reception desk with her keys, David Cutler approached her.

" Good afternoon, Mrs. Taite." It was exactly the polite formal tone he had used on Monday morning in the dining-room at Hythebourne. He held the soft brown hat in his hand in precisely the same way.

" Good afternoon." She added quickly : " I didn't expect to see you again."

" Well, no." He hesitated. " I was passing. . . . I wondered if you might be in."

" You've been waiting ? "

He glanced at his watch. " Only ten minutes."

She paused awkwardly, uncertain of his exact reason for calling, uncertain, too, of how far beyond mere formalities they would progress. One could stand for ever on the brink of intimacy with this man and never achieve it. Was it worthwhile, she questioned, to make the attempt on this last afternoon. She doubted that she would ever see him in her life again. There was something infinitely hopeless about making a contact which was doomed from the beginning. Could integrity permit the expenditure of energy on a lost cause ?

He solved it for her. " Could we find ourselves a seat somewhere ? I didn't think it was right to say good-bye quite so formally last night." Then he pressed it a little. " We've shared an experience, haven't we ? "

She stared at him, and he saw the hint of change in her. " I have a sitting-room. Come upstairs."

He followed her silently, but not meekly. In the sitting-room the table was spread with the letters left for Paul to sign. Cutler produced cigarettes for both, and they settled themselves in opposite chairs.

He had tossed aside his hat. It fell, a crushed brown object, to the floor. He leaned back in his seat and suddenly grinned. She thought he looked embarrassed.

"You know," he said, "I've come all the way up here, and I haven't a damn thing of any importance to say to you."

She laughed, because it was a relief to see his seriousness gone, to know that he could be other than polite and correct.

"You're lucky," she said, "if you always find something of importance to say. Most people never achieve an important remark in their whole lives."

"Yes," he said. And then, "How odd it's been."

"What's odd?"

With a wave of his hand he indicated their two selves. "All this business . . ."

"Hardly odd," she said. "Tragic perhaps."

"Yes, but from my point of view. Think of it. On Sunday morning I heard, quite by chance, that we were investigating Racey's trips. Now just that point alone. Probably in the next year I won't be in contact with the office again on a Sunday morning. But last Sunday I was . . . and out of it, all of this."

"Yes." Unwillingly she pursued his line of thought.

"And you, of course, being there, made it stranger still."

Deliberately she remained unconcerned. "Why so?"

"Well, surely. . . . The first time you've been in England for . . . how many years?"

"Six."

"Six years." He went on quickly: "Seeing Louis was a shock. He didn't recognise me."

She said dryly: "If it was a shock you certainly kept it to yourself."

Untouched by her tone he replied earnestly: "Yes, of course. It's my job."

She felt she had earned the rebuke.

"It hasn't been easy to take," he continued. More thoughtful now, his words came slowly. "The old man's death . . . and knowing that indirectly I was responsible."

She protested. "Oh, no . . ."

"I was," he said, "what one could call the remote cause."

The words made a deep impression upon her. He, like the rest of them, would never forget the days at Hythebourne. The passing experience had touched them separately, so that not even this man, almost an outsider to the group, had escaped it. He came here now only because he must talk of it, must seek this outlet for his troubled thoughts. Unreasonably he held himself responsible, and so were they all responsible in varying degrees, for the terrible ending to Lionel Taite's life. How swiftly and inevitably the innocent became involved. No use to struggle or to turn away, because each turning might be the beginning of a new and bewildering train of events.

"We were all," she said slowly, "responsible. Even in minor ways."

He leaned forward eagerly. "You do see it, don't you?" Then he plunged still further in. "That's why I wanted to talk to you. One can't . . ." He hesitated. "One mustn't let experiences slide without trying to sort out their meaning. Easier, perhaps, but not wise."

"These days have been more to you than routine?" She felt she need not have asked the question, but that he somehow expected it.

"Yes, that's it. That's what I wanted to say." He seemed grateful that she had expressed it for him. "Wherever you went, whatever happened to you, I wanted you to know that I wasn't untouched by it."

Her lips dropped a little apart in wonderment. "Why did you say 'wherever you went.' You know that I'm going to New York to-night."

His face clouded, and he didn't meet her gaze.

"Why?" she pressed.

Suddenly he looked directly at her. "Because I never did believe that you would go back. Forgive me for mentioning it now—it was quite wrong, I know. But down there, at Hythebourne, I was certain that you would stay."

" Are you still certain ? "

" You say you'll go—you say you're taking a plane this evening."

" Yes," she said evenly, " I am going."

He stood up. " Then I'm very sorry, Mrs. Taite. I've made a terrible blunder—believe me, I didn't come here with the intention of saying that." He stooped to pick up his hat. " Why is it that one always says too much when one begins talking ? I've kept my mouth shut for days only to end up making a complete fool of myself."

She rose also. " It's hardly as serious as that. I can't forget that you've been very helpful and perhaps have the right to say what you think."

" We none of us," he said, twisting his hat, " have the right to go blundering ahead into what we know little about and are less qualified to judge."

She walked with him to the door. " You're saying that somehow makes it all right."

He looked at her. " I've tried to believe that bit about ' Judge not that ye be not judged ' but it doesn't always make sense. I think that you've got to first make a judgment in order not to judge. After all, how many of us mistake indifference for tolerance. It's pretty easy to be tolerant if you just don't care."

" What are you trying to say—that you do care about what happens to me ? "

" Yes, that's about it."

She took his hand. " Thank you for that. I won't forget it."

" You don't think it was just plain, bloody interference ? "

" No."

" Then that's all right." He released his hold on her. " Good-bye, Susan."

" Good-bye, David."

She didn't watch him go, but behind the closed door listened for the sound of the lift. Then she lit another cigarette and sat down. Staring about the quiet room which the few scattered possessions of Paul made familiar, she tried to prepare her mind for Louis' visit which she knew with certainty would come.

At three-thirty she began to pack, and at twenty minutes to four the expected call came.

"Susan? Louis here. I'd like to see you."

"Of course. Come up right away."

While she waited she continued packing. There was no other way she could prepare for his coming save with this outward façade of calm. It was as good as any other, and it carried her well over these seconds when she heard the lift, and then his knock.

He entered slowly, and stood, his back against the door, surveying the open wardrobe, the dresses folded in tissue on the bed; the suitcases, standing about in that curiously urgent fashion. They were the strong reality of her departure.

Automatically, at his entrance, she had reached for her cigarettes, needing the feel of that tiny strip of paper, needing the defence against him which it provided.

"No, Susan," he said. "Have one of mine." She took it and watched his fingers as they tapped his own against his case, watched him carefully as he held the lighter close to her. He was handsome, she thought, in that same easy way of eight years ago. He and Racey had always behaved as if good looks and charm were a habit to which they were long accustomed, and had long ago forgotten about it. He smiled, but without self-consciousness.

He nodded towards the too-obtrusive suitcases.

"What time?"

She answered patiently: "About ten . . . perhaps a little later."

"Glad to be going?" He had seated himself precariously on the arm of a chair. His long legs sprawled languidly before him. "Or shouldn't I have asked?"

She evaded it. "One's always glad to be going home." And then: "Why shouldn't you ask?"

He grinned. "I might have forced you into a very

difficult corner. A polite lie, or a frank admission that you'd be only too glad to see the last of all of us."

With his head outlined against the window he was remarkably like Racey. And when he turned sideways and the light caught him, she could see the resemblance fade. She fidgeted with her cigarette. " Neither would have been necessary. I came over here to clear all the loose ends up —and now there's nothing more to do."

He laughed outright, but not unpleasantly, as if he found her statement diverting. " In most people's lives, Susan, this is a pretty important step. You're not trying to tell me that you've got it all parcelled up in your mind and labelled, ' Emotions Not Involved.' You've changed, but never so much as that."

She said quickly : " How did you know I've changed ? "

" I do know that much." He became serious. " Susan, can't you guess what it's been like ? Ever since the whole staggering business began to click on Friday night, each time I've seen you has been a little bit of pure hell. I've remembered so much more than I ever believed possible."

The talk had swung out into deep channels, and she knew that she must be pulled along with it. " Tell me," she commanded. It became imperative to know his conclusions; to see where, if at all, their thoughts might have run close together, perhaps even have reached agreement. " Tell me," she said again.

He leaned hard against the back of the chair. " How can either of us say exactly where we went wrong ? Can we either of us put a finger on the first time we might have spoken the few ordinary words of sympathy or help, and we just didn't bother. A war-time marriage has no spacious-ness to it, no room for growth. We had no chance for adjustments, no time to get used to each other, and become tolerant of inadequacies."

He stopped for a time, as if collecting his thoughts anew, She didn't interrupt him because she wanted to hear him through to the end in silence, to give him opportunity to develop each idea to its fullest. Only then could she judge by how much or how little they had missed concord. But missed it they had, somewhere, and perhaps at a stage when one small effort might have brought it within sight. And from that moment they had walked down dark passages alone, each in their secret thoughts accusing the other.

But he had picked up the thread again. "Ours could well have been a 'marriage of true minds,' Susan, if it hadn't been for the fact that one or other of us was always going or coming back from our job. That just turned our lives into a series of meetings between two comparative strangers."

She said, in a voice which was stiff and unfamiliar: "You didn't know even my appearance on Friday evening. Are you sure that your imagination hasn't helped you along with all of this?"

His face grew dark. "Losing one's memory is like having a wall drop down between you and the rest of the world. Once there's a gap forced anywhere it just keeps getting bigger and bigger. Seeing you and eventually remembering you was the final assault. Since Monday it's broken up completely." He looked at her with unrelenting stare. "There isn't time for dishonest imaginings, Susan. What I'm telling you, I'm quite sure about."

"Forgive me," she said.

Reflectively he listened to the words. "The tragedy of it is that we should have been so reluctant to say 'forgive me' to each other then. So many times we had the chance and didn't use it; so many times I've wanted to be honest with you and didn't dare—I didn't dare to trust your love enough to expose my own weakness."

Her hand gripped the side of the chair. "What didn't you dare to tell me?"

He didn't avoid her eyes when he spoke. "I used to tell you, didn't I, that flying was the only thing in life, that danger didn't exist except for the man who was a coward. That, Susan, was a fabrication of lies, a complete covering of deceit so thick that sometimes I myself couldn't see through it. Time after time I used to come home on leave to you, and want to spill it all out, the rottenness and the deceit. I wanted to tell you what it felt like to be sick with terror at the things I'd seen, so bloody crazy with fear that I'd thought of tipping myself into the Channel rather than have to go on facing it over and over again. Do you understand fear like that, Susan? Perhaps you do, but I couldn't tell you of it at the time. I played the fine hero until you must have been fed up to the teeth with it. I suffered that monster inside of me, but I didn't tell you."

She flung aside her cigarette, edging forward in her chair. " Why are you telling me now? "

" Because I want to. Because I think it's time things came straight between us. Not many people have the experience of waking up one day to find they remember exactly nothing. It's then that you discover you're stripped of everything but the few things that are lying so deep inside you'll never lose them. First you discover that you want to live—no matter how bad the pain is you want to go on living. And then, in this darkness where there's nothing to think about because there's nothing to remember, you start off by trusting those who are looking after you. Bit by bit it all adds up, until you've got a few beliefs, scratched from the substance of your mind as hard as rock, and they're the ones you cling to. Since that time I've loathed the idea of sham—sham of any kind. That's why I've told you this. You might as well go away with an idea of things as they really are."

He stood up. His face was stern and rigid, lines in it she had never seen there before. He looked exhausted. " I'm going now, Susan. Perhaps I've said too much. Probably I haven't said enough. Have you understood? Have I given you one single new thought that you'll carry away with you? Or are you going to forget it all—and me as well? "

Inwardly she cringed before him. " Of course I'll remember. Do you expect me to forget? "

" I expect nothing," he said wearily.

" Louis ? "

" What is it ? "

" Do you despise what you see in me now ? Do you hate me because I've been measured by the standards you've set up and I've fallen short of them ? "

He looked at her in astonishment. " What are you saying ? God in Heaven, you don't know what you're talking about ! You, as you are now, every imperfection, every inconsistency of you, I could get down and worship if you would let me. I could begin to love you now as I should have loved you seven—eight years ago."

Her body was weak and stunned, as if he kept striking giant blows at her, and her only thought was to remain upright until they should cease. Comprehension of what he was saying scarcely dawned on her. She was barely aware that he had risen from his seat and now stood behind her.

" For you, Susan, I've done incredible things. I've given you the child I wanted to keep with me. I've tried to make these days plain sailing for you—to stand down, to appear a weak-kneed fool beside Berkman, just because you were going to be happy with him. I've done what I could, every single thing that occurred to me, and then, last night, I saw Elizabeth—you remember Elizabeth, Susan ?—I saw her, and I made up my mind that I couldn't marry her."

" Why ? " The word was torn from her.

" Why ? " he repeated. " Why do you think ? Because of you. You never leave my thoughts for a second. We're fair to each other, Elizabeth and I. I've told her all of this because I won't have another marriage go on the rocks through lying and cheating."

She bent her head into her hands. " Louis, please stay. Don't go yet."

" Why should I stay ? " he said coldly. " There's no purpose in staying to hear the few consolations you will try to offer me. If I've grown to love you it's no fault of yours. It need not be your concern either."

She raised her face. " Louis, need you say it like that ? "

Unexpectedly he retracted. "I'm damned sorry, Susan. I've been unnecessarily brutal. Forgive me, if you can."

She called to him: "Stay a minute." And then, more urgently: "Louis . . . wait!"

But he went just the same, as if his conviction was stronger than any persuasion of hers. Her utter confusion made her powerless to stop him. He found his way through the orderly barrier of the suitcases, and didn't even turn in her direction before he closed the door. She remained in her seat, staring towards the window and the fading autumn light, and her thoughts drove her back over the conversation. That Louis should love her became more believable as she recalled in the past days how their thoughts had drawn together in a unity which both had tried to deny and later ignore. A unity of this kind brought with it an awareness of the other's physical presence so acute as to be painful, and to pretend to be untouched by it was a kind of agony she had not believed possible. They loved each other in a way that made it seem that all the years had been building up to this point, had been a long and slow preparation for it. And it was now a love based upon a sure knowledge for each other. Susan reflected that they could hardly have seen each other in harsher or more revealing lights than the events of the past days had provided. That he could recognise and love even the faults in her pointed that there was nothing of the old feeling left—what they had achieved was something new and quite distinct from their first attraction.

But she reminded herself of the truth she had confessed to Louis himself—one learned that one's own solution to a problem was not necessarily the right one. She knew that she could go on loving him and still return to New York with Paul, refusing to take the chance of a second and more disastrous failure. For another failure would wreck both of them. They would be unfit for each other and for anyone else. And Midge, older now, and more easily able to sense the disharmony, would be torn and buffeted between both. There was the joy, too, of her reunion with

Paul that morning to remember, the sweet freedom from doubt, the feeling of absolute certainty that to return to New York with him was right. And then his knowledge of her fear, his understanding of what she had experienced, made her doubts reasonable and expected, and not something whose existence could change her in any way. In his own particular fashion Paul needed her quite as badly as Louis—perhaps more. In the tight world of the press there was no place for the simplicity which he expressed in his love for her. It demanded expression for itself, and he would suffer in the loss of her.

Her gaze fell upon the cigarette still lying on the carpet and she picked it up and stubbed it carefully in the ash-tray, thinking all the time that her own feelings in the matter had entirely ceased to concern her. It was staggering but no less satisfying, to realise that, after a complete lifetime of suiting herself, finally Louis, Paul and Midge had now assumed a far greater importance. She was reaching towards the ultimate expression of herself, and the terror of it lay in the chance that she might yet choose wrongly. She might have gone on sitting there until Paul's return, her mind ruled by this awful confusion, if the demanding sound of the phone had not roused her.

A smooth feminine voice of an air-line clerk spoke to her. The liner of to-night's Atlantic flight was out of service, and all the bookings had been transferred to another company. They would land at Shannon and Gander, and would leave earlier. Could they be at the terminal at seven o'clock?

" Yes, we'll manage it," Susan said, and rang off.

She looked at the clock. A little more than two hours.

III

WHEN PAUL entered, the room wore a strange appearance of bareness. His glance took in the stripped dressing-table, the stack of luggage, Susan's loose coat laid ready over a chair. But all of this did not account for the sense of

247

desolation which hung over the brightly-lit space. As the door closed behind him, Susan moved away from the shadow of the long drapes at the window, and her face was a reflection of the barrenness about him. He searched it and could find nothing beyond a frightening kind of vacantness with which she seemed to hold back all animation.

He moved cautiously. "Packed already?"

She nodded, indicating the pad beside the phone. "There's been a message from the air-line. They switched planes. We'll be making a stop in Shannon as well as Gander."

He read it swiftly. "Seven o'clock." Glancing across at her he asked: "Have you had something to eat?"

She had turned back to the darkened square of window. "No. I hadn't thought of it."

He flung aside his coat and brief-case impatiently. Watching the projection of the scene in the glass, Susan could see him start across the room towards her.

"Susan?"

"Yes?"

He stood behind her. "There's something wrong. What is it?"

She sighed, and the slightest quiver seemed to pass through her body. "How tired you must be of hearing it, Paul."

"Hearing what?"

"Louis has been to see me." She turned around and faced him.

Before he spoke he went through the inevitable routine of bringing out his cigarette case, of lighting one for each of them. "Yes?" he said.

She held the cigarette just level with her face, and the grey smoke moved up between them. "Just that. Louis has been to see me."

He looked grave. "A bit more than that. What did he have to say?"

She shrugged. "Oh, Paul . . . Paul, can't you guess? What time-worn phrases do two people always use when they're breaking up like this? You must know it almost as well as I?"

"I don't think I do. I can't believe that any conventional phrases of Louis' would make you look like that. I can't believe either that he came to you to spill out platitudes."

She brushed past him, and went to where her handbag lay on the bed. "Why do you bother, Paul? There's nothing to be gained by asking further questions."

"Plenty to be lost."

His tones compelled her to face him once again. "What do you want to know?" she said. Her voice had dropped to little more than a whisper.

He said nothing for a while, but remained in his place by the window, gazing at her. She stood directly under a light, and the brightness threw shadows under her cheekbones and eyes. The blankness had left her, to be replaced with an expression of dread and apprehension. A strong inkling of the events of the afternoon had touched him the moment he had entered the room, and now, from her face, his guess was confirmed.

"I don't think I need to be told," he said, "but just one thing. Do you still love him?"

She shook her head. "I love you. I can't give that kind of love to two people."

The cigarette had gone dead in his hand. While he relit it she recognised the expression which he wore when a question or answer would not form readily for him. He snapped the lighter shut. "There isn't any limit, Susan, to the number of ways a mature person may love another. I don't doubt that you love me—but do you also love Louis?"

"How can I tell?" she answered softly. "I don't know."

An abrupt change came over his face. He struggled briefly with it, and she witnessed his struggle with compassion, but in the end his weariness and a kind of hopelessness showed upon his features. "That's it, you see. I would have given all I ever had to hear you say you thought no more about him. But since we're being honest, let's be thoroughly honest. What are you going to do about it?"

"Nothing."

"Nothing?"

"What is there to do? We'll go on ahead, just as we planned."

"No, we won't, Sue," he said quietly.

Her expression was suddenly alive and passionate. "So you mean to say you'll consider changing things just because I have a vague doubt about my feelings for Louis? You can't mean that!"

Quickly she came towards him until she was very near him. "Paul, I love you. Doesn't that mean anything to you?"

He said thickly: "It means a hell of a lot—more than you'll perhaps ever know." Then he shook his head, with much the same implication as he had a minute before. "But I haven't hung off marriage all this time in order to see it go bust in front of my eyes."

"Marriages don't go smash when there's a common foundation—your work, and my own."

Patiently he said: "That's not the idea. I want at least one thing in my life that's not business, not work. You aren't any use to me if you aren't a wife as well as a business woman. We've got to have a wider basis for marriage than just the work we both do. I don't gamble, Susan, on things that are important to me. On you, on our marriage, I can't afford to gamble. I can't risk this doubt of yours—can't stand round for years watching it growing, and know that I'd made a mistake."

She made no protest. "What will I do?"

"You must see Louis again. Right away."

She took a step back, her forehead creased in anxiety and bewilderment. "What good will it do? We have nothing more to say to each other. I've made my decision—I want to go with you. Whether I see Louis again or not, it can't alter that. I won't change my mind."

"Haven't you realised yet," he said gently, "that you

have very little to do with it? The decision is not yours any longer, it's Louis'."

He took her suddenly by the shoulders, and his hands, his gesture and his words all carried emphasis. "Understand me, Susan. Understand me once and for all. In you, in all of us, is the same desire to finish what we've begun. A tidy mind doesn't like loose ends. Your marriage to Louis is a loose end—a failure, if you like to put it that way. You'd like to go back and put it right if you could. Only you're not sure. You don't know. But Louis knows. And he'll tell you, too. Let him only say the word and you'll pick up your unfinished business and get cracking on it again. That's right, isn't it?"

"How do you know?"

"How do I know?" he repeated. "Look, I haven't been kicking round all this time without picking up a thing or two. I know what I'm talking about."

She hesitated, and then began slowly: "Then for you and me—at least—this is the finish. Is that what you mean?"

"Hell, no!" His eyebrows shot up. "Didn't I say this thing rested with Louis. He's only got to say he doesn't think it will work and you'll come back to me, and you won't have a doubt in the world that it was the right decision. Understand?"

"I begin to."

He said deliberately: "This is one of those rare phenomenon known as 'the sure thing.' I understand you pretty well, Susan, and it's either one way or the other with you. In this case—Louis or myself. Whatever he decides, you'll stick by it, and if it happens to be me, then I'm on to a sure thing, too."

"I can't do it, Paul. It's too much to expect."

"Nothing's too much to expect from the woman you're going to marry."

She said nothing.

"Look, Susan, get your coat and bags, and get yourself over to Carlton Mews right away. I'll expect you at the air-terminal before seven."

She spoke with difficulty, because she was beginning to perceive the extraordinary cold-bloodedness of the gamble.

" And what if I'm not there."

" If you're not there . . ." his shoulders moved in a barely perceptible shrug, " . . . that's that."

The taxi rumbled off Trafalgar Square to the entrance of the Mews and stopped. In the same moment Susan had got out. " Can you wait ? " she asked.

The driver turned to her, his face half-lost in the upturned collar of his coat and the peaked cap which the older ones seemed to favour. " What's that, miss ? "

" Can you wait ? " she repeated more loudly.

" Wait ? How long ? "

" A few minutes. Not long."

He nodded and didn't deign to give her a further answer. She turned and ran up the ramp. Below her the square of the Mews was bathed in sickly yellow from the lamp, all except the spot where a light from one of the flats, shining downwards, overlaced it with greater brilliance. There was a hint of mist in the air. It caught under the arch, and could be seen faintly against the wall the far end of the Mews. She grasped the knocker of Louis' door and let it drop insistently and heavily.

A woman, grey-haired, in an apron answered. She gazed curiously into Susan's face, and waited for her to speak.

" I'd like to see Mr. Taite. Is he in ? "

The woman held the door wider. " I think Mr. Taite is working, madam. Will you wait while I see ? "

Susan cut through her speech. " It's very urgent. I know he'll see me."

The woman's eyes had caught the sight of the cab below, the luggage piled upon the rack, and she stoutly defended her position. " Mr. Taite doesn't like being disturbed when he's writing, madam."

Impatience made her curt. " It's all right. I'm certain he'll see me." She stepped past the woman quickly and walked down the hall.

But he wasn't at the desk when she opened the door. He lay in a big chair, the black cat beside him, in an attitude of weariness, almost exhaustion. He opened his eyes reluctantly and turned in her direction. She had just a second in which to experience a full flood of thankfulness that he was at home and alone before he rose and spoke to her.

"Susan! Why . . .? Come in and close the door." She did as he told her. "Come and sit down."

She came close to him, but remained standing.

He looked at her closely. "You're out of breath." And then, "Why have you come?"

She clasped her hands together. Although they were cold to the touch, the sweat was already beginning to break on them.

"Louis," she said clearly, "will you have me back?"

His face remained cold and untouched. "What did you say?"

She drew in a breath. "I asked if you would have me back."

Over his features came an expression of sternness. He stared at her for perhaps half a minute with a gaze that was cautious and concentrated. She waited under his scrutiny, patient, and then as the seconds lengthened, suddenly restless: "Louis, do you understand?"

He seemed to take no account of her impassioned words. "That much I do understand," he said. "Now I want to know why you've decided to do this. What are the strings attached to it?"

"There are no strings to it. I want to come back to you."

He thrust his hands into his pockets. "You can't expect me to take it just like that, Susan. Marriage isn't something which is off one minute and on the next. There is a reason. Why?"

All the eagerness went from her. She faced an explanation more difficult than any yet presented to her. She couldn't stand before him any longer, seeing the coldness in his gaze. Listlessly she walked to the fireplace. On the mantel was the twin of the Dresden cup so incongruously placed in Racey's flat. "If you had stayed, Louis, this afternoon, when I begged you to, we wouldn't have been up against this now. You were right in thinking you'd said too much and yet not enough. Too much to allow me any doubt that you could love me, and not enough to assure me that I would be welcome if I wanted to come back to you. I've come here now because I think it's the right thing." She turned around and faced him. "Now I want to know your decision."

He began slowly to pace the room. "Does Paul know about this?"

"Of course."

She watched as he leaned back heavily against the desk, his forehead furrowed darkly. "God in Heaven, Susan, you can't expect me to make any decision while I know nothing! If you can come back to me so easily, why then the divorce in the first place."

"Because," she said calmly, "we didn't know each other. Divorce was the only thing."

His face tightened still more. "Then tell me what you know about me. Tell me what marriage is going to mean to you."

She began with difficulty. "All of us, Louis, long for the chance to go back to where we made our mistakes and try to pick up again. The opportunity is given to very few. We mostly carry round this unsatisfied desire, and at the back of our minds it nags, and the best we can do is to try to forget it. You and I, Louis, we have a child—and each other. That's a relationship which demands everything we've got, calls out every ounce of understanding and courage. I think I see in this a chance to win back my self-respect, and I want to take it."

He said nothing, and the rigid lines of his body never relaxed.

"I can't hope," she added, "to put into convenient words what is in my mind. If you can't understand what I mean by trying to win back my self-respect, then there's nothing doing. If we don't understand each other even this far, then it wouldn't be any use continuing."

The silence went on so long she began to believe that he never would break it. She knew quite well, that, behind her head, the hands of the clock were moving on towards seven. She thought of the taxi standing out in the mews, and then fixed her mind again on Louis' immovable silence.

At last he stirred. Even her thoughts seemed suspended while she waited to see in what direction he was moved. But he came towards her slowly, until they stood side by side against the mantel.

" Do you quite realise, Susan, what you're coming to ? Very little that's glamorous, much that's plain dull. Midge, won't, by any means, be the greatest of your problems. Suppose I decide to keep on Hythebourne ? Could you bear that ? Could you bear the routine, the sameness, the lack of excitement ? "

" Yes. Yes, I could."

" Why ? "

" Because one may only go on for a certain length of time expending energy and integrity on things unworthy of them. You and Midge, you're worth it—in a bigger way than Paul is. You need me more, as I need you. I know it won't be all roses, but it's worth it—it's worth everything I've got."

" Susan ! "

" Yes ? "

" Does all this include loving me as well ? "

" Yes."

He nodded, and then he smiled.

Susan thought, afterwards, that they might perhaps have said more to each other, have embellished the sparseness of their agreement with plans and promises, if the loud voices in the hall had not cut through.

She gestured towards the door. " I'm sorry. I've had a cab waiting."

The smile broke fully over his features. " My God, what a woman this is. Even a cab waiting to bear you away ! " Laughing softly, he went to the door and opened it.

The man took off his cap, looking past the woman who still held grimly to the door. " 'Ere, I just wanted to know if the young lady is going to be much longer. Can't wait all night, y'know."

" She won't be needing it any more," Louis said.

" Well, what about the luggage? Whole stack of it piled up."

" Luggage? " He glanced back to Susan.

" Yes," she said.

" I'll go down and get it."

She went to the door and watched them as they walked towards the ramp, Louis tall beside the bulky, coated figure of the cab-driver. The woman had slipped away; from the kitchen Susan could hear her voice, and Midge's in lighter tones in answer. Below, at the entrance to the mews, there was the clink of coins, and the deep and indistinct murmur of conversation as the cab-driver loaded Louis with the suitcases. And last of all, as he started back up the ramp, the sound of the taxi rumbling away to join the traffic in in Trafalgar Square.

THE END